Harper smiled when they walked past the study lined with books—where she stopped.

“Wow.” She stepped into the study. And, for the first time since she’d arrived, she looked excited. “I love books. That’s why I am—was—a librarian.”

A librarian? Why was she here—as a housekeeper?

“Books never let you down, you know?” She was scanning the shelves now, making little noises of approval or something else.

“Miss Harper.”

“Right.” She sighed. “We should go.” She ran her fingertips along the spines of several books. “Until later, books.”

Ames shook his head at that. First she was talking to herself, now she was talking to books. She was an odd duck. That’s all there was to it. He didn’t mind odd. Or unusual. Unusual he could handle.

But Harper? He wasn’t so sure about. There wasn’t anything about her that made sense. He liked things to make sense—liked to anticipate and understand things. Most of the folk on Crossroads had a past, and they didn’t like talking about it, either. Most of them had been in trouble with the law for some reason or other. Some had come here to find safety or, like him, brought here for shelter. Others had been left here and chosen to stay.

What category did Harper fall into?

Dear Reader,

I am so very excited to introduce you to Crossroads Ranch! Everyone there has a past, but the ranch owners, the Winston brothers, want Crossroads to be a place where everyone has the opportunity at a second chance.

Ames Paxton is the ranch foreman, and he takes an interest in all aspects of ranch operations. When his boss hires a woman with no experience to serve as the housekeeper, Ames doesn't expect Miss Harper Lynn to last the week.

Harper gave up her job as a librarian and her hometown for wide-open spaces and, hopefully, escape from her nightmares. She finds a new inner strength and acceptance amongst the hard-working folk of Crossroads. But Harper knows that when things seem too good to be true, they normally are. It hurts to think about leaving, but she won't let her past negatively impact the people she now considers family.

Welcome to Crossroads!

Sasha Summers xoxo

*A couple of notes:

The Texas Prison Rodeo program ended in the 1980s. The mentioned prison rodeo program, Graves Prison, Crossroads Ranch and most of the locations in the book are fictional.

Sensitive topics discussed include abuse and the aftermath/recovery from a mass shooting.

HER COWBOY PROTECTOR

SASHA SUMMERS

SPECIAL EDITION

Recycling programs for this product may not exist in your area.

ISBN-13: 978-1-335-18028-5

Her Cowboy Protector

For questions and comments about the quality of this book, please contact us at CustomerService@Harlequin.com.

Harlequin Enterprises ULC
22 Adelaide St. West, 41st Floor
Toronto, Ontario M5H 4E3, Canada
www.Harlequin.com

HarperCollins Publishers
Macken House, 39/40 Mayor Street Upper,
Dublin 1, D01 C9W8, Ireland
www.HarperCollins.com

Printed in Lithuania

USA TODAY bestselling author **Sasha Summers** writes stories that celebrate the ups and downs, loves and losses, and ordinary and extraordinary occurrences of life. Sasha pens fiction in multiple genres and hopes each and every book will draw readers in and set them on an emotional and rewarding journey. With a puppy on her lap and her favorite Thor mug full of coffee, Sasha is currently working on her next release. She adores hearing from fans and invites you to visit her online.

Books by Sasha Summers

Harlequin Special Edition

Texas Cowboys & K-9s

The Rancher's Forever Family
Their Rancher Protector
The Rancher's Baby Surprise
The Rancher's Full House
A Snowbound Christmas Cowboy
Love Letters from Her Cowboy

Harlequin Heartwarming

The Cowboys of Garrison, Texas

The Rebel Cowboy's Baby
The Wrong Cowboy
To Trust a Cowboy
Home to Her Cowboy
Her Cowboy Cupid
Her Texas Two-Step Cowboy

Visit the Author Profile page
at Harlequin.com for more titles.

Dedicated to the men in my life who taught me unconditional love and acceptance.

Papa, Daddy, and Larry, I love and miss you so very much! I wish there were more like you!

Chapter One

Harper had a long history of making bad first impressions. It wasn't intentional. She was just painfully shy. Which meant she was awkward, said too much or too little and was absolutely terrible at reading people. None of this was helpful during a job interview—and she really wanted this job. No, needed it. Her stomach—which had been roiling and growling all day—filled with lead and sank. And if she blew this, what then? Where would she go?

Going home isn't an option.

With a newfound resolve, she opened the car door. The first thing that hit her was the silence. No cars. No planes. No...sounds of anything man-made. Just nature. Birds, mostly. The balmy breeze whispering as it brushed over her cheek and ear.

How could something be peaceful and unsettling all at the same time? It was new, that's all. Different. It was change. The last six months had been all about that. Those changes had been horrible—this didn't have to be. This could break the pattern and be good.

She hoped.

Harper stepped out of the car, second-guessing everything. Her khaki slacks and short-sleeved button-down shirt were perfectly acceptable for work at the library. But this wasn't a library. This was a ranch. A real honest-to-goodness ranch. And it was *huge*. Once she'd driven under the Crossroads Ranch gate, it'd been another twenty minutes to get here, the HQ offices. She'd made it. She hadn't gotten lost. That was a victory in and of itself.

Oh, boy, but it was hot. Ridiculously hot. Illinois didn't get this kind of heat—ever. She plucked at the cotton fabric of her top and pushed her sunglasses into place. She was going to be red-faced and sweaty before she ever sat down for this interview. Not the best look but there wasn't much she could do about it.

When she reached back to close the car door, her backpack strap must have hooked on the car door handle. She didn't realize this so, when the door closed, the bag was yanked off her shoulder and hit the ground, spilling the contents all over the dusty ground.

"Of course," she murmured. Not getting lost had been the only bit of good luck she'd had on her trip here. "First the flat tire." She'd changed it on her own and there was a grease smear along the left leg of her slacks to prove it. "Then the soda." She'd swerved to miss a pothole in one of the country roads and spilled bloodred soda on her light yellow blouse. "I never drink red soda. Not ever." She eyed the red stain on her blouse, then dropped to her knees to collect her things.

"Breathe. Everything will be okay." She used her calm professional voice, the one she used when things got too noisy in the library. "You've come this far, Catherine Harper Moore. I mean, Harper Lynn." She shoved a notebook, assortment of pens, lip gloss and hand sanitizer back into her bag and stood to dust off the knees of her slacks. If it hadn't been for the tire blowing out, she'd have had time to change. As it was, she was on the cusp of running late, which, she'd been taught, was unforgivable.

She adjusted her glasses and shielded her eyes from the Texas sun to peer around her.

That's when she noticed the man. A cowboy—the hat said as much—who was watching her. He must have seen everything that had just happened. Had he heard her, too? She hoped not. *Talk about a first impression.*

The cowboy was tall and fit, his cowboy hat tipped forward. He looked exactly like a cowboy should look. Only, slightly intimidating. One elbow rested on a fence post, the other gloved hand rested on his hip. His shirt-sleeves were rolled up to reveal tanned forearms, while his shirtfront clung to his broad chest.

Sweaty from the heat. Because he was working outdoors. On a ranch. In Texas. *Where I am.* She took another deep breath. The heat wasn't the only thing that was going to take some getting used to. Pretty much everything was…different.

She raised a hand and waved awkwardly.

The cowboy nodded back.

The cream-and-tan dog that been lying on the ground nearby stood. Harper stopped waving. When the dog's ears perked and its whole body locked up, its eyes pinned on her, her sweating got worse. Another dog… Wait, what was that? A goat? She didn't know. The last time she'd seen a goat was at a petting zoo and that was years ago. But this creature resembled a goat or a sheep—one of the two. All that mattered was both the dog and the goat-sheep were staring her down and she didn't like it.

She cleared her throat. She couldn't just stand here…

"Hi." She waved again, catching the strap of her leather backpack before she dropped it again. "Are you Mr. Winston?"

He shook his head. Both the dog and the goat-sheep sat. Which was good.

"Oh… I'm looking for Mr. Winston." She took a deep, steadying breath. "Can you tell me where I can find him?"

The cowboy tipped his hat back, gave her a head-to-toe inspection and pointed at a path that disappeared over the hill behind her.

"That way?" she asked. She'd heard of the strong and silent type but this seemed a tad extreme. Still, she'd rather get out of the heat and not irritate the dog and goat-sheep. "Okay."

The cowboy nodded and reached for the shovel propped against the fence behind him.

She took another deep breath. "Thank you."

He touched the brim of his hat and went back to digging.

That was the most one-sided conversation she'd ever had. Since she'd gotten the answers she needed though, she had no complaints. The heat was too oppressive to linger so she adjusted the strap of her backpack and walked up and over the slight hill to see the cabin. Large wooden beams had been laid into the hill, providing steps down the steep hill. She was careful, eager to get inside without another incident. As soon as she stepped onto the small covered front porch, the door opened and a large man smiled down at her.

"Miss Lynn?" he asked.

She paused. Miss Lynn. Lying didn't come easy to her but applying under her real name, Catherine Harper

Moore, would make it easy to Google her past and why she was here. She'd always gone by Harper so that was no big deal. Lynn, however, was her mother's maiden name and would take some getting used to. "Yes." She nodded. "That's me. Miss Lynn. Or Miss Harper. Or just Harper."

He nodded. "Robert Winston. We spoke on the phone." Robert Winston reminded her of Santa Claus. A cowboy version, that is. He was probably in his mid-sixties but he had snow-white hair. He was a few inches taller than her but as solid as a brick wall. Well, except for his belly. He wasn't exactly intimidating—more assessing or shrewd. But instead of worrying over what he was thinking about her, she focused on his impressive handlebar mustache and kind eyes. "Ames point you in the right direction?"

"Who?"

"Ames." He nodded. "The fella over the hill. You'd have walked past him on your way here."

"Oh, yes. Ames, is it? He didn't tell me his name…" *Or say a word.* She took off her sunglasses and tucked them into her bag.

"He doesn't talk much." He chuckled. "Come in out of the heat." He closed the door after her. "This way." He led her down a short hallway into a surprisingly sizable room. Two large leather wingback chairs, a long sofa and a coffee table filled the middle of the room. On the far wall was a wood-burning stove, an office chair and an old wooden desk.

"Have a seat." He indicated one of the leather chairs.

"Thank you." She sat and tried not to fiddle with the leather pull-string of her backpack. When she was tense or stressed, she tended to fidget.

"You've come a long way." He sat in the oversize chair opposite her. "Illinois?"

She nodded. A very long way. She looked a mess, her nerves were frayed and she was beginning to worry she'd made a terrible mistake. But going back? *No.* She couldn't bear it.

"What made you apply for this position?"

She swallowed, hard. "I needed a fresh start." That was all she felt comfortable sharing.

The man gave her a long, inquisitive look. "Are you on the run from the law?" There was no judgment or accusation. In fact, he could have been asking her what her favorite color was or the day of the week. He sat back, resting his steepled hands on the swell of his belly. "I like to be prepared if the law shows up, asking questions about you."

Was he joking? She couldn't tell. "No… Mr. Winston, the law won't come looking for me." The only people who might care where she was were her parents—mostly her father. And that was a maybe. Had they even noticed she'd left?

"Call me Hoss. Everyone does." Then he nodded. "Anyone following you? Husband? Boyfriend? Girlfriend? Someone you owe money to? Might be looking to cause you harm?"

Her mouth was hanging open but, really, what sort of interview questions were these?

"A lot of the people that come here have a past they'd rather not talk about or have catching up with them—and I'm fine with that. Everyone needs a fresh start, like you said. The folk here all want a good, peaceful life. We all work hard, respect one another and view this place as a safe haven of sorts. That's why I like to know if there's a chance there could be trouble." He paused. "There are a lot of eyes and ears on this place. If they need to be on the alert, they can be."

Which, in a way, was oddly reassuring. Plenty of people hated her—including her stepmother. Some were even scared of her. But now that they'd no longer run into her on the street or the grocery store or the library—a constant reminder of the tragedy—she felt certain they'd all do their best to forget her. "No one will come looking for me. Or bring trouble here."

He studied her for a bit.

And she found herself studying him right back. Now that she'd had a chance to get a good look at him, she didn't feel intimidated. Probably because he did, truly, remind her of Santa Claus. A cowboy-boots-and-belt-buckle-wearing Santa. And then there was his handlebar mustache, not a beard. She knew that's what it was called because her little brother, Matt, had tried many times to grow one…

One memory of her brother was all it took for a vise to clamp down on her chest, squeeze all the air from her lungs and cause her to hold her backpack with a white-knuckled grip. Now was not the time to wander into that emotional minefield. She was in the middle of an interview, for crying out loud.

Pull it together, Harper. She cleared her throat and straightened her shoulders.

Hoss was still watching her. "You don't mind cleaning? Housework, mostly. Laundry—lots of laundry. Everyone tidies up their own messes but you'd do the deep cleaning. Might need you helping out at mealtimes once in a while—though we've got enough cooks. Some would say too many cooks in the kitchen." He sighed. "Might need to give Ames a hand with the animals, too. On occasion."

She hadn't expected that. The job posting she'd found online had been for a housekeeper, *not* an animal caregiver. She'd never seen a real cow. The one time she'd seen a mounted police officer patrolling the mall parking lot, the horse had been more threatening than the rider. "What sort of animals?"

He scratched along his jaw. "Oh, well, let's see. You name it and we probably have one on the place. Chickens, goats, llamas and cattle, of course. Horses. Dogs, cats and a couple of rabbits. One of the hands found a fawn whose mama got killed out on the highway and Ames raised her. She's free now but you might see her coming round for a visit."

Ames. The quiet cowboy. That was nice of him… But it wasn't exactly comforting for her. Which animals, exactly, would Harper be helping with? And what, exactly, did "give Ames a hand" mean? But, before she could ask, Mr. Winston was talking again.

"Crossroads is a working ranch but we're also a family. We take care of one another—of the animals and the land. It's a good life but it's not for everyone." He paused then, put on his reading glasses and picked up a piece of paper. He peered over the rim of his glasses at her. "Your résumé says you're a librarian? With a master's degree? That's a lot of college."

She glanced at her résumé, waiting for him to call her out for lying. Or maybe he hadn't called to verify her references. If he had, none of them would have known a

Harper Lynn—only Catherine Harper Moore. She swallowed and nodded, waiting.

"Got a teacher comes out two days a week to help any of the ranch hands wanting to finish their GED or some working on online college. Might see about you helping out with that down the road, if you like. If not, that's fine, too. But, for now, let's get you settled in the Big House and see about getting you a tour of the whole spread." He set her résumé aside, stood, pulled a well-worn tan cowboy hat off the hook behind him and set it atop his thick silver-and-white hair. "You ready?"

Ready? For what? He wasn't going to call her out over her résumé? Did he mean…? "I… I've got the job?" That was it? To be fair, she'd only had two real job interviews before but *this* was…different. The questions, especially. Very different.

"Well, you did come all this way." His smile was gentle. "And something tells me there's a reason for that. No one winds up here without a reason."

She had a reason—but she didn't even like thinking about it. Part of the appeal of this job was the sheer unfamiliarity of it all. There would be nothing to remind her about what had happened back home. That was all that she wanted. She followed him out of the office and outside, beneath the bright Texas sunshine. And even though it was still really hot, she didn't mind it as much. For the first time in months, she wouldn't have to hide from would-be friends or neighbors, have press camped out on the front lawn or get threatening phone calls at all hours. Maybe here, her every waking hour wouldn't be haunted by ghosts and her dreams would be nightmare-free.

* * *

Ames wiped his face with his handkerchief and paused what he was doing. Hoss was leading that woman back down the path to the ranch house. His boss had mentioned someone new might be moving onto the place, but this… Well, she wasn't the sort of person Ames had been expecting. This woman seemed…fragile.

"Ames." Hoss stopped. "This is Miss Harper."

"Harper is fine." She smiled and held out her hand. "Nice to meet you."

Ames pulled off his gloves, wiped his hand on his jeans and took her hand. "Ma'am," he murmured, wishing he could have washed his hands first.

"After me and my brother, Rooster, Ames has been on the place the longest. He's the foreman for HQ though he doesn't act like it. He's the Crossroads pilot, animal-whisperer and fixer of all things." Hoss smiled at him. "Not that you'll hear him bragging, Ames is the humble type. But if you have questions or need something and can't find me or my brother, Ames can get you taken care of."

Hoss's praise meant the world to Ames. He respected Hoss Winston more than any other person on the planet—he had since he was a boy. And, for over twenty years, Hoss had never given Ames any reason to question his decisions or actions. If he felt Harper belonged here, Ames would accept it and move on.

"I'll try not to be a bother," Harper said, looking at Hoss, then Ames.

Ames shied away from the woman's steady gaze. He'd do as Hoss asked but that didn't mean he'd like it. He had his way of doing things and his way was mostly on his own.

"It'll take some time getting you settled in," Hoss said to the woman. "But don't you worry about that. Everyone started out as you are—a greenhorn. No one will hold it against you."

Meaning Hoss would give them all a talking-to and make sure that didn't happen.

Ames glanced at the woman. He could tell she was a ball of nerves the second she'd stepped out of her car. When her backpack had hit the ground, he'd almost gone to help her. But then she'd started talking to herself and it felt wrong interrupting her pep talk.

Seeing her up close, she reminded him of a deer. Nervous. Thin. Almost dainty—and that wasn't a word Ames used…ever. Her large sunglasses covered up a bit but, from what he could see, she had a nice face. She'd braided her dark brown hair back and twisted it up into a knot on the back of her head. It looked like a lot of hair—like it'd be heavy and hot.

Miss Harper wasn't petite like Brandy, one of the ranch hands, or all colt-like and tall like Micah, Hoss's niece, either. But there was something small about her. Something in her posture. Like she was trying to blend in or hide. Disappear, even. It was familiar. Long ago, he'd done the same. He suspected his reasons were a whole hell of a lot different than Miss Lynn's, though.

When his dog, Copper, hopped up, ears and stubby tail alert, Harper went totally still.

He watched as Copper circled the woman. His dog was a herding dog by nature. Of all the dogs on the ranch, Copper was best at sniffing out stray cattle or goats and bringing them back to the herd. The way his dog was watching Harper, Ames got the feeling Copper was trying to figure out where, exactly, the woman belonged.

Same, Copper. Same.

Daisy, the goat, followed Copper. Everything Copper did, Daisy tried to do. The little goat had no idea she was, in fact, a goat. But he and Copper had raised her so it sort of made sense she'd act like a dog.

"Copper. Daisy." Hoss chuckled. "This is Harper." He patted his thigh. "Come on, now. Come say hello."

Harper didn't extend a hand.

Ames whistled, a low deep sound, and Copper was instantly at his side. Daisy, on the other hand, trotted up to Harper and headbutted her right in the thigh.

Harper took a step back.

Daisy did it again, an extra bounce in her step. She rarely got any of the other animals on the ranch to acknowledge her so she was delighted at this new turn of events.

"Daisy." Ames's tone was short.

Daisy bleated, gave Harper a long look, snorted and trotted to Copper, little tail flicking one way, then the other.

"Daisy," Hoss chastised the goat kid. "Where are your manners? Harper's a friend now." He shook his head. "Daisy here thinks she's a dog. She's a might unusual little thing. Then again, Ames tends to find the unusual ones." But Hoss's smile was approving.

"Castoffs." Considering he'd been one himself, Ames could always find room in his bunkhouse and his heart for one more of those. Always.

"That's nice." But Harper was watching Copper and Daisy warily.

As much as he'd like to reassure her neither animal was a threat, it would have to wait. Ames had learned to live with the sound of his voice but he knew it threw people off guard. One or two words and it wasn't so obvious. Anything more and there was no missing it. He'd been accused of faking the hoarse, rasping deepness a number of times. Like he wanted to sound this way. Like he enjoyed his halting speech pattern or the inability to speak up or the pitchiness of his voice. Or the reminder of what had happened to him.

"Right. Where were we?" Hoss asked, stroking his chin. "Schedules. Well, I'm only in the office from eight to ten in the mornings but my door is always open." He kept talking as he waved Harper to follow him. "You can't run a ranch from behind a desk. But, if you need anything, Penny's in the kitchen and she'll get you sorted out. You just came from my house. It's just me so I don't need much—except my own space." He stopped at the crest of the hill. "From here, you can see most everything."

Ames knew that view like the back of his hand. When Hoss brought him here, he'd been twelve years old. He'd taken one look and been able to breathe easier for the first time—maybe ever. When he'd had a rough day or was feeling down, that view had an almost healing power on him. This place—Hoss and Rooster—had saved his life. He'd never take that for granted.

What would Harper Lynn see and feel when she looked out and, in every direction, it was still Crossroads?

"Crossroads was founded in 1874 by my great-great-great-great-grandfather," Hoss was saying. "I'm proud to say we've kept ahold of most of the original land. The whole place is over two-hundred square miles in size.

We've got an airstrip with a plane and helicopter, a full-scale veterinarian clinic and one of the best equine centers in the West."

Miss Harper looked shocked by this announcement. Which was fair. But that was the thing about Crossroads—it was full of surprises. The place wasn't a ranch so much as a community. Working here wasn't a job—it was a way of life. It was hard to explain. It was something that had to be experienced.

"The place is divided into four quadrants." Hoss pointed as he spoke. "Northern Camp, Southern Camp, HQ—which is where we are—and the Equestrian Camp. There are bunkhouses in each camp but you'll be the housekeeper for the HQ."

Which drew Ames up short. Miss Harper was a housekeeper? He couldn't get his head wrapped around the idea of her making beds and scrubbing toilets in her tan slacks and soft yellow top. And those shoes… She had painted toenails. Pink. He shook his head.

"I won't bore you with all the details of this place's history now but—" Hoss chuckled "—I'll make sure to tell you all about it one night after supper. The last Friday of the month, we all gather round the firepits on Lookout Point." He pointed at the distant hill. "It'd be easy to get lonely out here so we do what we can to make sure that doesn't happen. On Lookout Point, we all catch up, share anything the rest of us need to know and stay connected. If there's a birthday or something special, you better believe there will be cake." He paused. "Oh, one thing you should know now. There's no alcohol on Crossroads. No hard liquor. No beer. No wine. Nothing like that."

Too many of the ranch hands were recovering alcoholics or addicts so it made more sense to keep the ranch temptation-free. After seeing how drink had affected his father and uncle, Ames had never had the slightest interest in tasting the stuff.

"I understand." Harper nodded. "I'm happy with tea and water."

"Good, good." Hoss smiled. "Anyhow, today's Monday but this Friday is the last Friday of the month so you'll get to meet everyone real soon. For now, let's get you to the Big House. I'll hand you over to Penny and the girls and they'll make sure you're all situated."

"Thank you," she said, looking like a deer in the headlights.

It was a lot to take in. The place and the people.

"The Big House is over there." Hoss pointed to the roof peeking through the ash and live oak trees. "It's a walk so I figure we should take your car. It'll be easier to unload your things."

Harper nodded. "Alright." She pulled a set of keys from her pocket. "I'll let you drive."

Hoss took the keys. "Rental car?"

She nodded.

"No sense in paying for it when we've got plenty of vehicles hereabouts you can use. Ames, you think you can take Miss Harper back into town so she can turn this car in?"

Did he want to spend two hours in a car with a stranger? No. Was there any hope for getting out of it? Also, no. "Yeah." He hadn't meant to sound quite so gruff—it was just the way it came out.

"Oh, there's no rush." Her gaze darted his way. "I can see you're busy."

"If you're waiting for Ames here to not be busy, you'll have a long wait." Hoss chuckled. "Don't you worry. Ames is all bark and no bite."

Once again, Harper didn't look convinced. "Well… thank you."

"We'll let you get back to work, Ames. Come on, Miss Harper, let me show you where you'll be staying." Hoss was walking to her car.

Harper took a step, tripped over his toolbox and started to fall.

Ames wasn't sure how he got to her in time, but he did. He slid an arm around her waist and pulled her upright so that her back pressed against his front. "Careful," he murmured, then set her on her feet. Now Ames knew she didn't just look fragile, she felt fragile, too.

"Thank you," she breathed, spinning to face him. "I… I'm a bit of a klutz. As you saw…earlier." She sighed, almost defeated. She looked defeated. Exhausted, too. "Nerves is all. But it won't happen again." Her attempt to square her shoulders was downright sad. "Anyway, thanks, again." She pressed her hands against her thighs, clearly nervous. "I guess I'll see you later?"

"Yes, ma'am." He watched the woman hurry to catch up to Hoss—wondering if she could make it to the car without incident. He wanted to give Hoss the benefit of the doubt *but* Ames was having doubts. And returning her rental car so soon? Bad idea. When she changed her mind about being here—and he felt confident that's what would happen—she was going to need the car to get back to wherever she'd come from.

Chapter Two

"Harper Lynn." She shook hands with Hoss Winston's sister-in-law, Penny. "It's nice to meet you." She could feel the eyes of the three other people in the kitchen on her.

"You too, honey. Boy, you sure are a skinny little thing." Penny's lips puckered and a V settled between her brows. "Wind gusts get too strong, you'll be blown into New Mexico."

Harper wasn't sure what to say to that.

The man leaning against the kitchen counter stopped chewing his apple and said, "Momma." The word was all disapproval. "She didn't mean anything by it. Most of what Momma thinks comes right on out her mouth. Takes some getting used to. Name's Calder." Calder nodded at Harper and offered her a friendly smile.

"Food is Penny's love language." Hoss chuckled.

"Don't be surprised if she tries to feed you—all the time." Calder took a bite of apple. "And that lovely lady over there is my sister, Micah."

Harper saw the look the siblings exchanged and felt a sharp stab in her chest. Now was not the time to think about Matt… Or…well, any of that.

Hoss smiled at the other woman in the room. "Micah is one hell of a good baker."

"Hoss always hands out compliments when he knows I've been making cookies." Micah pointed at the cooling tray on the other counter. "Help yourself, Hoss. You, too, Harper."

"Don't mind if I do." Hoss went around the counter and grabbed a cookie. "Still warm, too." He took a bite. "You like oatmeal raisin?"

Harper nodded and took the cookie he offered.

"I should head on out," Hoss said, grabbing another cookie. "But I'll leave you here with Penny and Micah. They'll take good care of you. Won't you, ladies?" His bushy brows elevated just enough until Penny and Micah nodded. "Good. Good. I'll see you at lunch." And with that, Hoss headed out the French doors at the back of the kitchen.

"Welcome to Crossroads," Calder said, following Hoss and closing the door behind him.

"So, what do you think?" Penny asked. "Of the place, I mean?"

Other than feeling overwhelmed, she wasn't sure what to think. "The place is huge. So is this house." Which was true. The Big House was just that—a big house. Hoss had said something about it being over ten thousand square feet of living space but she hadn't really understood how big that was until she'd seen it. Hoss had every reason to be proud of his family and all they'd built but Harper was going to have to ask someone to repeat a lot of what he'd told her.

"It is that," Penny agreed. "Like my kitchen." The room, and everything in it, was supersize: the stainless steel equipment, the wide granite counters, multiple ovens and a massive refrigerator. "But it has to be for an operation of this size. Are you coming from another ranch?"

"No." She winced, feeling painfully out of place as she said, "From a…library, actually."

Both Penny and Micah stopped to look at her, surprised.

"I am… I was a librarian." And she'd loved her job. Books had always been a source of joy. *Or escape.* She'd spent a lot of the last six months buried in a book for that very reason.

"Well, now." Penny nodded. "Isn't that…something."

Micah, however, was openly confused. And she stared at Harper long enough for it to get uncomfortable. But then she blinked and said, "I've got the time set on those rolls. I can show you to your bunk, Harper."

Bunk? As in bunk bed? The job posting had said room and board was included. She'd assumed… She didn't know what she'd assumed. She wasn't a ranch hand—a term in need of clarification—so bunkhouse hadn't been part of the equation. Until now. Privacy was important to her. Being an introvert meant needing people-free time. Which would be a challenge in a bunkhouse.

It's fine. It's good. It was too late now. She'd take whatever they offered. "Yes, please."

"Harper, you do what needs doing and come back here at eleven." Penny went back to chopping carrots. "Lunch will be ready." She gave Harper a smile. "I'll make sure you don't miss a meal but, so you know, breakfast at six, lunch at eleven. At two is snack. Now, either one of us will take snack out to the barn or they'll come collect it. Then, we all wash up and have dinner at six."

Harper nodded, silently repeating this information over

and over as she followed Micah from the kitchen. It wasn't a short walk—and she found herself exploring her new home. The walls of the long hallway were covered with sepia-toned photographs, framed certificates and awards, newspaper clippings and surveys of the property.

"The Winstons are mighty proud of their heritage." Micah paused when the hall forked. "If you go left here, it will take you to the stairs and wind-around to the bunkhouse. Straight will take you out the side door and into the vegetable garden. Right, where we're going, will take you to your room. And at the end of your hall is the walled garden. Real peaceful." She was tall so Harper had to move quickly to keep up.

"I might need a map." Harper was only kind of joking.

"It won't take long and you'll have it all figured out." Micah stopped at the end of the hall. Three doors. One on either side and one at the end.

Harper would definitely need a map.

"Door to the garden." Micah pointed at the door at the end of the hall. There were doors on either side of this hall, too. "This is you." She unlocked the room on the right and stepped inside. "Your bags are here. There are extra linens in here." She patted the built-in cabinet behind the door. "But if there's anything else you need, we can get it."

No bunkhouse? She breathed a sigh of relief. "Thank you." The enormity of the entire morning was finally starting to settle in.

"Don't mention it." Micah handed her the keys. "I'll see you at eleven." And, with a not entirely welcoming smile, she pulled the door shut behind her.

Harper sank onto the edge of the twin bed and pressed her

eyes shut. She'd done it. This was her room now. She lived here on Crossroads Ranch. And she was a…a housekeeper. All the nervous energy turning her insides to Jell-O drained away. For the first time in months, the weight on her shoulders felt just a tiny bit lighter.

And yet, she wasn't foolish enough to think it would be all smooth sailing moving forward. Her stepmother, Valerie, had been a textbook helicopter mom. Well, for Matt, anyway. He was *her* son. Harper was only her stepdaughter—and competition for her husband's affection. Harper's father had no idea how Valerie felt about her—he saw what he wanted to see. A loving wife. A doting mother to his two children. A meticulous housekeeper and cook and someone who enjoyed being home and taking care of her son and husband while tolerating Harper. Growing up, Harper might not have been loved by Valerie, but the woman had taken care of her. So much so that Harper wasn't all that equipped for her new position. She didn't have much hands-on experience with laundry or cleaning or anything a housekeeper should know. Luckily, her cleaning experience or job qualifications hadn't been one of the things they'd discussed during her anything but stereotypical interview. Lack of experience aside, she'd watched hours and hours of cleaning videos online. She could handle it. As long as nothing unusual came up, that is.

I can do this.

A fresh start. As of today, she had a whole new life where no one knew her or her family or her…brother. It was good, what she wanted—needed—but the hollow ache in her chest was still there. Maybe it was the long-suffering look Micah and Calder had exchanged over their mother but thoughts of Matt pressed in on her.

Mattie. Her little brother. *He's gone*.

She pressed her hands over her face, fighting the need to cry. Crying wouldn't help. She'd done enough to know that. The rage. The sadness. The guilt and disgust. And, always, the disbelief. It was too surreal—too nightmarish—to have *really* happened. But it had happened.

All she'd had to do was walk into her father's home office to be reminded of every horrible detail. There, on the walls, were all the photos from the crime scene and every newspaper clipping her father could get his hands on. Dad's determination to find out what had happened to his son had turned into an obsession. She'd tried to tell him he'd never find the answers he wanted—but he wouldn't let go. "He was my boy, Harper. How did I let him down this way?" He'd asked that too many times for her to count.

Matt. She shook her head. *Mattie*.

It would be one thing if she could summon all the good memories of her brother. She'd had twenty years of them. Twenty years of ordinary sibling interactions: teasing, fighting, laughing and supporting one another. But now, all she could see was that look on his face the last time she saw him.

His surprise.

The dawning realization of what was happening. The horror and fear.

The roar of the gun. The startling way his body had propelled forward from the force of the bullets. How he'd fallen next to her, crying, and reached for her hands, before he'd gone still. Lifeless. Some nights, she'd wake up with the feel of his blood on her hands.

She stood, wiping her hands on her slacks. "Enough."

The whole reason she'd come here was to get away from what had happened—not to sit and wallow in it. It was over and done with. Her parents refused to move forward but she had to. Or, like her parents, the whole ordeal would suck her under and pick away at any hope or goodness that remained in her world.

That wasn't going to happen. She wasn't going to let it.

She turned, inspecting the room. "Home sweet home." It reminded her a lot of the tiny studio apartment she'd had in college. She had everything she needed. It was a corner room so two walls had nice size windows that let in natural light and opened up the space. On one wall was a twin bed with drawers built into the base, a tiny closet, and a small side table. On the other wall was a loveseat and lamp. Between one of the windows and the door leading into the bathroom, a built-in bookshelf housed a microwave, electric kettle and dorm-sized refrigerator. "Nice."

The bathroom was perfectly acceptable, too. The tub wasn't made for long, leisurely bubble baths but the shower head had an array of settings—so that was something.

"Nothing to complain about." She opened up her suitcase and started unpacking. After she was unpacked, she'd shower and change and see about returning her rental car. With Ames…

Which brought her back to the whole "helping out with the animals" thing.

It wasn't that she minded animals—she'd just never had any. Her stepmother thought they were dirty and Matt had been allergic to everything. She'd managed to keep a goldfish for several years. But goldfish weren't intimidating—they didn't ram you with their heads. She rubbed her thigh. At least she knew now it was a goat. Daisy. *A goat that liked to ram people.*

She and Ames would be working together? He was the one she'd be helping out?

The man had said a grand total of seven words in her presence—not even to her. She knew this because she'd gone back through their conversation and counted. It was hard not to take all the side-eye assessing looks and brusque exchanges personally. Since he didn't know her, it didn't make sense for him not to like her but…he didn't seem to like her.

He doesn't have to like me. She'd prefer for Daisy to like her, though, if it prevented her from getting a bruised thigh.

A goat that thinks it's a dog. One of many new experiences.

She was smiling as she shook out a white cotton button-down shirt and a pair of jeans. Everyone she'd met had been wearing jeans so she might as well, too. She lay them across the twin bed and paused to admire the stitchwork of the quilt. Quilting was an art form. Her granny had been quite the quilter. When she'd passed, her closets had been full of colorful squares ready and waiting for use.

Valerie had no interest in quilting so she'd sold the patches. Harper suspected it had more to do with the fact that the quilting supplies belonged to Harper's biological mother's mother and, as such, a reminder. She didn't like to hear about Harper's mother or her husband's happy first marriage. In fact, she got upset whenever her father spoke fondly of his late first wife. To make his Valerie happy, he rarely mentioned Harper's mother—even to Harper. And since she'd been three when her mother died, Harper had only faded memories of the woman who'd birthed her.

Seeing the intricate needlework on the quilt now before her had her wishing she'd tried to save the quilt squares and learned to quilt—instead of taking up knitting. Knitting took up less space and was less expensive, according to her stepmother, anyway. But one of the smaller suitcases she'd brought with her was full of not-so-cheap yarn and other knitting supplies.

She peered out one of the windows, then opened the door on the outside wall.

"Wow," she whispered, surprised by the vibrant green of the garden. Flowering shrubs, honeysuckle vines, roses and primroses—even a lemon tree. It wasn't what she'd expected to find right outside her door. "It's lovely." Two steps down and she stood on a thick green carpet of grass. Beneath the sprawling limbs of an oak, a stone bench waited. After a long day of laundry and whatnot, this would be the perfect place to unwind and enjoy some evening knitting.

She glanced at her watch. Fifteen minutes until lunch—and meeting more coworkers. She'd shower, get dressed and do her best to make a better first impression on them than the one she'd made on Ames. *Oh, well.* It wasn't too late. She'd try again. For all she knew, he was quiet because he was shy—like her. Maybe, behind all that watchful silence, was someone who'd be happy to have a new friend. Between lunch and their drive into town together, she'd have plenty of time to find out.

* * *

Ames worked his way down the food line. He loved Penny's Cowboy Casserole so today was an extra treat. That and Micah's yeast rolls and cornbread and he might just make it to dinner without starving. Lunch was a casual affair—his favorite meal of the day. They were expected to serve themselves, then scrape and stack up their dishes when they were done. Best of all, they weren't expected to sit around the long table together like they did for breakfast and dinner. At lunch, he could take his plate outside, sit under a tree and keep to himself—the way he liked it.

"Table," Calder whispered, nudging him. "Hoss wants to make introductions. Let Harper meet the crew. Don't act like a pouty jackass through the whole meal."

"Fine." It wasn't a dig so much as a reminder. Ames didn't have the best poker face and everyone knew he preferred to keep to himself and, for the most part, they respected that. Today just wasn't his day. He sighed, stacked two rolls and two slices of cornbread on the edge of his plate and headed to the end of the table.

"Is this seat taken?"

Dammit. Of course, it had to be Harper. No one else would ask, they'd just sit. "Nope." He glanced up at her as she sat beside him.

She'd changed. Her hair wasn't braided back, for one. It was longer than he'd thought. Her yellow shirt had been swapped out for a more serviceable white cotton shirt, but it had a lot of small buttons and ruffled sleeves so it still wasn't what he'd consider ranch wear.

His gaze wandered to her plate. "Not hungry?" There was no way Penny was going to allow this woman to eat like a bird. She hadn't even taken any bread. Bread, according to Penny, was essential at every meal. And the dab of casserole on her plate looked more like a bite than a serving.

She tucked her hair behind her ear. "Not all that hungry. Nerves, remember? But, since I showered, I haven't tripped over anyone or dropped anything so things are looking up."

The way her smile faltered, uncertain, had him sighing again. She didn't need to look at him like that. Waiting for him to answer her—to have a conversation. He hadn't done or said a damn thing to make her think he'd want that, had he? He'd just been…him. "Good."

She nodded, her smile solidifying. "Hoss said I'd be helping you out with the animals? What does that mean, exactly?"

Hoss had said what now? His fork paused halfway to his mouth. He didn't need a hand—especially hands that looked like hers. Soft. Silky. Her nails were shaped and painted. Hands that were likely lotioned-up and massaged and whatever else needed doing to keep hands looking like that. He'd make peace with her being here but having her underfoot and in his business? He and Hoss were going to have to talk about that.

"Harper." Penny stood across the table, eyeing Harper's plate.

Ames knew that tone. But since he preferred to mind his own business, he took a bite of cornbread and sat back.

"Harper, honey." She shook her head, her red curls bouncing. "You're going to be doing some backbreaking work. You've got to eat—to keep your strength up. We need to get some meat on your bones."

Dammit all. Harper's smile vanished. Now she looked all beat-down and sad. Worse, she looked ashamed. He dropped his fork on his plate and scowled up at Penny. "She's fine," he snapped.

Penny's eyes widened. "Who asked you, Ames Paxton? I certainly didn't." She put her hands on her hips. "No one needs you stickin' your nose in their business, either." She was all fired up now. "Keep eating and hush up."

And this, right here, was why Ames preferred to keep to himself. He shoved more cornbread into his mouth.

"I… Well…" Harper leaned forward. "I'm a little nervous and, well, my stomach's upset so…"

Penny instantly melted. "That's understandable. How about I get you a roll? Some bread might settle your stomach. And Ames here can tell you Micah's rolls are delicious. He's eaten a half a dozen already."

Harper glanced his way.

Now she was looking to him for his opinion? He was frowning but he nodded.

"What did I tell you?" Penny smiled. "I'll get you one." And she hurried off.

"Thank you," Harper murmured. "I'm sorry. I didn't mean to cause a scene."

He scooped a bite of casserole into his mouth. What did she want from him? All he wanted was to enjoy his lunch. In peace and, preferably, quiet.

"Are you sure about this afternoon? Taking the car into town?" she asked.

Clearly, she didn't get that he wasn't much of a talker. Which was odd. Most people seemed to pick up on that pretty damn quick. "Yep."

She sipped her iced tea. "Hoss said you've been here

the longest. I don't suppose you'd be willing to show me around? If you're not too busy, of course."

He *was* too busy. Taking her into town meant he couldn't finish patching the roof on the chicken coop. And, with those damn coyotes sniffing around, he'd have to be on alert all night. "Can't."

"No. Right. Of course." She was staring at her plate, poking at her casserole with her fork.

"It's good." He nodded at her plate, his gaze settling on her face. It was a nice face. Pretty. Not that pretty was all that good for much.

"Okay." She scooped up a pitiful amount on the tip of her fork and put it in her mouth. "Mmm. You're right." She smiled his way.

He stabbed some casserole and scooped it into his mouth. Why was she smiling like that at him? He didn't make the food.

"Here, honey." Penny put a plate between him and Harper. "I brought a couple, just in case."

"Oh, goodness." Harper blinked. "Thank you, Penny. I didn't mean to cause any trouble."

"It's no trouble." Penny patted her on the shoulder. "Looks like we're all here now. I think Hoss was wanting to say something."

Ames couldn't help but notice the way Harper stiffened. The color in her cheeks faded and she clasped her hands in her lap. She looked white as a sheet as her gaze swept the now full dining room. He gave the room a once-over. He could imagine, as an outsider, just how rough around the edges they all looked. Truth be told, some of them were pretty rough individuals. But all of them were good people. If Harper was worrying over that, he could set her mind at ease. "Decent folks," he murmured.

She glanced at him, her smile tentative.

"I wanted to give you all a chance to welcome the newest member of the Crossroads team, Miss Harper Lynn. She'll be taking Rebecca's place here at HQ. I'd appreciate you all making her feel welcome and helping her get the lay of the land." Hoss paused, making sure he met the gaze of the ten other men and women in the room. "This is Miss Harper's first ranch so I expect you to go easy on her and give her grace as she adjusts."

Ames heard the slight hitch in Harper's breath, drawing his attention.

She'd gone from white as a sheet to beet red.

"I figured I'd give you time to come up with something useful to tell Miss Harper at dinner tonight. Some tips or tricks or advice you wished you'd gotten when you arrived at Crossroads." Hoss grinned. "I guess I'm giving you all homework. Eat up and we'll get back to it."

Penny, who'd remained beside Harper's chair, gave the woman another pat on the shoulder. "There now. You eat up."

Ames pushed the plate of rolls toward Harper.

Harper took one, tore it in half and—likely because both he and Penny were watching her—took a bite. That was all it took. The whole roll was gone in under a minute.

Ames chuckled.

Harper grinned, already reaching for another roll.

While he ate, Harper shook hands with at least a dozen ranch hands. While Gabe and Eddy seemed a little too eager and interested in Harper, the overall impression was of welcome. By the time he'd finished his lunch,

Harper's posture had eased. She no longer looked ready to run away—which he figured was an improvement. Or was it? Better she cut and run now.

"There's not a lot of us girls on the ranch," Athena was saying. "So we need to stick together."

"That's good to know. Do you bunk here?" Harper asked.

"Yep. Me and Brandy are the only two female ranch hands at HQ. Don't expect Brandy to be too friendly, though. She's like Ames here, quiet but *way* more prickly." But Athena winked at him.

Ames shook his head. Athena was like his little sister. She was a good big sister to Gabe, funny, told it like it was, and, most importantly, she was a hard worker.

"Prickly?" Harper glanced at him. Her hazel eyes were something. Bits of blue, gray, green—and rich. Warm. "He's been chatting my ear off all day." That had both her and Athena laughing.

Ames's sigh was dismissive but, damn, he wound up chuckling, too.

After lunch wrapped up, he knew there was no delaying the inevitable. "Ready?" he asked.

She nodded. "Let me get my purse. I'll be right back."

He watched as she left, a frown forming on his face. He got up and followed. Where was she…? He sighed. She was right across the hall from him. This was his hall. His space. Why had Hoss put her here? Why not put her with Brandy and Athena?

"Ames?" Harper paused when she saw him.

He pointed at the door opposite hers.

"Is that your room?" She smiled. "So we're neighbors?"

Well, hell. He wasn't sure that was something to smile about but… "Yep." He ran a hand along the back of his neck.

"Just a sec." She disappeared into her room and reappeared with her leather backpack. "Keys and stuff." She pulled her door shut. "Do I need to lock my door?" she asked, glancing at him.

He shrugged and cleared his throat. "Up to you." No pitch or rasping or growling. So far, so good. But it'd be easier to tell her. They'd have a full hour on the drive back and something told him talking was going to happen whether he liked it or not.

She was still smiling when they walked down the hallway, through the massive great room, past the study lined with books—where she stopped.

"Wow." She stepped into the study. "So many books." And, for the first time since she'd arrived, she looked excited. As if the expression on her face wasn't enough, she said, "I love books. That's why I am—was—a librarian."

A librarian? Ames had no idea. Which begged the question, why was she here—as a housekeeper?

"Books never let you down, you know? Well, I guess that's not entirely true. There are bad books." She wrinkled up her nose. "That's unfortunate, sure. But that's the great thing about books. You don't like one? Try again. There are so many to choose from." She was scanning the shelves now, making little noises of approval or something else.

"Miss Harper." If they didn't get a move on, the shops would close and Penny had told him to take her to Winston Creek Ranch and Tack or Main Street Mercantile for proper ranch wear.

"Right." She sighed. "We should go." She ran her fingertips along the spines of several books. "Until later, books."

Ames shook his head at that. First she was talking to herself, now she was talking to books. She was an odd duck. That's all there was to it. He didn't mind odd. Or, as Hoss put it, unusual. Unusual he could handle.

But Harper he wasn't so sure about. There wasn't anything about her that made sense. He liked things to make sense—liked to anticipate and understand things. Most of the folk on Crossroads had a past, and most of them didn't like talking about it, either. Most of them had been in trouble with the law for some reason or other. Some had come here to find safety or, like him, been brought here for shelter. Others had been left here and chosen to stay.

What category did Harper fall into? Harper, the librarian.

"I guess I'll follow you?" Harper asked once they'd reached her car.

He nodded and headed for the ranch truck parked nearby.

"Can I ask one question?"

He turned to face her.

"Is it me?" She swallowed. "The not talking thing. Is it because you don't want to talk to *me* or do you just not like talking? Because I can understand the not talking part. That's part of the reason I chose the career I did. More books, more quiet—less talking. But, if it is me, then I'd like to fix it. I mean, you don't have to talk to me. I'll respect that. I just mean, that if there's something I've done or said that makes you not want to talk to me, I'd like to fix…*that*."

Ames was struck by how uncertain Harper Lynn was. Here she was, an educated, attractive woman, ready to apologize to him for nothing. "It's not you." He spun the keys in his hand.

"Oh." She nodded, letting out a slow breath. "Okay." She got into the car.

He'd almost reached the truck when Copper came trotting up, Daisy at her heels. "You two can't come."

Copper barked once. Daisy snorted, stomping and sassy.

"I said no." He tipped his cowboy hat back, grinning down at the two of them in spite of himself.

Copper whimpered and swatted the air. Daisy bleated, long and loud.

"You two are spoiled, you know that?" He stooped to give them both a scratch behind the ear. "It's a long drive into town and back. Too long for you." He tapped Daisy on the nose. "Copper, you keep an eye on her. I'll be back."

Copper gave a final whimper of protest but sat. Daisy sat beside Copper, flicking her ears but staying silent.

"Behave." Ames climbed into his truck, waited for Harper to pull up behind him and started the long trek into Winston Creek. He made the trip maybe twice a month, once if he could help it. He glanced in the rearview mirror to see Harper's fingers tapping on the steering wheel. From the looks of it, she was singing. She must have noticed him watching her because, suddenly, she smiled and waved at him.

And, damn fool that he was, Ames found himself waving back.

Chapter Three

After they left her rental car with a nearly toothless man named Cal at the local garage, they drove a bit more.

"Town." Ames said as they drove down a street. "Main Street."

This was a town? It was one street with, maybe, a dozen shops. Was this all there was to it? Harper lingered on the sidewalk out front of the shop. From the looks of it, not all the storefronts were occupied. "What's the name of the town?"

"Winston Creek."

"Winston? As in Hoss and Rooster Winston?" She was trying to wrap her head around this.

He nodded, his gaze drifting over the storefronts. "Nothing else." He cleared his throat. "For miles." He held the shop door open for her, then followed her inside.

"Afternoon, Ames." The man behind the counter greeted them as they walked into the Main Street shop. "Miss Penny called in, said to expect you all. You must be Miss Lynn?"

Harper nodded, glancing at Ames for clarification. This was news to her. Miss Penny had called to tell this man about her? Why?

Ames didn't say a word.

"Nice to meet you. I'm Rupert Castillo and this is my place. Welcome to Winston Creek and Crossroads Ranch." He smiled.

"Thank you." Harper was still trying to piece together why Penny had called this man and why he'd been expecting them. "Are we supposed to pick up something for Miss Penny?"

Rupert smiled. "No, ma'am. She said Ames was going to get you set up with whatever you might need for your job. I pulled a few things already."

That made sense. "Oh?" She glanced at Ames again.

Ames shrugged, then nodded.

"What am I going to need?" she asked.

Ames headed to a rack of women's clothes, flipping through the long-sleeved plaid button-up shirts.

She joined him at the rack. "I have clothes." These were not her style. She might be a housekeeper on a ranch, but she wasn't a cowgirl—cow person—whatever.

He glanced at her shirt.

Harper tugged at her cotton shirt. She'd left most of her work clothes at home. Librarians needed business professional attire but she suspected ranch housekeepers would not. She'd left her array of nice slacks and pastel-colored blouses and packed all of her jeans and casual, yet tasteful, tops. "What's wrong with my shirt?"

From the look on his face, a whole lot.

"That's just rude." She moved on to another rack. They all looked the same. Each shirt was snap-front, lightweight and long-sleeved. "Plaid. Plaid." She slid another hanger aside. "And...plaid." After digging through two more racks, she'd found two subdued flower prints. "Better?"

He ran his hand along the back of his neck. "Yep." But

he pulled two more—plaid—from the rack and added them to the ones she had. “Jeans.” He pointed.

When it was all said and done, she was standing in front of a mirror—laughing. Never in her wildest dreams had she imagined looking like…this. A cowboy hat. Boots. Cowboy-cut jeans that fit very differently from the ones she was used to wearing. And those shirts. All the snaps and plaid and… Ugh. Was he serious about this? She glanced in the mirror at Ames. “Really?”

He gave her a thumbs-up.

Apparently, he was serious. She gave herself another once-over. “Okay, then.” She giggled at her reflection one more time, handed Ames the hat and headed back into the dressing room to change. When she walked back out, Ames put the cowboy hat on her head again.

At the counter, Ames added a stack of thick socks and six navy blue T-shirts. “These, too.” He placed two navy blue caps sporting the Crossroads Ranch brand on top of the shirts.

She sighed. “I need six navy blue T-shirts?”

Ames turned and popped open the buttons on his shirt to reveal a navy blue T-shirt underneath. The Crossroads Ranch brand was stitched on to the breast pocket. “Yep.”

She was laughing all over again. But, sure enough, the brand was on the shirts Mr. Castillo was scanning. “We’re going to be twinning, huh?”

Ames, however, looked confused.

“Dressing alike?” She watched as Rupert Castillo folded up the plaid shirts. “Maybe I should exchange those for ones that match yours?”

Rupert paused.

Ames snorted. “We’re good,” he said to Rupert.

Harper saw the number going higher and higher on the register. "The boots are how much?" She swallowed.

"Good leather boots will last you years, Miss Lynn. These are a bargain, too. We always give Crossroads employees a deep discount." Rupert Castillo was quick to defend his prices.

"I appreciate that." She held her breath. Money wasn't a problem—she had plenty of savings. But she'd rather spend it on things she wanted versus…this stuff.

When she reached into her purse for her credit card, Ames was already handing a card to Rupert.

"Oh, but…"

"Your uniform." Ames adjusted the cowboy hat on her head. "Feel right?"

She blew a strand of hair from her face. "It might surprise you to know that I've never worn a cowboy hat before." She blew again at the same strand. "But, I guess it feels fine."

"Move around." He watched as she did. "Jump."

She did. "Well, it doesn't move so I don't think it'll fall off." Which, she assumed, was the point.

He nodded.

"It's been a real pleasure doing business with you today, Miss Lynn." Rupert Castillo handed over the two brown paper bags, full of Harper's new ranch-approved wardrobe. "Always a pleasure to see you, Ames."

Ames took the bags in one hand and touched the brim of his hat. "Take care."

Harper had seen actors do that in movies and on television but she'd never seen it in person. "You're a real cowboy, aren't you, Ames?" she asked once they were outside.

"I guess." He glanced at her questioningly.

"The hat thing." She mimicked what he did.

He was fighting against it but wound up grinning.

She smiled, too. Ames was totally candid. He didn't need to say a lot—what he did say was enough. If there were any blanks to fill in, Ames's expressions said the rest. Like now. "I look funny doing it?"

He shrugged but kept on grinning. "Yeah."

"Then I'll leave that to you." She followed him down the sidewalk to the waiting ranch truck. "Winston Creek is a little place, isn't it?" From where she stood, she could see either end of Main Street. The store offerings were limited—but sufficient. Considering the town's population wasn't that big, there was no need for a bunch of touristy boutiques or fancy restaurants.

"Big enough." He hefted the two bags.

"You're right." She nodded. "We got everything we needed. And some things I didn't know I needed." She ran her fingertips along the brim of her hat. "Anything else?" She glanced up at Ames—to find him watching her.

At lunch, she'd noticed he was attractive. Anyone with eyes could see that. There was something wary about him—but she didn't think he was unwelcoming so much as cautious. Or maybe, probably, she was projecting what she hoped was the case. She couldn't help but notice a scar that ran down the side of his neck. It only added to the whole rugged cowboy mystique. Now that his brown eyes were pinned on her, her estimation went from attractive to *hello, handsome…* He was tall. Broad. And *really* handsome.

And he was currently giving her a look she couldn't quite figure out.

"What?" she whispered.

He shook his head but kept on looking at her.

"The hat?" she asked, heat creeping up her neck. "It's a bad hat?" Like she needed to ask? She'd seen her reflection. She looked like a kid playing dress-up. Heck, she felt like a kid playing dress-up.

He shook his head, opened the passenger door for her and slammed it once she'd climbed into the truck.

She watched him walk around the front of the truck, wondering what had just happened. He was upset—the whole truck had bounced from the force of the door slam. But, before that, he'd been fine, hadn't he? He'd been thinking something when he was looking at her. Did that mean he'd been thinking *of* her? Since he was looking at her? She nibbled on the inside of her lip.

The first ten minutes of the trip were silent. If he was already upset with her, she didn't want to do anything that might anger him more. And it had been her intention to stay silent—since that's what he'd prefer. But the minutes were dragging and the silence was anything but peaceful. She tried, but words were building up until they forced their way out. "What brought you to Crossroads, Ames?"

He glanced at her and cleared his throat. "I could ask you the same question." The muscle in his jaw clenched tight.

She swallowed. "Fair enough."

Ames's brows rose, but he nodded his head.

"Moving on," she murmured. She didn't want to tell Ames, or anyone at Crossroads, about her brother. She didn't think she could even get the words out: *My brother and I were shot in a mass shooting.* Nope. Besides, there was more to it. The truth was too horrible to say out loud. So she wouldn't.

She pressed her eyes shut, pressing against the scar in her side. Like Ames, she bore scars. One on her side and one in her right thigh. But she'd been lucky. Both bullets had gone clean through and neither had hit any vital organs. Neither hurt anymore but, at times, she could remember how it felt—like a phantom echo of that searing, hot pain.

Why had she opened that door? Ames hadn't asked so she'd been snared by a trap of her own making. So much so that the truck cab felt like an oven—an oven that seemed to be shrinking and pressing in on her.

"Hey." Ames's tone was especially gruff.

Her eyes popped open. "Yes?" She blotted at the sweat along her brow and upper lip.

"You good?" He was watching her intently, a deep V between his brows.

She nodded. "Stuffy." She pressed the button to roll down the window. That didn't help. The heat from outside buffeted her face, making her already flushed skin feel feverish.

Ames reached over and turned up the AC before closing her window. "Better?"

"Yes. Thanks." She took a deep, steadying breath. "Sorry." She pressed her hands to her thighs and tried to think of something, anything, to say. Something neutral. Not too personal or too prying. *Got it.* "Do you like books?" For some reason, it was really important that he did.

He nodded.

She smiled, instantly relieved. "Any particular type? Mystery? Thriller? Western? Biographies? Nonfiction?"

He shrugged. "Whatever—" he cleared his throat "—looks good."

"I'm the same." She turned in her seat. "If there's a book I'm on the fence about, I'll read reviews to help me decide. The last book I read was pretty good—if you like high fantasy?" She waited for his one-shouldered shrug. "It was about dragons. Well, dragon-riders. There was a lot of politics and battles and I stayed up all night reading it."

"All night?" He shot her a disbelieving look.

"Even though I was exhausted the next day, it was worth it." She sighed. "What was the last book you read?"

He shrugged. "Been a while." He coughed and took a sip from his water bottle. "Never read…overnight."

"Never?" She'd done it plenty of times. "I can't imagine that. Really. That sounds like a challenge to me, Ames. I'm going to have to find that book—the one you can't put down."

"Can't." He shook his head. "Work."

"You never get a night off? Come on, Ames." She wasn't going to be deterred. "You don't know what you're missing. For all you know, I could find you something life-changing. If I can find you the right book, you'll read all night without even knowing it."

He shook his head, chuckling. "Doubt it."

"All right, mister, that *is* a challenge." She rubbed her hands together. Maybe she was being silly—she probably was—but it was just the sort of thing to keep her mind occupied. She'd work hard all day, search the surprisingly well-stocked study for a good book for Ames and knit when sleep still eluded her. Anything to keep her thoughts from going back to that day—walking along the path she'd walked oh-so-many times—and the sound of gunshots.

Ames had spent a lot of time learning people over the years. Once people stopped expecting you to talk, they started talking over you—almost like he wasn't there. It was fine by him. He knew more about most people than he'd like but, as it was none of his business, he didn't worry over it too much. If anything, it helped him understand that person in a way he might not have otherwise.

That hadn't happened with Harper yet.

Whatever was eating at her was right there, under the surface. At least twice today he'd seen her eyes take on a faraway look. Wherever she'd gone, it wasn't a happy place. He got that from the way her hands shook. When that happened, she pressed her hands together or played with the tie on her backpack, but that didn't stop them from shaking.

He was a man who liked things to make sense. He liked cause and effect. But Harper being here stumped him. A highly educated woman looking for a job on a remote ranch—as a housekeeper? He glanced at her lily-white, smooth hands.

Yeah, no, something didn't add up. And while her motivation or story shouldn't matter to him, it did. That might be the most troubling part of this.

It wasn't that he was worried about her, per se. More that whatever she was hiding might be bigger than what any of them expected. She was unusual—it followed that her reasoning for being here would likely be unusual, too.

He glanced at her. Now that he'd turned the radio on, she was humming along and staring out the window. So far she'd pointed out a longhorn, a bison and a zebra with equal wide-eyed wonder.

"I expected the longhorn, it being Texas and all, but buffalo? Zebra?" She shook her head. "Those were surprises."

"Bison," he murmured. "Lotta imported game." He cleared his throat. "Lotta open spaces."

"Oh, I've noticed." She lifted her Stetson, tucked the hair behind her ear and put the hat back on. "Is there a difference between a bison and buffalo?"

"Yep." He couldn't help but notice she looked cute in a cowboy hat. She did.

She looked at him. "What is it? The difference?"

Explaining that was going to take a whole lot more words than he was prepared to say so he shrugged.

"Okay… Are there any on Crossroads?" She smothered a yawn with the back of her hand. "Bison-not-buffalo?"

He nodded. The Winston brothers had a small herd on the place—participating in one of the restorative efforts through the National Parks and Wildlife Department.

"Anything else? Zebras or lions or anything?"

"Mountain lions." He saw her eyes widen and chuckled. "They're native."

"Are they dangerous?" She paused, shook her head, then said, "Of course they're dangerous, they're mountain lions." She faced him. "Are there a lot of them?"

He shook his head. The last time a mountain lion had caused any trouble with the herd had been a couple of years back. Since it had only taken an older cow or calf now and then, the decision was made to leave the animal be. The Winston brothers liked leaving nature to nature—or at least that's what Hoss liked to say. A mountain lion can be a nuisance. It can also help take care of other nuisances like feral pigs, coyotes or the like.

"That's good." She took a deep breath.

Ames swallowed against the tightening of his throat but it didn't ease. Every now and then, his vocal cords would spasm and tighten up. It was a pain but it normally didn't last too long. He cleared his throat but wound up reaching for his water bottle. He took a long drink, waited, then took another.

"Are you okay?"

He nodded but avoided her gaze. No point in putting it off. "Accident." He pulled his shirt back so she could see his scar.

"Ouch." She winced, leaning closer to him to inspect the raised line, which extended from under his jaw to beneath his clavicle. Thankfully she couldn't see that part of it. Since he'd had no medical treatment until Hoss had arrived—weeks after he'd been injured—the scar that formed was a jagged, twisted mess. After a pause, she asked, "Does it hurt?"

He shrugged. "Mostly talk funny, is all." The fact that the sentence ended on a broken wheeze only reinforced what he'd said. "Takes effort."

She nodded, her expression searching. Finally, she said, "Guess it's a good thing you're not much of a talker, then." Her smile was sympathetic.

Sympathy he could take. Pity, he could not. He'd felt pitiful—pathetic—for too many years. He wasn't. Not anymore. And he didn't want people thinking of him that way now.

To his surprise, she let it be. Instead of asking questions, she went back to humming, so Ames's mind wandered to the never-ending list of tasks waiting for him at the ranch. The chicken coop took top priority. After that, the latch on the south pasture needed replacing, he needed to check the maintenance logs on all the HQ equipment, and two of the roads were in need of regrading.

In the distance, a pair of mule deer ran across an open field. Harper leaned forward in her seat, watching them.

In a lot of ways, Harper reminded him of the deer. More like a fawn, though. Gangly and awkward, stumbling over her own feet, but trying all the same. He glanced her way after a little while—to find her sound asleep. Her head rested against the bench-seat back and her hat rested in her lap. It was just as well. They had a good thirty minutes left and she'd had a big day.

As best as he could tell, she was a city girl. She was too fascinated by every little thing to have spent much time in the country. From her fair complexion and soft skin, he figured she preferred reading her books indoors. And she didn't get things like the long-sleeved shirts were moisture-wicking—drawing the heat and sweat away from her body when she worked. Or that the hat protected her from the sun, boots prevented her toes getting crushed by a misplaced hoof, and jeans—well, they were jeans. What else was there to wear? Put all that together and it meant she didn't spend a lot of time sweating or working in the outdoors.

Most of the Crossroads folks had some sort of foundation in ranching. Either they grew up doing it, took up rodeo in prison or were used to physical work. Ranching—and Crossroads—was a good fit for them.

Still, he hadn't had a lick of ranching know-how when he'd arrived. He'd been all knees and Adam's apple—at least that's how Hoss had described him. All Ames remembered before coming to Crossroads was fear.

His father? The bastard had haunted his dreams for years long after he was no longer a part of Ames's life. But he'd never forget his father. His uncle, too. His father had been mean, but his uncle had been evil. He'd put enough marks on Ames's body that there was no forgetting him, either.

Eventually, Child Protective Services took him from his uncle and handed him over to Hoss Winston.

Ames had had no idea how different his life was about to become. He'd trailed after Hoss like Copper and Daisy followed him. Wherever Hoss was, whatever he was doing, Ames was right there watching and learning and trying to prove he was worth Hoss's time and energy.

Hoss had never judged him or punished him or made him feel foolish over his mistakes—and he'd made plenty of them back then. Hoss had taught him what it meant to be a good man. His father and uncle had too, in their own way. Hoss had been an example of what he should strive to be—the other two had been an example of what he'd never be.

Harper mumbled something, pulling his eyes her way. Her face was drawn tight. She was murmuring something—her tone panicked—and her head shaking.

It wasn't a good dream.

He frowned. "Harper?" His voice was too low, too weak for her name to reach her. He cleared his throat and tried again. "Harper." No better.

He reached over and gave her shoulder a gentle shake.

She only stiffened and jerked away from him. But it was the sounds she was making—and the tears on her face that had him taking her hand in his.

"Harper." He forced the word out. It was louder than he'd expected, jarring both of them.

But her eyes were open now—that was something. Even if there were tears running down her cheeks. And there were. There was no sign of them stopping, either. Harper was shaking something fierce, too. She wasn't okay.

Dammit all.

He took a quick look in the rearview before he pulled the truck off into the grass alongside the road. Then he sat, his hand gripped in both of hers, until she looked at him.

She opened her mouth, then shook her head.

"It's okay." But it sounded more like an order, not the offer of comfort he'd intended.

"I'm sorry," she whispered, wiping at her cheeks with one hand and clinging to his with the other.

"No need." He shook his head. He knew what it meant to be haunted. The look in her eyes said she was, too. By what, he didn't know. And it didn't matter. Not really. All that mattered was her knowing she was here, now, not stuck wherever she'd been in her dreams.

"You're mad." Her voice wavered.

"I'm not." Well, dammit, he *sounded* mad. In fact, he sounded riled up and ready to fight. He sighed and pointed at his throat. "I'm not."

"Oh." She sniffed, her eyes lingering on his scar.

It took all of his concentration to temper his tone as he said, "You're okay."

Her light gaze met his and held. There was a hell of a

lot going on in those eyes. "I will be." The words were all determination.

Good. She had to believe it—to want it—to get there. "I believe you." He nodded. But the more she kept looking at him, the more uncomfortable he got. Here she was, a fine-looking woman holding his hand and making things mighty uncomfortable—for him, anyway. Why was he staring right back at her? Like a damn fool. He wasn't made out of stone. He tried to be—getting emotional or feeling things made things messy. He didn't like messy. Recognizing that Harper Lynn was attractive, for example, would make things messy. So he wouldn't. "You ready?" He untangled his hand from hers.

"Yes. I just..." She sniffed and took a deep breath. "I'm sorry. That... Well, that won't happen again."

He didn't argue with her but, in his experience, it wasn't that simple. If turning off the torment of the past was like a light switch, half the people on Crossroads wouldn't be there. It wasn't. It was a process. And, from what he could see, Harper was likely in the thick of that process.

So, instead of getting distracted by how pretty she was or getting rattled by how good she looked in her cowboy hat, he'd see her for what she truly was. A broken person trying to put herself back together again. That he understood—but he couldn't really help with. This was something Harper would have to figure out herself.

And yet... It's not like he'd just sit there and do nothing if she started crying again. Tears were too much for him to bear. But, other than that, she was on her own.

Chapter Four

Harper needed to get out of her head. She'd made a fool of herself—now she had to do damage control. How? Ask questions? She had plenty of them. When it came to Ames… Ames what? She didn't even know his last name. How could that be? She wracked her brain but, as far as she could remember, when Hoss had made the introductions he'd just said Ames.

"What's your last name?" she asked.

Ames looked rather intimidating as he asked, "Why?" It was a borderline scowl, really.

"Oh." She blinked. "Hoss didn't mention it and I… Well… You know mine." She waited but his expression remained hard. "It's not a big deal." She shrugged. "Never mind."

Maybe asking questions was a bad idea. Silence. Silence was better.

He was irritated with her and she couldn't blame him. Talking too much and crying and asking what were probably prying questions…

He also didn't seem interested in helping her get to know him. Since he balked at giving her his last name, he wasn't going to tell her how he'd wound up with such an angry scar. The raised twist of the linear scar had extended beneath the collar of his shirt. How far, she didn't know. Whatever had happened, it might be traumatic for him to think or talk about. Or, like her scars, painful, too.

She took a deep breath and glanced at him from the corner of her eye. He seemed entirely focused on driving and content with the silence. He had a nice profile. Strong, like the rest of him. And, even though he was on the brusque side, it had been kind of him to wake her from her nightmare—and let her cling to his hand.

After all that, he probably had questions for her—like she did for him. She'd love to know if vocal injury was why he was as surly as he was? Or was the injury in addition to him being surly?

It doesn't matter.

That was his business, his past. She'd respect his privacy and hope that he'd do the same for her. Now was the time for her to be less curious—at least when it came to people. When it came to her job and the *who*'s and *what*'s it required, there was plenty to be curious about.

"I heard I was replacing Rebecca?" She waited for his nod. "We didn't get into the nuts and bolts of my job during the interview. Would you happen to know what Rebecca did? You know, her daily schedule, when she helped out with you and the animals, that sort of thing."

Ames glanced her way. "She didn't."

"Didn't what?" She waited.

"Help me." He cleared his throat. "What did you and Hoss talk about?"

Now that he'd told her about his voice, she could hear a marked change from his first word to his last. His tone was gruffer, kind of raspy, like he'd been running or couldn't quite catch his breath. "Mostly if I was wanted by the law or if there was someone coming after me that he'd need to be aware of." She held up her hands. "To clarify, I'm not and there's no one." She shifted on the seat so she was facing him. "Hoss did mention I'd be the housekeeper for the Big House—laundry and cleaning—but no daily schedule or specifics or anything like that."

He shook his head, his sigh filling the cabin.

"What?" She'd irritated him again, she could tell. "He told me to ask you if he wasn't around. You were there when he said that. Remember?"

He nodded. "Yeah, well… Ask Penny."

"Is she in charge of the kitchen or the whole house?" The older woman had the energy and confidence Harper could only dream of.

"The *ranch*." He chuckled. "That's how she sees it." He glanced at her. "Most times, Rooster and Hoss let her, too."

"Rooster?" She had yet to meet someone named Rooster.

"Hoss's brother, Penny's husband." He paused. "He's at the Horse Camp today."

"Hoss and Rooster are brothers. And they own the place—"

"And Miss Janie." He blew out a whistle. "Their sister. Visits now and then."

Harper had never seen such a perfect example of *long-suffering* as the look on Ames's face. From his furrowed brow to the downturn of his mouth to the tic in his jaw muscle. "I'm sensing Miss Janie is a…*character*?"

His sudden smile changed his entire demeanor. "Sums her up, alright." His gaze landed on her. "Best avoid her. She's nosy." He paused, then said, "*Real* nosy."

She wasn't sure what "now and then" meant about Janie's visits, but maybe they were infrequent enough that she wouldn't have to worry. Ames was still watching her so she said, "I'll duck and cover when she's around."

"Good." He was back to frowning. "She gossips, too." He rolled his neck, like he was working some kinks out. "Don't tell her anything you don't want *everyone* knowin'." Most of the sentence was a hoarse whisper, but Harper got the message.

"Okay." She started again. "Hoss, Rooster and Miss Janie own the ranch." She waited for his nod. "Penny is Rooster's wife and runs the house—"

"Unless Miss Janie's there." He shook his head. "They butt heads."

"Lovely." Harper avoided conflict at all costs so she'd see about hiding in her room when Miss Janie visited. "Rooster and Penny's son, Calder, works on the ranch. Micah, their daughter, is a cook at the Big House. Am I missing anyone in that family?"

"Ellie. Penny's youngest." He cleared his throat. "Vet at the Horse Camp."

Penny's youngest. Not Penny and Rooster's youngest? She wanted to ask but, with the whispers and throat clearing, she didn't want to strain his voice.

"Then there's Eddy, Logan, Gabe, Resse, Brandy and Athena." She went back through all the names and faces of the people she'd met at lunch. "Are they all ranch hands?" Other than what she'd looked up online and the movies she'd seen, she didn't really know what being a ranch hand entailed. "Hoss and Penny said you can do pretty much anything. You fly planes *and* you're the foreman. What does a foreman do?"

"Keep everything runnin', mostly." Ames shrugged.

Harper got the feeling there was more to it than that. But since he didn't want to talk about that, she'd try again later. "Hoss mentioned the get-together at Lookout Point. I guess I'll meet more people then." She closed her eyes, doing her best to connect names and faces she'd be seeing on a daily basis. So far, everyone seemed nice. Maybe not Brandy, but other than shooting Harper a hard look, she'd ignored her. Micah was a bit distant—but no more so than Ames. In time, maybe the two of them would warm up to her, too.

At the same time, she was fine flying under the radar. She'd been mostly invisible her whole life. It wasn't a bad thing. Recently, she'd missed being able to blend into the background. The last six months, she hadn't been able to go to the gas station without getting looks or being whispered about. She'd be fine keeping her head down, doing her job and enjoying some peace.

But…it would be nice to have one friend, at least.

It was hard to tell if Ames liked her—even a little bit. He *was* talking to her. According to the others, he didn't talk so, surely, that was a good sign. It was early yet but, since they'd be working together, there was a chance they'd become friends, wasn't there? And since neither of them wanted to talk about what brought them to Crossroads Ranch, there was no reason she and Ames couldn't have a straightforward, uncomplicated, stress-free friendship. At least she hoped so. He might be guarded and big and gruff, but something about him was also steady and calming. That was it. There was something about Ames that put her at ease. Now all she had to do was figure out how to hold on to that feeling without having to…hold on to Ames.

* * *

Ames climbed out of the truck and stretched. He didn't like sitting still for long. The drive to and from Winston Creek just about exceeded his limit. He'd done something that needed doing, but he hadn't touched the list of things he'd needed to do today.

Things like the chicken coop.

He glanced up at the sky. If he hurried, he might just get the coop roof patched. If he didn't, he and Copper would be camping out. Between the coyotes, foxes, hawks and owls, there were plenty of predators who'd happily use the hole in the roof to devour the inhabitants of the coop. He needed to get that patch done. And soon.

At the sound of Copper's bark, he was smiling. The dog came speeding across the packed dirt, little Daisy following as fast as she could. When she was close enough, Copper launched herself at him. He caught Copper in his arms. "I'm back."

Copper leaned into him and rested her head on his shoulder, making the softest whimper.

"Miss me?" He dropped a kiss on her head and put her down. "You, too?" He lifted Daisy into his arms and rubbed on her back. "You're gonna get too big for this soon."

Daisy bleated in protest.

"All better?" He kissed Daisy on the head, too, then sat her on the ground beside Copper.

Daisy bleated again, hopped over Copper one way, then the other. As soon as Copper snorted, Daisy sat. To Daisy, Copper was Mom and if Mom said behave, she behaved. It was enough to have him laughing. "You two."

He spun his keys around his finger and turned to find Harper watching them.

"They sure are devoted to you." Her tone was surprised more than anything. Between the way her eyes continually darted between the dog and goat and the fact that she stayed where she was, with the truck bed between them, he was more certain than ever that her experience with animals was limited.

"I feed them." But that wasn't the half of it. They were his family. He spent more time with them than just about any other living thing on the ranch. Their unconditional love was something he'd never experienced before. They didn't judge him for being a grump, give him grief when his voice cracked or wheezed, or leave him the minute someone else was available.

"I think it's more than that." Still, she didn't move.

"They won't bite." He put his hands on his hips, getting offended on their behalf.

"That one did ram me." She pointed at Daisy.

"Daisy?" The goat heard her name and peered up at him. "That's what goat kids do." He grinned down at the small goat. "She was playing." Right about then, his phone started ringing. "Yep."

"Are you still in Winston Creek?" It was Penny. "I need you to pick up that replacement bobbin I ordered for the sewing machine."

"Already back." He tipped his hat back on his forehead, watching Harper. She was holding herself so rigid he almost wondered if she was breathing.

Penny's sigh was all disappointment. "*Already*? You coulda taken some time to show Harper around the town, Ames. It's the last bit of civilization she's going to get for a while. I don't think that poor thing has any idea how lonely it can get here."

Lonely? Ames thought about how crowded the table was for breakfast and dinner but kept his opinions to himself.

"Did you at least get her rental car squared away? And her work gear taken care of?"

"Yes, ma'am." He was surprised to see Harper coming around the truck. In her hand was a piece of the beef jerky and the apple she'd bought at the convenience store next door to where they'd dropped off the car. She was moving slowly but she was moving with a purpose—toward Copper and Daisy.

"Good. Good." Penny sighed again. "I guess I'll let you get back to work then. Send her in when you can so I can show her the washhouse. We're already getting backed up on sheets."

"Will do." He hung up, shoved his phone into his back pocket and waited to see how this was going to play out with Harper and the animals. If she was aware of him, there was no sign of it. She was too focused on Copper and Daisy. "Watch it," he murmured.

She paused.

"Root." He nodded at the root she was about to trip over.

"Oh." She blinked. "Thanks." She knelt where she was. "I brought you something." She held out the jerky to Copper. "I figure you'd like this."

Copper had been sitting and waiting, her ears cocked up and her head at the slightest angle. Now, Ames knew his dog didn't have a mean bone in her body—but Harper didn't. Copper would take to her if Harper said a kind word or offered a scratch behind the ear. Jerky? Copper's loyalty to him might be tested after all.

"Copper." Harper's voice was soft and gentle, with just enough coaxing to get Copper up and walking toward the woman.

Copper trotted right up to Harper, sniffed the jerky and sat.

"You don't want it?" Harper held the jerky closer. "I won't eat it. I'm pretty sure Daisy won't, either."

Daisy heard her name and came trotting to Copper's side. She sniffed at the jerky and sneezed.

Harper giggled. "This is for you." She put a bit of apple on the ground. "I hope you're not a germophobe, I had to bite it into pieces."

Ames shook his head. She had taken the time to bite the apple into bite-size pieces for Daisy? And she was talking to Copper and Daisy like they understood her—like they might talk back, even. He didn't know what to make of Harper Lynn. He'd never met anyone quite like her before. She was…different. In a good way. Gentle. Uncertain. Eager. And kind. All the women in these parts tended to be opinionated and on the sassy side. He'd never thought much of it before.

Daisy gobbled up the apple.

"There's more." She set a handful of apple bites on the ground. "Would you rather have apple?" she asked Copper.

He chuckled. "Copper's got good manners. She won't take it from you."

"Oh." Harper laid the jerky on the ground close to the dog's feet. "Sorry. I wasn't trying to tease her."

"I don't think she's holding any grudges." Ames grinned as Copper chowed down on the beef jerky.

"Good." She gave Daisy a pat on the head. "Friends?"

Daisy put her front hooves on Harper's knees and sniffed her chest, throat and face—then bleated loudly.

"Yes?" Harper asked him.

"I'd say so." He nodded.

Now that Copper and Daisy had decided Harper was one of them, they sniffed and pawed and showered her with appreciation.

"Okay, now." Ames walked over to Harper and offered her his hand. "Harper's got work. So do I." He'd held her hand in the truck earlier but he'd been too stunned to feel just how silky her skin was. Soft, uncalloused hands. Not working hands—like his. He helped her to her feet but let go right away. He wasn't sure why but he was hesitant to part ways.

"Thank you." She smiled up at him. "For everything, Ames." She took a deep breath. "It's nice to know I've made a friend here."

They were friends now? At least, she thought so. It seemed sorta fast but he wasn't exactly the friendly type so what did he know? He wasn't against the idea.

"Rather friend*s*." Her voice was light and sweet. "Copper *and* Daisy."

Hold on, now. She'd been talking about Copper and Daisy? He caught himself before he asked, "Not me?" And now she was wasting a real pretty smile on his dog and his goat. *His* dog and *his* goat. "Them?"

"Well." Her hazel gaze locked with his. "I—I don't know what you think…" Her cheeks turned rosy and she clasped her hands in front of her. "Do you want to be my friend, Ames?"

He stared at her. Did people really ask that question? Whether or not *people* did, Harper had. Because she did things her own way. She'd caught him off guard more than once today—not including now. He wasn't sure how he felt about that or her. And now she was waiting and watching for him to give her some sort of answer.

"That was silly." Her hands flailed awkwardly, like she was trying to wave away what she'd said. "Forget I asked, Ames." Her smile was sad. "I'll see you at dinner." She headed down the path to the front door and disappeared inside the Big House seconds later.

Ames stood there for another solid minute staring after her. What the hell just happened? First, she'd thrown him off by asking such a question, then she'd done it again by looking the way she did when he hadn't answered her. He hadn't done a thing to make her sad, dammit.

"This is why I avoid people." He shook his head and gave Daisy and Copper a whistle and headed for the chicken coop. "Come on." He'd have peace and quiet for the next hour or so and he was oh-so-grateful for it.

First things first. He had to get the supplies. He waited for Copper and Daisy to jump into his truck, climbed in beside them, and drove to the storehouse. While he pulled the corrugated tin, nails and caulk together, Daisy munched grass and Copper had her nose to the ground—sniffing out who knows what. The sun was already making its way to the horizon when he'd loaded everything into the truck bed.

"You two up for a campout?" He didn't see a way around it. Might do him some good to sleep out under the stars and sort himself out. He peered up at the cloudless sky. "There will be plenty of stars."

As he was driving to the lumber yard to get spare boards, his mind wandered. Today had been a whole lot of strange. And, since dinner was fast approaching, it wasn't over yet. Who knew what might happen the next time he ran into Harper Lynn? If he was being honest with himself, there was a part of him that couldn't wait to find out.

Chapter Five

Harper stared at the massive washer and dryer. She'd never seen a washing machine that big. Ever. She hadn't known a washing machine this size existed. And, yet, here she was, face-to-face with one. It was taller than her and wider than her and looked more like something you'd see helping launch a rocket into outer space.

"They're on the older side. Nineteen eighty-eight, to be exact." Penny laughed. "Probably older than you are."

Harper nodded. "I guess it was built to last."

"I wouldn't say that." Penny cocked an eyebrow and glared at the massive washer and dryer. "Sometimes they do what they're supposed to do and sometimes you have to…improvise."

"Improvise?" This was not the sort of news Harper was hoping for.

"Oh, you know, give it a good kick. Pull out the ol' screwdriver and see what's popped loose. That sort of thing." She shrugged. "We've kept two of those ol' time rotary line spinner racks to hang-dry things on—whenever the dryer acts up."

Harper had no idea what Penny was talking about.

"Those laundry racks aren't the prettiest thing in the world but a couple of hours under the Texas sun will dry just about anything." Penny nodded and turned to face her. "You don't need to look so panicked, honey. Ames is the foreman for a reason. He keeps the ranch hands in line—mostly—and he was real good at fixing things, too. So, if one of these clunkers gives you a problem you can't fix, give him a holler. He can."

Ames. When she'd headed inside, he'd still been staring after her like she was growing a second head. It wasn't his fault, though. She was the one who'd stuck her foot in it. What, was she five? Honestly. She might as well have written him a note, drawn a box for yes and a box for no, then folded it into some fancy shape before handing it to him—like they'd done back in elementary school.

He'd be thrilled to learn she'd been told to come to him for help. Again. *Not.* She'd like to think she'd figure this out without his help but these machines were nothing like the ones she'd watched the how-to videos on. These were big, had lots of knobs, several doors and tubes and pipes running out the top and bottom. There was a lot going on and none of it made sense.

"Your wash days are all day Tuesday and Thursday afternoon. You'll have extra help this week, don't you fret." Penny handed her a clipboard that had been hanging on the wall by the gargantuan dryer. "This is the washhouse schedule Martha came up with. She's got seniority so she's someone you can call on if you need a hand. She's married to Virgil Kelly—meaning she has the patience of a saint and a *real* good sense of humor. She'd have to, to put up with that man." Penny rolled her eyes. "Of course, Rooster and Hoss swear Virgil is the only one that can put up with all the bachelors in South Camp…" She turned to Harper then, her brows rising. "Well, you'll meet them all Friday. Don't be discouraged by a lot of these men's pasts. If they're here, it's because they're striving to be their best selves. And, if one does catch your eye, you let me know and I'll fill you in on anything you should know about him. That way, you won't be in for any…surprises."

Harper was concentrating too hard on reading the detailed, if faded, instructions attached to the side of the machine to comprehend what Penny was saying. It was only when the woman fell silent that Harper stopped reading. She tried to pick up on what Penny might be waiting for. "Let you know?"

"I was saying if one of the cowboys here catches your eye, I could help." The older woman shook her head. "But I guess I should be happy you're more focused on your work than anything else. Less drama, that's for sure." But she sounded disappointed instead of happy.

"Oh. Um… I appreciate the offer but I'm not looking for…romance." Her shrug was awkward. Considering she'd been here for less than twenty-four hours, she wasn't the least bit comfortable with this line of conversation.

"You know what they say, don't you? Love finds you when you least expect it." Penny winked. "Well, that's it for now. I've got to get back to the kitchen. If you have any questions, jot them down and you can ask Martha on Friday. She'll be happy to help." She waved. "I'll let you poke around on your own a bit. Don't be late to dinner or I can't promise you'll get a taste of everything."

And just like that, Harper was left alone with the two colossal, slightly menacing boxes of faded teal metal. She'd ask Martha if they still had the owner's manuals—then she wouldn't have to worry about going to Ames for help.

"How much laundry can there possibly be?" she murmured, clutching the clipboard to her chest.

Lucky for her, laundry was only a small part of her job. Penny had handed over Rebecca's daily schedule and checklist. It was concise and detailed and exactly what Harper was hoping for. Before Penny had led her inside the washhouse, she'd let Harper explore around the cleaning pantry. She'd been surprised to learn that the cleaning pantry was actually a mini-barn, painted rust red to match the rest of the buildings on the ranch. It was fully stocked—resembling the cleaning aisle in one of the big wholesale warehouse stores her stepmother loved shopping in.

Saturdays used to consist of the four of them, walking slowly down each aisle, eating samples, laughing together and filling up their basket with a whole lot of stuff that was never on their grocery list. Those memories she'd begun to treasure, memories of her parents and life *before* Matt's death—when there'd still been laughter in the house.

The day Matt died, the world had become a dark place. After that, no matter where Harper had turned, she'd been trapped in the nightmarish aftermath. While Valerie blamed Harper for not protecting Matt, her father had defended Harper—but only until Valerie threatened to leave him. Harper was the only one who accepted the truth: Matt was dead. Until her dad and Valerie accepted that, they would never have peace.

She'd had no choice. Stay and she'd remain stuck and subjected to her stepmother's hatred and accusations and her father's fixation, fielding reporters' phone calls or questions from those waiting along the sidewalk lining their front yard, and enduring the looks and whispers from people she, and Matt, had known and loved for years.

Her best friends had gone from being sympathetic to too busy to not responding to her calls or texts. At least her boyfriend, Walt, had been honest when he'd broken up with her. He told her outright that he couldn't deal with having what happened be a part of his daily life anymore. After two years together, it had hurt but she'd appreciated his honesty all the same.

She hated what happened, hated how sick and anxious those memories made her, but she had refused to let the rest of her life be consumed by what had happened.

Leaving had been her only choice.

And now she was here—staring at two monster machines that would be a substantial part of her job. In a few days, she was going to have to use this thing. "I can figure it out."

She stood like Penny had, hands on her hips, legs akimbo, stiff posture—pure confidence and know-how. Only she didn't feel confident or capable. "Maybe I need to practice," she murmured.

But practice would have to wait. It was five forty-five so she only had fifteen minutes to clean up for dinner. Fifteen minutes to mentally prepare herself to go back through the names and faces of the people she'd be sitting down to enjoy dinner with. One of the things she loved about working at the library? Books always had a title and author name right there on the cover and spine of the book. Plus, library cards had the patron's name on them. Meaning, she rarely had to worry about remembering a name.

I'll come up with a mnemonic or acronym for everyone. That had always helped her in school.

She waved goodbye to the washing machine and dryer, closed up the washhouse and headed for the main house. By the time she was inside, sweat was running down her back and pooling between her boobs in her sports bra. All in all, she needed to rinse off and change into some dry clothes—again. At the rate she was going through clothes, she was going to have to figure out those machines pretty quick. But as this was only the second time she'd seen most of these people, she wanted to make an effort so the others would want her to be part of the team.

Just because Ames wasn't receptive to being friends didn't mean everyone would feel that way. Surely, there'd be someone on Crossroads Ranch who would want to be friends.

Ames stepped into the dining room at five minutes past six. Nothing like getting stung six times by a bunch of angry wasps to put him in a bad mood. And he was in a *real* bad mood. But, he had no one to blame but himself.

Pretty damn stupid. Letting himself get distracted. If he'd been thinking about what needed doing, he'd have checked for pests before tossing boards around and disturbing them. But he hadn't. That's why he'd been stung *and* chased out of the lumber storehouse by an angry swarm of wasps.

Damn foolish.

That, plus a splinter. It was stuck, deep, in the skin between his thumb and pointer finger. He'd got it from one of the rough boards he'd been carrying *while* he'd been running from the wasps. His attempt to get the damn thing out had only made it worse.

All the running around this afternoon had thrown off his routine, left him out of sorts and put him behind for the rest of the day. But, grumpy or not, he couldn't go without dinner. If he sat at the far end of the table by Hoss, it wouldn't be too bad. Hoss was pretty good at picking up on Ames's moods—he'd let Ames eat in peace. But being five minutes late had cost him. The single empty seat at the long table was between Penny and Brandy.

Sonofabitch.

Penny had too many opinions and loved to hear herself telling everyone what they were. Brandy lived to pick and tease and get a rise out of whoever was in her line of sight. Eating beside either one of them on a *good* day could lead to indigestion. But both of them? On a craptastic day like this one had turned into?

Was he really *that* hungry?

"Almost started eating without you." Gabe Lopez, the youngest ranch hand—who also enjoyed pushing buttons—nodded at the open chair. "Glad you made it."

Ames was careful to keep his face expressionless as he crossed the room and sat. Gabe, Eddy and Logan were all watching and grinning at him—he could feel it. This was going to go one of two ways. The first, and preferred scenario, was the three of them behaved and he'd do his best to keep his temper in check, eat and leave. The second, and more likely scenario, was them deciding to have some fun and make his dinner as miserable as possible.

Evening meal was family style so there was a lot of plate-passing, cup-filling and getting settled. He didn't say a word when Penny added an extra serving of brussels sprouts to his plate—and he hated brussels sprouts. As long as he stayed quiet, avoided making eye contact, maybe neither woman would notice he was there? It was a long shot but he was willing to take it.

He glanced around the table, wanting a couple more rolls, when his gaze landed on Harper. It didn't help that she was sitting directly across from him—with Eddy and Gabe sitting on either side of her. The two of them were adding food to her plate, shooting smiles her way and being about as subtle as the damn wasps had been when they started stinging him.

Well, hell.

She looked pretty. That was a…problem. For one thing, she was wearing some pale green top that made her eyes look bigger. And her hair was loose, all shiny and soft-looking, hanging over one shoulder and down her back. Plus her shy smile was—

He stared down at his plate, silently cursing himself.

This, right here, was how he'd wound up getting stung by wasps. Because of *her*. Harper. Because of how damn guilty he'd felt last he'd seen her. Her face—looking so sad. As if he'd done something—like it was his fault… But how did that make sense? And what was he guilty of, exactly? Not answering her question? Being confused?

Enough of that. He concentrated on loading up his plate with food. He'd keep his head down, avoid looking at or thinking about Harper, eat and, bam, he'd be done and free to go.

"As most of you know, Miss Janie will be coming in this weekend." Hoss's attempt to sound enthusiastic had a few of them chuckling.

"Of course she is. Doesn't want to miss out on any of the gossip at Lookout Point ," Penny whispered.

Who Penny was talking to, Ames didn't know but, out of sheer self-preservation, he pretended like he hadn't heard her.

He wasn't exactly thrilled about Miss Janie's visit. She liked to drop in with as little notice as possible. Ames was pretty sure she did it just to piss Penny off, too. The woman was a pot-stirrer, no doubt about it. And she was all about knowing *everything* about the people working her family's ranch. Which was why a lot of her visits coincided with the Lookout Point gatherings.

He tried to fight it but—knowing just how pushy and intimidating the woman could be—he found himself glancing Harper's way.

It chapped his hide.

Why was he feeling this way? So, dammit, protective almost. He'd spent less than eight hours with her—he barely knew the woman. She sure as hell wasn't his responsibility.

She was Hoss's responsibility. Rooster and Penny's, too. They should be the ones worrying over the pinched look she was currently wearing, not him. Or the way Gabe and Eddy were being, all in all, too much with their attentions.

He had no business worrying over her.

He shouldn't be thinking she was pretty, either. What did it matter? Brandy was pretty, so was Athena. When Micah smiled, she was downright gorgeous. So what? He didn't get hung up on them—he wasn't about to get hung up on Harper. She could be pretty all she wanted, he didn't care.

Clearly, Eddy and Gabe did care and that's why they were acting like idiots—all but tripping over themselves to make a good impression on her. He frowned, rolling his neck against the tension building at the base of his head. If she asked them to be her friend, they'd say yes without missing a beat.

He took a big bite of roll and started chewing, watching as Eddy winked at her—then how Gabe rested his arm along her chair and leaned forward. How was she supposed to eat when they were crowding in on her like that? What were they trying to do? Outdo each other in the tomfoolery department?

Harper didn't look all that impressed. If anything, she looked uncomfortable.

He glanced at Hoss, then Rooster and then Penny. Didn't they see that? Shouldn't they do something? If one of them told those two jackasses to knock it off or stop talking to her or leave her alone, period, they'd do it—right away, too.

Not that two grown men should be told how to act. They should know better. He took another bite of roll, glaring at Eddy and Gabe.

"I'll need one of you to pick her up at the airstrip around noon on Friday." With that, Hoss turned to Eddy and Gabe—ending the whole fawning-over-Harper episode.

Ames shoved the rest of his roll into his mouth and very nearly smiled.

"Can't you send Logan?" Eddy nudged Logan. "Janie likes him best."

"Folks say it's 'cause you're pretty." Gabe gave Logan

an assessing look and shook his head. "I don't see it but..." He shrugged.

"There you go, lyin' to yourself." Logan rolled his eyes. "I can't help it that I look the way I do. And you two look...the way you do."

This caused a ripple of laughter from around the table.

"Logan is not going." Rooster's tone brooked no argument. "You two sort it out but don't be late. You know how she is about being on time." He pointed between the two of them with his fork.

"'If you're not ten minutes early, you're late.'" Gabe and Eddy recited in unison.

Ames saw Harper smile at that—he smiled, too. Miss Janie said it a lot, so much so that they'd started keeping a running tally to keep track of it.

"I'll go," Gabe said, as he shrugged.

"I can do it." But Eddy's drawn-out sigh said he wasn't happy about it.

"I said I'll go. Now you want to?" Gabe shook his head.

"I don't want to hear you complaining about it, later." Eddy cocked an eyebrow at Gabe.

"No need to fight over the lady, boys, she'll be here the whole weekend." Logan was laughing then.

"At least you don't have to share the bunkhouse with her." Brandy turned to Penny. "I can't sleep when she's here, Miss Penny. She uses all sorts of perfumes and creams and stinks up the whole place."

Ames slowly leaned back against his chair so he wasn't blocking their conversation.

"I know, I know. This is her home and she can come and go as she pleases. But..." Penny slapped her hand on the table, then paused for effect. She was *real* big on pauses. "She cannot come in here and disrupt the whole dang operation whenever she feels like it. If Brandy and Athena don't get any sleep, how are they supposed to do their jobs? Working sleep-deprived is downright dangerous. And how can you all function if you're down two ranch hands?"

This wasn't a new argument. Miss Janie liked to visit "to stay in touch with the needs and wants of the people that worked the ranch." Why she thought sleeping in Athena and Brandy's bunkhouse was a way to do that, no one quite knew or had been brave enough to ask her, either. Miss Janie called herself eccentric but mostly, she was just oblivious to the realities of a working ranch. Those who worked the ranch were of interest until she'd caught up on all the gossip—after that, she'd leave pretty quick.

One thing everyone knew about Miss Janie: she had a temper. While there was no predicting what might rub the woman the wrong way, once she got riled up, there was no smoothing things over. All anyone could do was batten down the hatches and ride out the storm.

"I can talk to her." Hoss ran a hand over his face.

"We should talk to her together." Rooster set his jaw, resigned.

Thanks to all the talk about Miss Janie's arrival, he might just escape from the dinner table unscathed.

"Or she could sleep in Harper's room?" Brandy suggested. "And Harper can stay with us." She leveled one of her "dare me" looks at Harper.

"If that's easiest, I'm fine with that." Harper nodded, her smile for Brandy genuine and warm.

Ames wasn't sure whether Harper had either entirely

missed Brandy's intended challenge or decided not to take the bait. Either way, her response eased the tension in the room.

"Or she could stay in *her* room." Clearly, Penny wasn't ready to move on. "You know, the one with the massive en suite bathroom she had completely remodeled what, five years ago? Along with her special mattress and allergen-free bedding and towels? And don't forget that newfangled air purifier she insisted on that cost so much Rooster saw the bill and turned a shade of red I'd never seen before."

"All right, now, darlin'. I hear you." Rooster reached over and covered his wife's hand. "We'll sort it out."

Ames watched the couple. In the years since Penny had come to the ranch, Ames had seen a new side to Rooster Winston. Before he married Penny, he'd been distant and just as short-tempered and irrational as Miss Janie. After marrying her, his heart had softened. Now it took a whole hell of a lot to get him angry and he no longer kept people at arm's length. He, like Hoss, saw the people around this table and those living and working the other camps on the ranch, as their family. As such, they were concerned about the total well-being and safety of each and every person on Crossroads Ranch.

Once again, he found himself looking across the table at Harper.

It must be hard for her—probably feeling left out. It wasn't intentional. They'd all been here for years, their relationships and habits set. In time, she'd become a part of that, too.

If she stayed. He shook his head.

And, even though it had been less than a day, he

couldn't see that happening. She didn't fit here. Harper Lynn was too sweet, too soft and too pretty to become a permanent fixture on Crossroads Ranch. It was true. She *didn't* belong here. But, for some reason, thinking that bothered him a whole lot… And he didn't know why.

Chapter Six

It was quiet.

Quiet-quiet. Eerily so.

Like, she could hear herself breathing.

The first scratch on the wall, outside, had her pulling her blankets up and over her head. But the scratches kept coming… As someone who read a lot of books, Harper had an abundance of imagination. Meaning each and every scratch elicited some new and terrifying potential reason for the scratching. Most were the sorts of things that didn't exist outside the pages of a book, but still.

After ten minutes of smothering herself with her sheets, she sat up. "Stop being ridiculous," she said loudly.

It helped. She leaped from her bed and searched for some sort of weapon. Armed with the large metal flashlight she'd found stowed under her bathroom sink, she took a deep breath and threw her exterior door wide. No mountain lions or coyotes or bears or some other creature with scary, scratchy claws. Nope. It was a low-lying branch of one of the nearby trees.

She cradled the flashlight against her chest and leaned against the doorframe, the fear draining away. She took a deep breath and glanced up.

"Holy cow." She had never seen a sky so full of stars.

So many, so bright. It was awe-inspiring. Logically, she knew these were the same stars that shone over Illinois, but they seemed different somehow. The sky was bigger, wider, richer in color and…deep. A bottomless ocean of midnight blue with bits of scattered gemstones left to shine from the depths.

She took a deep breath, pulling the surprisingly chilly night air into her lungs.

After sweating most of the day, she hadn't expected to get goose bumps from the chill night air. Her thin white lawn nightgown wasn't cutting it. Not that she had much else for sleeping. According to the internet, this place was going to be hot so packing her thermal pj's hadn't even been a consideration. She'd left her robe, too.

The robe might have come in handy right about now.

She sat on the steps and leaned against the metal handrailing. While the inner courtyard was green and lush, with a carpet of thick grass and an astonishing variety of flowers, the land surrounding the Big House was not. It looked exactly how she'd pictured the place. Wide-open. Empty.

And quiet.

Other than the low of the cattle in some pasture nearby, there wasn't much to hear. An owl hooted. Once, then again. There was a whole chorus of crickets singing up a storm, too. They fit. Those were the sort of things you'd expect to hear out here.

Not a man laughing.

She turned toward the sound. There was a wrought iron gate in the far side of the garden—so she headed for it.

Someone, a man presumably, was lying next to a campfire. Which, considering the surroundings, wasn't all that surprising. Cowboys loved being outside, didn't they? Her father had discovered an all-Western retro streaming channel and that had been it. He'd watch them all—it didn't matter how bad they were—and most of them were dated and on the wince-y side. One thing they had all agreed upon: a cowboy liked sleeping under the stars.

Apparently, that's true.

If it hadn't been for Daisy, she would have stayed put and enjoyed her stargazing. But Daisy was gleefully hopping around the man lying on the ground so the man, laughing, had to be Ames. If she'd thought it through, she still would have stayed where she was. She would have taken the time to remember he didn't want to be friends. She would have also remembered how diligently he'd avoided making eye contact at the dinner table. But, at the moment, she was still shaking off her unease, and Daisy's prancing and Ames's laughter—plus the whole beauty of the night—offered some sort of comfort. Which she needed.

She pushed through the gate, careful to close it behind her, and headed their way.

Copper must have sensed her because she stood, ears alert, until she seemed to recognize Harper—and trotted over to give her hand a sniff in greeting.

"I'm sorry, I didn't bring any jerky with me." She smiled down at the dog. "An oversight on my part." She made a note to keep some jerky in her pocket from now on—she needed to keep the only friends she had on this place happy.

"Harper?" Ames sat up, running his fingers through his thick dirty-blond hair.

"Hi." She waved. "I can't sleep." She shrugged. "New

place. Too quiet. The sky is just…wow." She pointed up. *Like he needs help finding the sky?* "The stars."

He nodded.

"What are you doing out here?" She noticed the rolled-up sleeping bag he'd been leaning against. "Camping out?"

He nodded at the chicken coop. "Coyotes."

"Here?" she whispered, her heart slamming to a stop. "Now? Are they dangerous?" She peered into the dark. "I've seen videos of them taking dogs out of people's backyards. They look like wolves, baring their teeth and growling. Scary stuff." Lucky for her, she saw no glowing yellow eyes peering back at her from the dark.

"Yeah." Ames lifted a rifle. "A real nuisance." He nodded at the chicken coop. "Gotta protect 'em."

But Harper couldn't stop staring at the rifle. Big and menacing—the flames' reflection glinting off the weapon's long black metal barrel.

This gun wasn't as lethal a weapon as the weapons that had been used that day but it was still a gun. Some nights, her dreams were full of rapid gunfire echoing. She could feel the searing pain in her side from the first bullet. Then the fire and burn as the second lodged itself in her thigh and knocked her to the ground. All around her, the screams of people as they tried to run away.

They'd used bigger guns, military-like, with large scopes attached to the tops and big clips that held lots of bullets. She only knew that much because of Matt's affinity for first-person shooter video games. He'd been pretty good at gaming. Police said that might have been why he'd had such good aim…

She pressed a hand to her side, fighting against the remembered pain. It was no use. For a minute, the sounds, the smells, the sense of impending doom, all came crashing over her with more clarity than any nightmare.

"Harper?" Ames was standing in front of her, the gun strap held loosely in one hand. When he reached for her, she instantly recoiled.

She should turn and run. Or drop to the ground and curl into a ball. But she couldn't—she was frozen. Sweat was pouring off her, her heart was skittering all over the place and her lungs weren't pulling in air.

"Okay." He moved very slowly, setting the gun on the ground—on the other side of his sleeping bag. "Better?" He held his hands up so she could see they were empty.

And while she couldn't see the gun, she knew it was there. "I think so." She couldn't be sure she'd actually said the words. In her head she had but, from the look on Ames's face, she wasn't so sure.

"Guns are a problem?" he whispered.

She nodded. "I… I was shot. Twice." She shook her head. Why had she shared that? Because she was acting unhinged and she knew it.

Ames was silent for a moment, then said, "Okay." He took her hand. "Let's warm you up."

"I'm not cold." Her feet were still too leaden to move.

"No?" He was watching her closely.

That's when she realized she *was* shivering. Violently. "Oh." How had she not felt it? She didn't resist when he guided her to the fire.

"Here." He tossed a folded-up blanket on the ground.

She sat on the blanket and stared into the flames. If she concentrated on the fire and warmth, the flashes of images and sounds cycling through her mind would fade.

It was a technique she'd learned with her therapist. After Matt's death, she'd been diligent about her regular therapy sessions. No one was equipped for what she'd been through, period. Dr. Weisbaum had been amazing. He still was. He was always there when she needed him. When he'd moved his practice, he'd offered her weekly tele sessions so she wouldn't have to start all over with someone new…

I'll text him in the morning. She had a lot to tell him.

Copper sat beside her, resting her head on the edge of the blanket.

"Hungry?" Ames held out a candy bar. "It's good."

"Thank you. Almond Joy is one of my favorites."

He took her hand and put the candy bar in it.

Daisy came trotting up until they were almost nose-to-nose. Then she bleated and licked her lips.

"No, ma'am." Ames's voice was stern but there was a hint of a smile there.

And it helped drain some of the tension from her shoulders. Yes, there was a gun right over there but… Ames was here, Daisy was begging for a bite of her candy bar, and Copper had managed to press her warm body along Harper's side to rest her head in Harper's lap. While Daisy continued to stare, unblinking, from her face to the candy bar, Copper's eyes were closed and her posture suggested the dog had dozed off.

She eyed the candy bar. Her stomach was a jumble of knots—too jumbled to eat Ames's gift. "I know chocolate is bad for dogs. Is it bad for goats?"

"Best not to try." Ames shrugged. "She's spoiled enough."

"You heard that?" She reached up to pat Daisy's head.

"Your daddy said no. Not me. Him. So you can't be mad at me. Okay?"

Daisy's short, soft bleat sounded almost like a hiccup.

"Good. I'll bring you something more goat-friendly tomorrow, okay?" She tucked the candy bar under her other leg—away from Copper.

Daisy snorted, stomped her front hoof and backed up.

"No, ma'am," Ames repeated.

Daisy glanced at Ames, bleated long and loud, then snorted again, her head swaying back and forth.

"Is she arguing with you?" Harper couldn't help it—she laughed.

"You picked up on that?" Ames's gaze locked with hers.

The solid weight of his eyes on her face was oddly calming. And…not. Now that her shock was fading it was hard to miss that Ames was so good-looking. The thing was, most good-looking men looked right through her. She was a mouse—that had been her nickname. Even Walt had called her that. *Little mouse.* Timid, quiet, trying to avoid notice while staying busy to do what needed doing. She'd never minded the comparison, really. So for Ames, who was most certainly the most masculine man she'd ever interacted with, to continue to look at her and *see* her was…

She blinked. He'd said something. He'd asked a question, hadn't he? Possibly. But…but she had no idea what. It took effort to tear her eyes from his and, once she did, she felt the cold night air acutely.

"What a day," she murmured. She'd shown up, made a scene, babbled in town and all the way home, made a complete fool of herself over the whole friendship thing, and now here she was—in her nightgown—dealing with her PTSD. With a goat. And a dog. And a man with a gun, sitting around a campfire. "I can only imagine what you think of me." She glanced at him. "Actually, I probably know. You're thinking, that Harper is a real mess." She glanced at him again. "And you'd be right. I *am* a mess." She swallowed, staring into the flames. "But I won't let that get in the way of my work." She couldn't. If she messed up, where would she go? Going back home wasn't an option. Finding another job with room and board that paid decently and was far away from all the things she wanted to leave behind? That wouldn't be easy. "I promise." She met his gaze again, doing her best to infuse her words with as much confidence as she could muster.

Ames was shook. Harper had been shot—twice? He had a whole lot of questions but figured she wasn't in a place to answer any of them. Seeing his rifle had triggered terror inside the woman. He knew it because he'd been through it himself. For him, it wasn't a gun—it'd been a bottle of whiskey. Or pretty much any liquor bottle. Seeing one would have him looking for a place to hide. When drinking started, only bad things would follow. He could remember the hateful words and the blows to his body all too well if he lingered on such thoughts. So, he didn't.

Now, it didn't bother him too much.

He couldn't say the same for Harper. Whatever was eatin' at her was still raw.

She'd taken one look at his rifle and started trembling like a newborn foal, dripping sweat, shaking her head back and forth, pressing her hands to her side—covering something? Her posture had been so rigid, he worried she'd break into a million shards of glass.

Now she was trying to act like she was fine by staring him down and sticking her chin out?

Yeah, that isn't going to work.

He knew better. He knew all the defensive tactics to avoid dealing with what needed dealing with. Not that now was the best time for her to deal with anything. Only Harper could determine what she needed and when. In his experience, psychological wounds were much harder to heal than those inflicted on the body.

"I mean it." At least she sounded like she meant it this time.

"Okay." He nodded, his gaze sweeping over her.

"Okay," she murmured, staring into the fire. Every now and then, she shivered.

Because she was wearing a nightgown. Some white, frilly thing with little white flowers stitched all over it that tied at her shoulders and hung down to her bare feet. No sleeves. No shoes. And her hair hung all around her, the firelight showing off hints of red and gold and—

Sonofabitch. He pressed his eyes shut and shook his head. What the hell was wrong with him?

He swallowed against the tightness of his throat, casting a wary glance at the woman. Penny was right about Harper being on the slight side. Her collarbone was prominent and her arms were on the bony side. All in all, with those wide eyes and the way she sat with her knees drawn up into a defensive huddle, she looked downright breakable.

And Ames was feeling it. All kinds of protective. Protective of her. Powerfully so.

Knock that shit off.

But when another shiver rolled over Harper, he was up, around the fire, and draping his fleece-lined denim jacket around her shoulders.

"Your hand." She grabbed hold of his hand.

His hand? Hell, he'd all but forgotten the damn splinter. "It's nothin'." He tried to pull away but she held on.

"Ames..." She frowned up at him, holding his hand closer to the fire and leaning in for a better look. "When something is swollen and red like this, it is something. I can see it—a splinter. It could get infected." She sucked in a sharp breath, her touch featherlight on his skin.

He tried not to think too much about how fair her hand looked next to his. Or how smooth her skin was—while his was tough as leather. As different as night and day. Too different. He frowned, gently, but firmly, pulling his hand from hers. "It'll wait."

He knew he needed to get the thing out—that's why he'd spent a while digging at it with his pocketknife. Damn thing was in too deep. And since he didn't want to start hacking away at his hand, he'd have to wait until morning to use the tweezers in the first aid kit inside. "You got medical training, too?"

"I have—had a little brother... So, sort of." Her gaze fell from him and she tugged his jacket closer around her.

That made him pause. *Had?* Not have, but had. Past tense. What happened to her brother?

Hold up, now. Did he want to know? Yeah, dammit, he did.

He returned to his spot on the other side of the fire and sat, feeling all sorts of frustration. At her? At himself? At knowing someone had hurt her so badly? At what? He didn't know what the hell was going on. And *that* pissed him off.

"Thank you." She was watching him with those big round eyes of hers. "For the coat."

"Mmm-hmm." He tore his gaze from her and poked at the fire with a long stick, letting the crackle and snap from the dry wood cover the awkward silence.

But the longer the silence stretched on, the more irritable he got.

Why was she here, at Crossroads, making things uncomfortable for him? Something about her made him mighty uncomfortable. Her showing up—being here... His sigh was long and loud, but he didn't care. He was working here, dammit. It might not seem like it but he was. He wasn't camping out for fun. And her being here was a problem. If a coyote did show up, how was he supposed to get rid of the thing knowing she'd fall apart at the sight of a gun?

After hearing what she'd been through, why in the hell had she taken a job where a gun might be a necessary tool? It didn't make much sense. But then, there was a whole lot about Harper that didn't make sense to him.

Had she come out here thinking Crossroads would be like one of those ranching TV shows Athena and Miss Janie liked to watch? Those shows made ranching life look downright glamorous. Everyone was rich, someone was always throwin' some sort of party and no one ever did any actual work or got their hands dirty. If that's what Harper had been expecting, she was in for a rude awakening.

It'd make more sense if that's what she thought—coming here without a stitch of practical clothing. What was she going to wear if he hadn't taken to get her outfitted today? Some ruffled shirt and nice white tennis shoes?

His eyes shifted to her feet. Bare feet.

And that's another thing. Who walked outside at night barefoot, for crying out loud? Didn't she know there were snakes? Cactus? Scorpions? And more. Chances are, she did *not* know to think about such things.

Instead, she was worrying over his hand.

Which only compounded his mounting frustration.

That she seemed to be watching him now didn't do a thing to help, either. Sitting at *his* fire, cuddling *his* dog and upsetting *his* calm. Up 'til now, folk figured out he liked to be on his own pretty damn quick. So why hadn't she?

"You're mad." It wasn't a question.

Hell, yes, I'm mad. He might not know why, but he was. He ran a hand along the back of his neck but kept his mouth shut.

And, dammit all, she kept right on staring at him. Even in the firelight, he could tell there was a whole lot going on in those eyes of hers. But what—

No. He sighed. *I don't give a rat's ass what she is thinking.* She could be worrying over his hand or picking him apart or composing some damn poem about him—he didn't care. And he didn't want to know. Harper's thoughts or actions or needs were none of his business and he wanted to keep it that way.

This protective thing for her he was all caught up in? That was gonna stop. Now. *Right now.*

He cleared his throat and turned to face her. Space. He needed space. Tonight was supposed to clear his head, not scramble it up even more. The longer she stayed here, the harder it was for him to focus on his work. That wouldn't do. She had to go. "You should turn in." He bit out the words, pointing at the gate.

"Oh." She blinked, clearly surprised by his gruff announcement.

Okay, maybe that was too harsh but he wasn't going to take it back. And the pointing thing was an asshole move, he knew that. What was she? A dog? He'd acted like a right bastard tonight—something he'd never done before.

"Okay." She stood and walked around the fire to him. "I… Thank you." She held out his coat.

He took it, hating that his fingers brushed hers in the process. Hating that, now that she was heading toward the gate, he was worried over her bare feet. Why wasn't she watching where she was going? He'd seen her trip and almost fall twice today already…

He closed his eyes and took a deep breath.

Enough, already.

He'd been downright rude and he didn't like it. His insides were knotted up over the whole damn exchange. But barking at her that way was probably the best thing that could have happened. After tonight, she wouldn't be so eager to see him—or spend time with him.

This is good. Hell, this is great.

He could breathe easier once he heard the garden gate latch close behind her.

"That was a real show of Texas hospitality, Ames." There was laughter in the familiar voice coming up behind him.

He ignored the man's dig. "What are you doing out here, Calder?" Ames glanced up at the man.

"Gabe was snoring so loud I figured I should leave the bunkhouse before I smothered him with my pillow." He squatted by the fire and held out his hands. "You?"

"Coyotes." He sighed. "Didn't patch the coop roof so..."

Calder nodded. "Yeah, Ma will chew you up and spit you out if you let any of her precious Silkies get eaten."

A couple of years back, Penny got some wild idea to bring home some Silkie chickens. She'd heard they were real sweet. Ames wasn't so sure that was a good thing—seeing how the birds might eventually end up deep-fried or in a soup. But, what did he know. Penny wanted "pet" chickens so Rooster got 'em for her. And, yes, they were some of the most docile birds he'd ever seen but that didn't make them any better than the other chickens in the coop. Since they didn't lay as many eggs as their Rhode Island Reds or White Leghorns, Ames wasn't impressed. Penny, however, did not see things that way. She cooed and cuddled those birds like they were her babies. If something happened to one of those birds? It wouldn't be pretty. "Thanks for the reminder."

"Anytime." Calder chuckled and sat on the ground, stretching his legs out toward the fire. "I never knew you were such a ladies' man, Ames. So...what was that about?" He nodded in the direction Harper had gone.

Ames shrugged. He'd been sitting here minding his own business and she walked up. That was all but, for some reason, that'd been more than enough to rile him up.

"What do you think of her?" Calder tossed another branch onto the fire.

He had a whole lot of thoughts about Harper. Too many. And none that he'd share. He shrugged again.

"She's not giving off serial killer vibes, so that's good." Calder glanced his way. "At least, not to me. You picking up on something shifty?"

Ames would keep what he'd learned tonight to himself. Harper was a victim—and was still struggling with what had happened to her. "No." His chest felt thick and heavy at the fear in her eyes.

"But you don't like her?" He tipped his hat back on his head.

Ames shot him a look.

"You made it pretty obvious at the table tonight." He yawned. "Figured she'd done or said something to have you scowling at her like that. Something bad, too, since she's only been here a day."

Ames had done what now? As far as he could remember, he'd been focused on dodging Penny and Brandy's attention. He hadn't been scowling at anyone. "You were seein' things."

Calder snorted. "Uh-huh." He shrugged. "Whatever. Just making sure there wasn't something I should know before I try to get to know her. Hell, Gabe and Eddy won't shut up about her."

Get to know her? Meaning, what? Or… Did he want to know?

"What's that look for? If I don't, one of the others is gonna try. She seems real sweet and she's easy on the eyes so…" Calder took the blanket Harper had used for a seat and rolled it up. "In case you hadn't noticed, there's not a whole lot of single ladies around."

Nothing Calder had just said was wrong but none of it was all that reassuring, either.

"You snore?" Calder leaned back and propped his head on the blanket roll.

"Not that I know of."

"Good." Calder yawned and closed his eyes. "Might get some sleep after all."

Now that the blanket had been taken, Copper trotted over and settled down beside him. Daisy, who'd been leaning against Copper to sleep, bleated and followed. After a whole lot of snuffling and snorting, the two animals went back to sleep and Ames finally had quiet.

The stars were bright, the air was clean and Copper was too at ease for there to be any coyotes around. All of that was good news.

So why wasn't he relaxing? His insides were hollow and he was more restless than ever. Copper must have sensed it because she opened one eye and rested a paw on his leg. He smiled down at the dog and gave her a scratch behind the ear.

"It's fine," he murmured.

As a man of routine, today had been anything but. That was enough to have him feeling out of sorts. Tomorrow would be back to normal. He'd be too busy to think about Harper or Calder or what, exactly, his intentions might be toward the woman. He'd mind his own business, get the coop fixed and, by the time it was Friday, he'd be able to enjoy himself at Lookout Point with everyone else on the ranch. At least, he sure as hell hoped that's what would happen.

Chapter Seven

Harper lay on her bed and stared up at the ceiling overhead. She'd done it—she'd made it through the week. Her arms and legs felt like wet noodles, but her back was the worst of it. She'd spent so much time bent or stooped or leaning forward to get each speck of dust or cobweb that every muscle in her back was protesting. As proud as she was of all the work she'd done, she was hoping the aches and pains would ebb in time.

She turned her head, making sure the bathtub wasn't overflowing.

So far, so good.

If it had been overflowing, she'd be in real trouble—she wasn't moving all that fast.

"Might as well head that way." With a groan, she rolled onto her side. She tried to sit up, winced and lay back down. "Come on, Harper," she mumbled. "This is your job now. Get over it. Brandy wouldn't lay here whining. Neither would Athena. Or Penny." And with that, she sat up and forced herself to her feet. Surprisingly, it felt better to stand than it did to lie down.

"Maybe the bath is a bad idea?" Too late now. The tub was almost full. Besides, it smelled amazing. She'd found some Epsom salts under the bathroom sink and had poured a liberal amount into the tub. Hopefully, a nice long soak would ease some of the kinks out and give her a much-needed energy boost for tonight.

Over breakfast, everyone had been talking about tonight's barbecue on Lookout Point. It was obvious the once-a-month get-together was a big deal for everyone—it was the first time Harper had seen Brandy smile.

Well, maybe not everyone. Ames hadn't seemed all that thrilled. He was puffy-eyed at the table—not uttering a word or looking her way. Just like he'd been all week. Not a word. No eye contact. Like she didn't exist, really. Which, after the way he'd talked to her Monday night, shouldn't be a surprise.

She'd never had someone talk to her that way. And the pointing, telling her to leave, had been incredibly demeaning. And hurtful. Like she was being dismissed. Like he couldn't wait for her to leave. There'd been no misunderstanding him. He didn't want anything to do with her so, from now on, she'd do her best to stay out of his way. And she had—all week.

That was fine. Ames wasn't the only person on Crossroads Ranch. It was his loss, not hers. Why would she want to be friends with someone who'd talk to her that way, anyway?

I don't want to be his friend.

Though she was sad she hadn't been able to spend any more time with Copper and Daisy.

Tonight would be fun. Harper wanted to believe that. She wanted to be excited, but the idea of the long ride there, then a lot of talking and socializing didn't sound all that appealing. Neither did the chance of having to see or interact with Ames. She really, really didn't want to see the man.

So stop thinking about him.

She sank into the tub, sighing as hot water wrapped around her body. "Mmm." Okay, maybe this would do the trick.

Cleaning, it turns out, was a full-body workout. Standing, bending, climbing and crawling had been required as she worked her way through the two bunkhouses. They weren't actually separate houses, but they did take up an entire wing of the Main House. Women's bunkhouse on the second floor, men on the third—directly above her and Ames.

Her brother's room had always been a disaster zone so Harper had braced herself for what she'd find. She'd been pleasantly surprised to find the male ranch hands seemed, as a whole, to be tidy people. As far as she knew, there were only five ranch hands at HQ. Since there were six single beds lined along one side of the long, hall-like room, maybe that hadn't always been the case. On the opposite wall were six two-drawer dressers and a small mirror hanging on the wooden beam walls. At one end of the room was a massive arched window—on the other end was the entrance to the bathroom.

She hadn't given herself much time to admire the space—there'd been too much to do. Thankfully, her predecessor had left another checklist for Harper to follow. First up, putting fresh sheets on the already stripped beds. Emptying the trash. Sweeping the hardwood floors, dusting every surface and putting clean white towels on the end of each ranch hand's bed.

Then she'd moved on to the bathroom. Three shower

stalls, three urinals and three enclosed toilet stalls for privacy. She'd scrubbed and mopped every inch of the place—leaving the men's bunkhouse smelling like lemons and disinfectant.

The women's bunkhouse was a different story. Like the men's quarters, there were six beds and six dressers, but there were only two female ranch hands. Harper had assumed that meant she'd have less work. She was wrong. Four of the six beds were a mess—none had been stripped. There were empty soda cans, granola bar wrappers and dirty clothes on the floor. And the bathroom? She was considering ordering a hazmat suit for the next time she had to clean that bathroom.

She owed Micah and Penny big-time for helping her out with the laundry this week. There'd been mountains of sheets and towels.

She didn't want to think about cleaning anymore tonight. Instead, she covered her face with a steaming washcloth and rested her head against the wall.

Peace and quiet—

The pounding on her door was a surprise.

"Harper? Harper, honey." It was Penny. "Hello in there. It's Penny."

"Oh…" She reached for a towel. "I'm in the bath."

"I'm letting myself in. But I won't look."

Harper was up, a towel wrapped around her, when Penny stepped into the bathroom.

"I swear, I don't think I have ever seen the place looking so clean, Harper Lynn." Penny was beaming at her. "I'm impressed. And that's not easy to do. You must be worn plumb out after this week." She held up a jar of ointment. "I figured, after all that, you might be on the sore side. This might help some. And it smells like peppermint. My daughter, Micah, swears by the stuff."

"Well…thank you." She stepped out of the bath. "My back's a little sore but, otherwise, I'm fine." She'd be even better if the woman set down the Mentholatum and left her to get dressed.

"I bet. We're going to be leaving for Lookout Point soon so why don't you let me help? You don't want to miss out on tonight. It's a real good time." She led Harper to the bed. "Sit, honey. Let me mom you a bit." She chuckled. "*And* it'll give me time to tell you who you're going to want to avoid tonight."

Harper sat, uncertain whether to protest or not. *Mom* her? She smiled. Even though Valerie had become her stepmother when Harper was four, she'd always been Valerie, never Mom. In the beginning, Valerie had tried but it had never felt sincere. But after three years and numerous miscarriages, Valerie saw Harper as a reminder of something she'd never have: her own child. The harder Harper tried to please her, the more distant Valerie became. Matt was born two days before Harper's eighth birthday. Even though her birthday was forgotten, Harper had been okay with it because, finally, Valerie seemed happy—which made it easier on everyone. The older Matt got, the more invisible Harper felt. She'd never blamed her stepmother for being so devoted to Matt—after all the woman's heartache and loss, Harper had understood why Matt was the center of her stepmother's universe. Matt had been her son, Harper her stepdaughter. After the shooting? Valerie hated her for surviving when Matt had not. At first, Harper had empathized with the woman and blamed grief for some of the things she'd said and done to Harper. But time passed and Valerie seemed more determined than ever to lay blame for the horrors of that day on Harper.

"Now, you've already heard about Miss Janie." Thankfully, Penny's voice interrupted Harper's train of thought. "But what you heard doesn't scratch the surface." As Penny talked, her firm hands worked the ointment into Harper's back. "That woman is as sly as they come. Oh, she's got her brothers fooled for the most part. She's charming enough with the menfolk. But when it comes to other women…" Penny clucked her tongue.

"Why is that?" Harper was too caught up in all Penny was saying to care about the awkwardness of the situation.

"Let's put it this way—she likes to be the center of attention. All the time. For everyone. She's a shameless gossip, too." Penny sighed. "You be real careful about what you tell her, you hear? Hoss told Rooster that your past is off-limits and that's enough for all of us, here. I'd say most folk here feel the same. But Janie? She'll likely try to pester information out of you her entire stay."

Harper swallowed. "What am I supposed to say—if she asks?"

"Lie, I suppose. You could make something up to satisfy her curiosity. She'll never know whether or not it's true." She paused. "Honestly, just avoid being alone with her. Better yet, avoid her in general."

Avoidance was better than lying. Harper didn't want to lie but…she wasn't going to share what she'd left behind. People looked at her differently once they knew about the shooting and Matt. Maybe, like Valerie, they blamed her somehow. Or, maybe, her involvement in something so violent and horrible would unnerve them? At the very least, they'd talk about it. It didn't matter. No one here needed to know. Especially Miss Janie. "I appreciate the heads-up, Penny."

"Of course." Penny patted her shoulder. "How's that? Your back any better?"

"Yes." It really did feel better so Harper smiled up at the woman. "Thank you."

"Oh, honey, you don't have to thank me. You're one of my little chicks, now. Not blood kin, but kin all the same, don't you know? You got aches and pains, you come see me. Don't delay, either, okay?" She waited for Harper to nod. "Out here, we have to look out for one another—take care of each other. Otherwise, it'd be a hard and lonely life."

But Harper had learned that, even surrounded by loved ones, she could be lonely. The last six months had been the loneliest of her life. "What about the ranch hands here? Is there anything I need to know about Brandy? I don't think she likes me."

Penny cocked her head to one side, looking thoughtful. "Well, Brandy won't like you for at least six months—she's real suspicious of people. After that, she won't be hostile but she's still sharp-tongued. That's not going to change." She chuckled. "Then there's Gabe. He's the baby. Only twenty-four. They all treat him like he's their kid brother. Poor boy." She laughed. "He and his big sister, Athena, came here after being tangled up in some nasty gang stuff. Easygoing and good-natured, the both of them." She shook her head. "Eddy, well, Eddy came here after losing his family. He's all right. Just thoughtless with his words sometimes."

Harper almost wished she was taking notes.

"Logan." Penny giggled. "He's a looker and, boy, does

he know it. Could charm the birds down from the trees. He was part of the Prison Rodeo Rehabilitation Program when Hoss met him—for some drunk and disorderly nonsense." She paused. "And you know Ames so who else?"

Did she? Really? She wasn't so sure about that. "I think that's everyone." It didn't feel right to ask about Calder or Micah since they were Penny's own children.

"Good. Now—" Penny turned and opened her closet "—what are you wearing? It's your first time to Lookout Point and there is a whole stable full of handsome single fellas to meet. I've got a few in mind for you, don't you worry. You never know, one might make your heart skip a beat… Or get you a little hot and bothered." She whispered that last part. "Nothing wrong with that, either, I say. A woman's got needs, just like any man. More, I think."

Growing up, her father had been the talkative one in their family. But her father had been decidedly less free with his words. If anything, Penny's ongoing dialogue almost felt like Harper was listening in on the other woman's stream of consciousness.

"Oh, now, this is nice." Penny held out a bright pink blouse. "Just the sort of pretty, feminine top that'll draw them in—like a bee to honey. Eye-catching."

"Do I want that? With Miss Janie being around?" Harper frowned at the top. Penny's desire to find her a good man and her assertion that she needed to avoid Miss Janie at all costs were in direct opposition to one another.

"Oh." Penny deflated. "I guess not. I tell you, that woman ruins all the fun. Well, we'll save this for next time. Miss Janie doesn't come to every Lookout Point. Thank heavens for that." She pulled out another top. "This one is nice, too." It was a plain, short-sleeved pale blue button-down. "With your pretty face and sweet smile, you don't need a frilly top to catch a man's eye anyway. You'll see."

Harper hoped not. "I'm not really—"

"Oh, I know. I know." Penny waved her aside. "You're not looking for any romance. I heard you the first time, honey. But, the way I see it, you're so young and pretty, romance is bound to come looking for you." She grinned.

And Harper smiled back.

"There now." Penny nodded. "That smile is a winner." She laid the blouse on the bed, nodded and stepped back. "I'll let you get ready. Don't forget, we've got—" she glanced at her watch "—oh, my, about eight minutes." She opened the door. "No time to dawdle." With another smile, she was gone.

Harper stared at the closed door, stunned by the sudden silence. "Wow." Penny Winston was probably in her mid-fifties but she had more energy than a woman half her age—character, too. And yet, Harper liked her. The same could be said of Hoss and Rooster. With their well-lined, weathered faces and gray-and-white hair, they could be anywhere from early sixties to early seventies but they worked just as hard as the ranch hands.

She stretched her back, rolled her shoulders and felt far more optimistic about making it through the night. She dressed, brushed out her hair, dabbed on some lip gloss and put on her small gold hoop earrings. After a day of jeans and boots, she decided to wear her own clothing. With her blue button-down, she wore a lightweight cotton khaki skirt and tan espadrille flats.

Her reflection was nothing remarkable. "Plain old

Harper. At her mousy best." Which was fine with her. A mouse was good at hiding—which seemed to be the goal for tonight. Not only was she hiding from Miss Janie but also from any of the "good men" Penny might try to send her way. Part of her was curious to know who Penny might have in mind for her and if, maybe, she should tell her to take Ames Paxton off the list. In case Penny hadn't picked up on the way he'd been treating her all week, that is.

She shook her head. No more thinking of Ames. He was on her "to be avoided at all costs" list. Right up there with Miss Janie, tied for the top slot. If she was going to have any fun tonight, she'd do her best to steer clear of both of them.

Ames sat at one of the firepits—one picked as far as possible from the grills or tables or dance floor. He wanted to enjoy tonight and people watching was one of his favorite pastimes. Maybe it was because talking too much could make things awkward when his voice did its own thing. And since he'd never learned how to make small talk, watching was more fun.

Plus, Miss Janie was here and in rare form. She seemed louder than normal. Which was saying something since Ames already considered her the loudest person he knew. Something about bringing in new investors to help out with the grasslands management project they were wanting to start had her all fired up.

The Winston siblings were all in their sixties, but that didn't stop them from being committed to environmentally conscious practices, from helping with the bison repopulation program to installing solar panels. Every little thing helped.

"Another?" Lars Christensen, a South Camp ranch hand, sat in the chair opposite Ames. He had the cooler open and tilted forward in case Ames wanted another bottle of soda.

"I'm good." Ames smiled. "But thanks."

"She always talking." Lars nodded at Miss Janie, then sat back in his chair. "Talk-talk-talk. On and on. So much." English wasn't Lars's native language—but he was pretty good at making himself clear.

"Agreed." Ames laughed.

"Give my head to aching." He pressed the bottle of soda to his temple.

Ames chuckled again.

There was a lull in conversation, which Ames was fine with—but it didn't last for long.

Lars shared how one of the pregnant mares was coming along, that Tobias and Maverick—two more South Camp hands—had gotten into another fistfight, and that he was learning some new songs on the guitar.

Ames mostly nodded in response but, really, he was only half listening. The whole time Lars was talking, he found himself tracking Harper's movements. It wasn't intentional—it just sort of happened. All the time. Every meal, all damn week. Meaning he couldn't blame it on Miss Janie being here.

So far tonight, Harper had done a good job of avoiding the older woman. Once, Harper had spun around on her heel and hid behind one of the support columns of the pavilion when Miss Janie walked by. Not exactly stealthy, but effective enough. Plus, it'd made Ames laugh.

"The truck blew up," Lars was saying.

That caught Ames's attention. "What now?"

"The engine smoking and clicking." Lars shook his head.

"Overheated?" Ames was pretty sure he'd have heard about a truck blowing up.

"Yeah, yeah, that." Lars chuckled. "So I take it to the shop—"

Ames watched as Gabe and Eddy made their way to Harper. He had to give it to them—they'd been on their best behavior all week. But they weren't the only ones circling Harper tonight. Milo Cruz, from Horse Camp, and North Camp's Javi weren't far behind. He sighed and took a long sip off his root beer. The damn fools were all vying for her attention but, even from this distance, Ames could tell she didn't like having them fawn all over her. Her smile was forced and she seemed…wary. Everything about her posture had him tensing up, wondering if she was okay.

Aw, come on. Dammit all.

There it was. That protective thing. Rising up, grabbing him by the throat and kicking the ground out from under him. He'd been fighting against the feeling all damn week but there was no stopping it. Because of Harper, his own instincts were working against him.

And, just like Monday night, he was pissed off all over again.

It wasn't fair. Why *this* woman? If he was going to get derailed by this peculiar tangle of emotions, why couldn't it have been someone else? Anyone else? Athena? Ellie? Hell, even Brandy. Well, maybe not Brandy—she'd punch him in the face for even thinking such a thing.

He shook his head.

This had nothing to do with Harper being a woman and everything to do with how vulnerable and lost she looked. Just like Copper or Daisy had been when he'd found them. He was feeling protective of her, like he'd felt for them. It had nothing to do with her being a woman.

And he was going to keep telling himself that until he believed it.

"Gotta go." Lars stood. "Warming up the guitar time."

"Good luck." Ames watched the man walk through the crowd to where the musicians were gathering.

Lookout Point was all about good food, good music and good company. Hoss and Rooster believed in hard work but they also understood that in order to keep this place running smoothly, having a close-knit and strong community was essential. Tonight, any one of them could get up and air a grievance or make a suggestion and expect to be heard. They were all invested in this place and Hoss and Rooster never took that for granted.

Ames got roped into helping with the barbecue shortly thereafter. He made three trips from the large pit grills to the pavilion, carrying large foil pans stacked high with smoked brisket, turkey, chicken, sausage and ribs.

Penny was there, directing everyone. With all the salads, side dishes, breads, sauces and condiments and meat, everything had to be arranged just so.

"Right there, Ames." Penny gave him a smile—but her eyes were narrowed enough to make Ames hesitate when she said, "I need you for a sec."

He was hungry so he hoped whatever she needed wouldn't take long. "Ma'am."

"Why are you shooting Harper Lynn the stink eye? Avoiding her like the plague?"

Ames stared down at the woman, momentarily thrown off. "What…? I—I'm not."

"I'm seeing things, then?" She crossed her arms over her chest. "You were doing it five minutes ago, over there." She nodded where he'd been sitting. "And this morning at breakfast, too. All week—starting Tuesday, I reckon."

He sighed.

"I was hoping you'd snap out of it but you didn't. And I'm disappointed in you, Ames." She shook her head. "I asked Calder why you were acting like a jackass and he tells me something happened Monday night? Right before you started acting up."

Calder? Really? Ames resisted the urge to run a hand over his face. Instead, he looked over the woman's head, scanning until he found Calder—who was grinning at him, completely unapologetic. Ames itched to shoot the man the bird but knew Penny would just love that. More like, she'd box his ears. "Nothin' happened."

"You being rude is something, Ames Paxton." She wagged her finger at him, like he was some kid needing a talking-to. "You know the others take cues from you."

What now? That was just about the biggest steaming pile of horse crap he'd ever heard.

"That sweet thing is barely holding on, Ames." Penny grabbed his forearm.

It was a relief to know he wasn't the only one who had picked up on Harper's fragility but he didn't like how Penny was acting like he had something to do with it.

And he needed to say so, carefully. "She is." He forced the words out. "Could be she's not meant for Crossroads."

"Is that so?" She snapped. "So Hoss should send her packing? Just like that? You don't think she deserves any grace—no matter what she's been through?"

Hearing it put that way made him feel like a real bastard. "Wait." Did Penny know Harper's past? "You know—"

"I will not wait." She had her hands on her hips now. "You know how hard she worked this week? Never once complained." She was openly scowling at him. "And what if Hoss had given up on you one week in? Or Logan? Or Tripp? Or any number of folks now calling Crossroads their home?"

"Logan or Tripp—hell, anyone living here now didn't need babysitting when they got here. Or protecting." He cleared his throat and nodded at Harper's pinched expression and her entourage of ranch hands. "She's too nice to tell 'em off." The way Gabe was looking at Harper, appreciative and far too eager, had Ames gritting his teeth. "She's not like you, Brandy or Athena. She's not tough or thick-skinned."

"That's the problem? She's too nice? That she might need someone to show her the ropes—teach her it's okay to stand up for herself?" Penny waited but he knew better than to answer that. "There's likely a reason she's timid like that, Ames. You know that."

He did and he wouldn't let himself think about it. The last thing he needed was another reason to get worked up and into protector mode.

"This is a whole new world for her, poor thing. Lonely,

I imagine. Probably wants a friend is all. What's so wrong with that?" She shook her head.

Do you want to be my friend, Ames? He could still hear her, still see her, asking him that.

He'd been a bastard for not answering. Even more so for pushing her away Monday night. Treating her like a dog—telling her to leave. Penny was right to be disappointed in him.

"I'm not sure why you dislike her but you need to accept she's one of us now." Penny's tone brooked no argument.

He didn't dislike Harper. It was just…her being here was a real problem. For him. "She… I…" There was nothing left to say—when it came to Harper, anyway. He broke off, ran a hand along the back of his neck and asked, "Did you need me to do somethin'?"

She stared up at him for a long time. "I need you to sort yourself out. And if you see Harper is uncomfortable and you won't step in, come tell me, Hoss or Rooster and *we* will take care of it." She clicked. "Now stop standing there and go get more food." She waved him off.

Seconds later, he saw Penny disentangling Harper from her moony-eyed fanboys. Penny would keep an eye on her so he didn't have to. He'd stay busy and not worry about anything… Or anyone.

For the most part, that worked. Dinner was a lively affair. Clean-up was too. Once that was done, cookies and ice cream were served to anyone wanting dessert and the announcements began.

"Not much on the list tonight. We've the Horsemanship Clinic coming up in a couple of months and—" Hoss read off a list of things from the tablet in his hand, then said, "And, lastly, we want to welcome Harper Lynn to Crossroads. I hope you'll all take some time to introduce yourselves and make her feel at home. That'll be all. Let's get to dancing."

Ames shoved the last of his cookie into his mouth. There'd been no hope for it—Hoss had to introduce her. But, by doing that, he'd put a big ol' target on Harper's back. A quick search showed Miss Janie had, yep, perked right up and was scanning the crowd.

Dammit. Dammit all.

The music was starting and the crush of people heading to the dance floor gave him a minute to find Harper. She was hanging back, her arms wrapped around her waist, staring up at the star-filled sky. It was like she'd never seen the night sky before. She was so caught up in it that she didn't see Miss Janie making a beeline in her direction.

Ames did and that's what set him in motion. There was no time to find Gabe or Eddy to intercept the woman. He'd have to do it. About the time he wondered if he should run, Martha Kelly waved Miss Janie over—buying Ames some much-needed time.

He was out of breath by the time he reached Harper. "Harper." Her name shot out, deep and gruff and downright aggressive, but there was no help for it.

Harper jumped, facing him with wide-eyed surprise, her hand pressed to her chest.

From the corner of his eye, he could see Janie and Martha were still chatting. He hadn't thought this far ahead. Now what? Getting her away from Janie Winston was the goal so… "Dance with me?"

"You want to dance with me?" Her confusion was almost comical. Almost.

Hell, no. But he nodded.

"*You?* Want to dance with *me*?" She repeated.

"Yes." This time, he managed not to snap.

She tucked a strand of her long hair behind her ear. "I can't dance."

Time was up—Janie was headed for them.

"I'll teach you." He grabbed her arm and tugged her toward the dance floor. He half expected her to yank loose and tell him off—that's what he deserved. But, as he'd witnessed earlier, she was too polite to make a scene. And he was counting on that. As soon as they stepped onto the dance floor, she stared up at him and he realized he'd trapped himself.

"Ready?" he mumbled.

She nodded.

That makes one of us. Hell, it was a dance. Just one. Nothing to get him worked up over.

He took a deep breath and stepped forward, releasing her wrist to take her hand. No point letting himself get distracted by the fit of her hand in his. Or that she smelled like peppermint, either. Or that, when he rested his hand at her waist, he thought he heard her breath hitch and that sound had his stomach go tight.

It was fine.

It was good.

They were moving to the music, like two normal people having fun.

Only she wasn't smiling at him. She was watching him—but not smiling.

And, dammit, he couldn't smile at her. He was just…

feeling… So many things. Mostly, it was an ache. Raw. Hollow. It was too strong to ignore. He was getting all twisted up inside. His heart was thundering faster than was healthy and breathing meant drawing in her scent that had him damn near tripping over his own feet. The longer he spent staring down at her, the more it felt like he was trying to keep his head above water. Because, any minute, there was a real possibility he was about to get sucked into the undertow and drown in her eyes.

He didn't care that they weren't keeping time with the music—he considered it a victory he was moving at all. She was moving with him—following his lead. If what he was doing could be called leading?

Focus, man.

Not on her, but on the music.

Not on the folk likely watching him make an ass of himself, but on getting through the song.

Not that he liked her hand clinging to his. Or that he was so damn aware of the slight weight of her other hand resting on his chest. Everything about this moment made him want to keep her right where she was. Close to him. In his arms. Looking at him like, maybe, she felt this pull between them, too.

He swallowed hard. He had to stop thinking like this. So why couldn't he?

Dammit all to hell. He was in trouble.

Chapter Eight

Harper knew she had a white-knuckled grip on Ames's shirt but it was the only thing keeping her upright. That and his hand at her waist. It wasn't just resting there now—he was holding her and pulling her closer to him. Which made it incredibly hard to breathe or think or keep herself balanced and steady. Nothing felt balanced. Or steady.

Ames stared at her. Unflinching and overwhelming. She wasn't sure which of them threaded their hands together—only that the warmth of his rough fingers sliding between hers set every hair on her body upright. How could such a simple touch feel so…intimate? It did. So much so that a tremor shot from the tips of her fingers to race up the length of her spine. What would he do if she melted against him? At this point, it was a very real possibility. But she didn't want to do anything that might sever the electrified threads binding them to one another.

Ames's brown gaze shifted to her mouth and the tiniest noise slipped from her. It was involuntary but…no man had ever looked at her that way and she was more than a little rattled by all of this. By him. He wanted her—looked ready to devour her, really. That was it. That was exactly how he was looking at her. Like she was dessert. A burning throb started, low in her belly.

Did he want to kiss her right now?

Did she want him to kiss her?

Yes. She did.

Which was a surprise. A delightful surprise.

Everything felt magnified. The worn fabric of his shirt as she gripped it tight. The press of his big hand at her waist. The brush of his calloused thumb along the back of her hand… And that shudder that rolled over her?

"Harper…" The way her name slipped from him had her shuddering all over again.

But there was a loud crash behind them, breaking the threads pulling them together and jolting her, firmly, back to reality.

Something had changed… People were gathering on the edge of the dance floor. No one was dancing? Because… "The music has stopped," she whispered. How long had they been standing here like this? "Should we—"

"Come with me?" Ames was staring at the commotion behind her, the muscle in his jaw flexing. "Harper?" He glanced at her, his hand slipping from her waist as he stepped back.

But he didn't let go of her hand.

She nodded, letting him lead her past the people, through the pavilion, and out on the other side. It was much quieter here, cooler and darker, too. But the flames from a deserted firepit he was leading her towards hadn't entirely flickered out.

"You know…" He paused, his pace slowing. "You need to be careful. At night. Real careful. Out here." His words were rushed, running into one another.

She wasn't sure what she'd been expecting him to say but that was not it. "Oh?"

"Snakes. Javelina. Cactus." He took a deep breath. "Don't go off alone."

She gave his hand a squeeze in case he needed reminding. "I'm not."

He nodded, glancing down at their joined hands. A furrow settled between his brows.

She tended to avoid conflict and awkward conversations, and she'd never been the assertive type. But she was tired and confused, her body was still recovering from the live-wire experience that had happened on the dance floor, and she needed to understand what was happening between them. "You don't want to hold my hand?" she asked.

"Maybe. I don't know. This… It's…different." He sighed.

Well, that wasn't exactly a happy sound. She tugged her hand free from his. "The whole man of mystery thing makes for an interesting character in books or movies but, in real life, it turns out I'm not a fan." She peered up at him but couldn't make out his features in the dark. "You…you're like a human roller coaster ride, Ames. Up and down and *all* over. I don't know what's coming next. And I'm a little scared."

"Scared?"

She nodded. "Monday you told me to get lost. You ignored me all week. Tonight you ask me to dance." She ticked off each statement on her fingers. "What happens tomorrow?" Now that she'd asked the question, it worried her.

"Is that all that tonight was?" He shoved his hands into

his pockets and moved closer to the firepit, kicking at a rock. When he glanced at her, the fire cast just enough light to see him. He looked…troubled. "A dance?"

No. But the word got stuck.

"I—" He cleared his throat, his gaze falling from her. "I get real…protective around you." He took off his hat and ran his fingers through his hair. "There's no stopping it."

She was stunned by this announcement. *Protective?*

"I thought space—between us—would help. Didn't." He spun his hat in his hands. "I was wrong." He paused. "I can't shake this…whatever this is."

She swallowed against the tightening in her throat. What exactly was he trying to say? Was this good? Bad? "But you would? Shake this—I mean. If you could?"

He stared at her for a long time before running his fingers through his hair again. "When I saw Miss Janie heading your way tonight, I had to step in—"

"That's why you asked me to dance?" That stung. And left her second-guessing every second she'd spent getting all swoony and rubber-kneed in his arms. "You were on some sort of rescue mission?"

"No." He shook his head. "Yes. Hold up." He stepped closer. "It was an excuse—I wanted to go after you." He cleared his throat. Twice. "I've been an asshole… Saying and doing everythin' wrong." He paused. "I'm sorry."

But his words were replaying through her mind to scramble up her insides all over again. Maybe she'd heard wrong? How could a man say so much while saying so little? She shook her head. "To clarify, when you say you feel *protective* of me… Do you mean protective like an older sibling protective? Or uncle or some other family member or close friend that should be protective in a purely platonic sort of way?"

The corner of his mouth kicked up. "Is that what you think I mean?"

"I—I don't know what to think." She threw her hands up. "My whole life, I've been the mouse. So much so it became my actual nickname. I am quiet and shy, and, for the most part, invisible. And I'm fine with that." She gestured to him. "And men—especially big manly handsome ones—have never seen me. Again, I'm okay with it. I'm used to it. But tonight… You. And this." She pointed between the two of them. "I don't know what to…think."

He stared at her, wearing an almost puzzled expression. With a slight shake of his head, he took another step and erased any space between them. "I *see* you, Harper." Slowly, he traced his fingers along the side of her cheek. "Even when I try not to, I do."

"You do?" She broke off, trying to wrap her head around what he was saying.

He tilted her chin up so their gazes locked. "You felt it, same as me." His voice was delightfully gruff as he said, "Wanting you is taking some getting used to."

Oh, my. She swallowed. "You. Want… Me?" The last word was more of a squeak.

He smiled at her then.

The fire in his eyes wiped out any lingering doubts. It didn't make sense for him to want her but she wasn't going to point that out to him. Maybe it was wrong or selfish but she'd like him to look at her like this for a while longer. She'd never been desired before—not like this anyway. She liked it. She liked being desired by Ames. "Do you want to kiss me?"

"If you're asking." His other hand came up to cradle her face.

His fingers might be calloused but his touch was surprisingly tender. When he bent his head toward hers, Harper's anticipation had her teetering forward to rest her hands on his chest. She pressed her eyes closed, the brush of Ames's breath on her cheek knocking the air from her lungs.

It was the barest brush of his mouth on hers. Hardly a kiss, really. But it was a promising beginning.

His kisses started out gently. Light and soft—almost teasing. But when her lips parted just enough for his breath to mingle with hers, Harper was undone. She couldn't stop the small groan that slipped from her any more than she could stop herself from sliding her arms around his neck and pressing herself against him.

This is what it feels like to really, truly want. She'd read about it in books but this was a first for her… It turned out really, truly wanting someone was an all-consuming experience. She wanted the steel bands of his arms to pull her more tightly against him. She was gasping with want for his lips and tongue. She wanted to stay entirely caught up in his scent and feel and touch.

"Harper." The way he basically growled her name did nothing to tamp down this hunger. "This is too fast."

"Is it?" She didn't think so. She was on fire for this man—and more than content to stay that way for the foreseeable future. So she stood on tiptoe and pressed a kiss against the side of his neck. He was delicious.

He groaned. "I didn't bring you out here for this…"

"I don't mind." She tried to reach his earlobe.

His hands rested on her shoulders. "I do." He was

breathing hard as he stopped her advances. "I want you—"

"I want you, Ames. I've never wanted anyone or anything like this. Ever." She froze, slammed a hand over her mouth and shook her head. *No-no-no.* She'd said that. Out loud. And there was no way—no way—he hadn't heard her.

"You okay?" He sounded concerned but she couldn't be sure because she was still covering her face.

"Mmm-hmm," she murmured. Absolutely horrified that what she'd been thinking came pouring out of her mouth but, otherwise, she was okay.

"You sure?" He sighed. "I didn't mean for things—" he cleared his throat "—to get out of control."

"It's not your fault. I was the one trying to climb you like a tree." She took a deep breath and peered up at him. Luckily, thoroughly humiliating herself had knocked her hunger from raging to tepid at best.

"A tree, huh?" He grinned.

It was a devastating grin. Borderline lethal, really. Was it any wonder she'd lost control? Look at him. He was so… Ames. She sighed.

He shook his head. "What?"

"This." She pressed against his chest. "This isn't how I usually spend my Friday nights."

"No?" He pulled her into a loose hug.

"No. No dancing or barbecue or making out with cowboys." She rested her head against his chest, savoring the rapid thump of his heart beneath her ear.

"Not with cowboys?" He chuckled.

"Or…anybody. I wasn't kidding about the whole mouse thing." She looked up at him.

He kept on smiling. “Don’t see it.” He smoothed her hair back.

“Really?”

He nodded, studying her—in that unique Ames way of studying her.

“And tomorrow… What happens then?” She almost wished she hadn’t asked the question. She hurried on, trying to make light of it. “Is this one of those Cinderella moments? Over at midnight?”

His smile faded. “Is that what you want?”

She shook her head. “I’m giving you an out.”

“I was thinking I’d stay close to you.” He was watching her, waiting.

“Hmm.” She shrugged. “I guess I’m okay with it.”

He ran his fingers along her jaw, then took a deep breath. “You ready to head home?”

“Yes.” And since it was at least a forty-minute drive back to the Big House, she’d get to spend more time with him.

“Let’s go.” He took her hand in his.

She didn’t know how he navigated in the dark, but he did—managing to avoid the rest of the Crossroads residents, too. Now that she was clear-headed, she acknowledged he was right—they should slow down. Even though he’d said he was going to stay close, there was a part of her that knew she’d wake up in the morning and all of this—Ames, the hunger in his eyes and his kisses—would all be a dream.

Ames glanced at the clock on the kitchen wall. It was pushing six fifteen and there was still no sign of Harper. Sleeping in on weekends was expected. After five days of hard work, those extra hours in bed had been earned. He didn't begrudge her that right—only that he might not get to see her before he rode out this morning.

Weekends at Crossroads moved at a slower pace. Saturdays meant washing their own clothes and rotating essential tasks. There was no day off from things like feeding the animals, moving livestock, any maintenance that might unexpectedly arise or anything Hoss or Rooster deemed necessary. This weekend was his weekend on call—well, his and Calder's.

Meals were more leisurely, too. Kitchen duties, like the rest, rotated through the hands and residents of the ranch. One person for cooking and one person for cleaning. Brandy was the acting cook and, from the way she was wielding those metal tongs, it was obvious she wasn't thrilled about it. Gabe was in charge of cleanup so he was propped against the kitchen counter, half asleep, the dishwasher open and ready for loading. As far as weekend jobs went, kitchen duty was lightweight work. Penny and Micah made it real easy, cooking up all the weekend meals so whoever was acting as cook didn't have to do more than warm it up and set it out.

Breakfast this morning consisted of individually foil-wrapped breakfast burritos, biscuits and gravy, coffee and juice.

"Morning." Calder pulled out the chair next to Ames and sat. "You eat?" He nodded at Ames's plate.

He nodded.

"Eyes bigger than your stomach?" Calder eyed the wrapped burrito with raised brows. "If Ma sees you throwin' out food, she'll chew you a new one."

He knew. They all knew. Wasting food was frowned

on. But the burrito was for Harper, not him. He'd been worried there'd be nothing left by the time she got there. What he hadn't known when he'd taken the extra burrito was there was a whole other full tray in the oven—keeping warm.

Calder elbowed him. "You gonna be all uptight and quiet all day?"

Ames glanced at him. "You gonna eat or talk?"

Calder chuckled, unwrapping his food. "Looks good." He took a sniff, then pointed at the burrito on Ames's plate. "That for her?"

Ames could pretend he didn't understand but Calder had already figured things out, so what was the point. "Yep."

"You're not gonna thank me?" Calder shook his head. "I got my ass handed to me for knocking over that table last night. Ma is still sore about it. But that was the only reason you two didn't get caught making doe eyes at each other."

"Thank you." Ames nodded.

Calder paused, reached up to jiggle his ear, then yawned. "Did I hear that right? Did you say—"

"Thank you." Ames turned to face him. "You going to hold this against me?"

Calder took a big bite of burrito and shrugged, smiling.

"Figured." But Ames wasn't all that upset. He was grateful to Calder for causing a distraction at Lookout Point. If it hadn't been for the noise and commotion he didn't know how things would have played out.

Calder took a sip of coffee. "You two a thing now?"

Ames shot him a look.

"Don't give me a look. You were the one tripping

all over your tongue—in public—not me." He took another bite.

Ames ran a hand over his face.

"Morning, Harper." Athena called out as she pulled out the chair opposite him and Calder.

Ames looked up to see Harper standing just inside the kitchen. Seeing her did a whole lot of things he hadn't expected. His heart sort of stuttered, then kicked into high gear. His chest felt puffed up and warm from the inside. And, somehow, the morning seemed…brighter.

"Morning." Harper's voice was light and cheery.

"Don't let Brandy scare you off with those tongs." Athena pointed. "And get some biscuits and gravy, too."

For a second, Harper's hazel eyes met his. Her cheeks went pink and she smiled the sweetest smile and knowing all that was just for him had him grinning like a damn fool.

Ames knew Calder was watching him—he could feel it. That was the only reason he didn't jump up and wave Harper over. Then again, maybe he should be thankful to Calder for that, too. He wasn't so sure about letting the rest of Crossroads know about the two of them yet.

The two of them. *Us*. He grinned.

Calder saw his grin—and rolled his eyes. "Don't make me choke, man," he grumbled, emptying his cup of coffee. "Be back."

Ames braced himself as Calder walked over to Harper and Brandy. He said something that made Harper laugh and Brandy slam a burrito onto Harper's plate. Ames was used to Brandy's constant foul mood but Harper wasn't. He hoped she wouldn't take it too personally. Brandy made it her personal mission to make others as uncomfortable as possible.

"Ames," Athena whispered. "You need to be careful."

"Sorry?" Ames wasn't so sure he'd heard her.

"Dude. I saw you." Athena fanned herself. "I helped Calder flip that table, too. It was heavier than expected."

She what now? He wasn't sure what to say.

"If word gets out you like Harper, it'll cause a whole *thing*. My brother and Eddy and, well, probably all of them, will turn it into some stupid competition. They're way too competitive for their own good. You know it. I know it. And I wouldn't do that to Harper. She's too sweet to get caught up in some tug-of-war game like that." She rolled her eyes.

He wasn't feeling any better when she finished talking. Because Athena was right—about all of it. "I appreciate it."

"I won't even say you owe me one *or* hold it over you." Athena grinned. "Calder is totally going to, by the way. But *my* lips are sealed." She pretended to lock her lips.

About that time, Calder and Harper joined them.

"Here you go." Calder pulled out a chair so Harper could sit.

"Thank you." Harper put her plate on the table and sat. "Morning, Ames." Her voice wobbled when she said his name.

He heard it and liked it.

But, from the corner of his eye he saw Athena and Calder glance at each other and make a face.

Yeah, this was going to work out real well.

"What's your plan for Saturday?" Athena used her

fork to cut off a piece of biscuit. "Since you've got some free time."

"Hmm..." Harper unwrapped the burrito. "I could knit. Or...peruse the library." Her gaze darted his way. "I'm on the hunt for a good read. The kind that keeps you up all night."

Ames remembered what she'd said—she'd taken it as a personal challenge to find him a book he'd want to stay up reading all night. The book she was hunting was for him? He smiled.

"No offense but that sounds...boring." Athena wrinkled her nose.

"Oh? Okay." Harper shook a piece of tinfoil free from her finger. "What do you recommend I do?"

"Come swimming with me. There's a freshwater pool that's always icy cold—perfect for days like this." Athena smiled. "It's kinda like a mini-Balmorhea."

Harper shook her head. "Am I supposed to know what that means?" She glanced at each of them. "Is it a ranch thing?"

"No." Calder chuckled. "It's a Texas thing. Some big-ass spring-fed pool in west Texas full of clear water and fish and stuff. Ours is nothing like that."

"It's smaller but it's fed by a creek. And there are fish and turtles. And the water is clear and cold." Athena pointed at Calder with her fork. "Don't be such a negative Nelly, Calder. Or I won't invite you to come."

"Can't." Calder sat back. "Ames and I are on duty."

"On duty?" Harper picked up her burrito and turned it one way, paused, then turned it over. She set it back on her plate and picked up her fork and knife.

Ames watched, finding it impossible not to smile. He'd

never seen anyone use a fork and knife to cut up a breakfast burrito before.

"Weekends the hands rotate and get done what needs to get done. But there should still be time to swim, after." Calder shoved the rest of his burrito into his mouth.

"Are we supposed to wait and go after you're done?" Athena propped an elbow on the table.

"You could ride out with us." Ames suggested.

"Ride?" Harper's fork paused on its way to her mouth. "As in…horses?"

Ames, Calder and Athena all looked at her.

"That's what cowboys ride." Calder chuckled. "No cowboys where you come from?"

"Only when there's a rodeo in town." Harper shrugged, finally taking a bite of her burrito.

"Ricky Rodeos don't count." Calder snorted.

Watching Harper eat was entertaining. Her first bite had been hesitant but now she was chowing down and enjoying every bite.

"Are horses a problem?" Athena asked Harper. "You can ride with one of us, if you want. Might make it easier."

"Yeah, that's a good idea." Calder nodded. "You should ride with Ames. He's got that thing with animals… You know? Keeps 'em calm." He shrugged. "They like him, I guess."

"Better than you? Wow, what a surprise, Calder." Athena rolled her eyes. "But, I agree. Ames is real steady in the saddle."

Ames shot them both a look.

Harper looked at him, still chewing on a big bite of food, and raised her eyebrows—like she was asking a question.

"If you want?" Ames wasn't going to force her. He remembered how she'd reacted to Copper and Daisy. A horse was a whole lot bigger.

She swallowed. "I'm…not sure."

"Fair." He offered what he hoped was an understanding smile.

Her cheeks went that pretty shade of pink all over again.

It struck him, deep in his belly, to know that he had that sort of effect on her. That he was the one who put the color in her cheeks and that smile on her face.

"That's okay." Athena patted her shoulder. "We can walk out and see the horses. Who knows—maybe it'll change your mind."

Harper put another bite of burrito into her mouth and nodded.

"You gonna eat that?" Calder asked Ames—reaching for the extra burrito on his plate.

"Nope." Ames let him take the burrito.

"Not hungry?" Harper asked. "It's really delicious. I'm going to gain so much weight." But she didn't look bothered by that.

He was glad, too. She could use a little meat on her bones. "Already ate two. And biscuits and gravy. I'm good."

"That wasn't for him, it was for—" Calder broke off with a hiss. *"Ouch."* He jumped. "Dammit, Athena."

What the hell? Ames wasn't sure what to make of the narrow-eyed look Athena sent Calder. Or the way Calder leaned over to rub his calf.

Hold on. Athena had kicked him? It was hard for Ames not to laugh.

"You're wearing steel-toed boots. That hurt." Calder scowled at her. "Not cool."

"You're the one that's not being cool." Athena crossed her arms over her chest.

The two fell silent, locked in a silent standoff where neither of them appeared willing to blink or be the first to look away.

"Is something wrong?" Harper stopped eating, glancing back and forth between Athena and Calder.

Athena and Calder both looked at him. So Harper did, too.

"Well…uh…" He cleared his throat. "Last night… They saw us…" Ames swallowed, hard.

"And we knocked over the table so no one else noticed you two all hot and bothered over each other." Calder chuckled.

Ames frowned at Calder but it was too late, the damage was done. Harper wasn't laughing or smiling—she was embarrassed. She pressed a hand to her cheek but that didn't stop her face from turning bright red. Ames wasn't sure whether to kick Calder for being such a jackass himself or say something to make her feel better. Kicking was easy. Coming up with the right thing to say? Words had never come easy to him. But, he was gonna have to try.

Chapter Nine

Hot and bothered. Harper wasn't sure how to feel about Calder's pronouncement. She'd all but floated in for breakfast she'd been so giddy. But now… Was that all this was? Between her and Ames? Granted, it was very… sudden. They didn't know one another well. Not really. Not yet. But that would come in time, wouldn't it?

As her only real relationship was with a man she'd known since elementary school, her experience was limited. She and Walt had been friends for years before either of them had considered the other romantically. And even when that had happened, they'd had a discussion that included a pros and cons list and a five-year plan.

She had never, ever wanted to climb Walt like a tree. And trying to imagine how he would have reacted if she had acted with such uncharacteristic abandon was impossible.

When she'd been with Ames, even before last night, there'd been a pull between them that was both unnerving and exhilarating…

Which begged the question, was she romanticizing something that was based purely on physical attraction? Since she'd never had such a primal response to a man before, it was possible. She took a deep breath. But being so overwhelmingly attracted to a person didn't mean something more couldn't develop, did it? There were a lot of questions she didn't have answers to but one thing was certain—the way Calder was talking about them cheapened what had been a special evening. It had been special for her, anyway.

She avoided looking at Ames. She wasn't sure how she'd react if Ames agreed with Calder. There was a chance the burrito she'd devoured would come back up right here at the kitchen table.

"Ignore him, Harper. I always do. And don't worry. Y'all's secret is safe with us." Athena waved a hand dismissively in Calder's direction.

"Don't listen to him." Ames agreed.

"Aw, see." Athena sighed. "Honestly, I think you make a sweet couple."

Harper took a sip of her water, willing the churning of her stomach to stop.

"Couple?" Calder chuckled. "It's been what—a whole five minutes? I wouldn't start picking out wedding flowers yet, Athena." He leaned forward and said, "You two best be careful."

"Why?" Careful? She felt heat scorching her cheeks. He was not reminding them to have safe sex, was he? But the rational side of her brain kicked in and she realized there was a perfectly normal reason for the warning that was entirely work-related. "Is there an anti-fraternization policy for employees?" Hoss hadn't mentioned anything at her interview but there'd been a lot they hadn't discussed. Lots of companies had no-dating policies. And, out here, it made sense. They lived in close quarters so there was the potential for things to get messy or disruptive. It was a valid concern—and something else she hadn't really thought about last night when she was happily tangled up in Ames. "I… Will you get in trouble?" She'd only meant to glance at Ames. Now she was staring.

"Oh, give me a break with the staring and the smiling and all that." Calder sighed.

"Shut it." Athena shushed him. "If you were smart, you'd be taking notes."

Calder snorted.

If Ames heard the two of them, he didn't acknowledge it. He was doing that thing he did—staring at her the way that instantly melted her. "No rules broken, Harper."

His voice was low and gruff and enough to turn her into a boneless puddle. Lucky for her, she was sitting down so his effect on her wasn't apparent. "Good." She tore her gaze from his, desperate to get hold of her emotions before his effect on her *was* apparent to everyone else.

"Ames," Hoss called from the other side of the room, waving Ames to the table where he and Rooster were sitting. "We need a sec."

Ames hesitated, his gaze bouncing between Harper and Calder.

"I've got this." Athena smiled at him. "Don't keep the bosses waiting."

Ames hesitated, his brown eyes sweeping over Harper's face. "I'll see you later."

The crooked smile he sent her way was just as lethal this morning as it had been last night but Harper still managed to nod in answer. Disheartened, she watched him walk away. This morning was not going the way she'd dreamed. And, last night, all of her dreams had been about Ames.

"Rules wouldn't stop him, anyway," Calder mumbled. "But I was talkin' about them." He pointed at Gabe, propped against the wall sleeping, and Eddy and Logan at the buffet table—pushing each other and laughing. "You might have caught the eye of one or two others, Harper. It's likely they won't give up without a fight."

"A fight?" All Harper could do was stare at him—stunned. "A literal fight?"

"Not a *fight*-fight." Athena rolled her eyes. "For cryin' out loud, Calder. Has anyone ever told you you're melodramatic—like your mother? Eat your food and hush, will you?" She ignored his offended expression and smiled at Harper. "What he means is these boys, yes I said *boys*, get *real* competitive. You and Ames being a thing, might start some contest to win you away from him." Athena sighed. "Because getting into mischief is more fun than finding something useful to do." She rolled her eyes. "Like I said—boys. That includes my little brother. But Gabe has an excuse. He's still young."

"Are you serious?" Harper was waiting for them to all laugh. Athena was kidding, right? So was Calder? Being competitive wasn't the issue. Mattie had had a competitive streak but she couldn't imagine him pursuing a girl just because some other guy was. Then again, he'd done a lot of things she'd never suspected him of… She shook her head. The issue was—these were grown men. She couldn't believe a grown man would compete with his friends for the same woman. But the thing that guaranteed this discussion was a joke that had gone on a little too long: *she* was the woman these men would be competing for. It was so ridiculous, she laughed.

"I know." Athena laughed along with her. "They're stupid. What can I say?"

"It'd liven the place up a bit. Make things...interesting." Calder rubbed his hands together. "Course, if you two just...you know what I mean—" he bobbed his eyebrows so they all knew *exactly* what he meant.

Harper winced at the suggestion.

Seconds later, Calder bent over and started rubbing his calf. "Dammit, Athena. Stop kickin' me."

"You're an ass, you know that? Do you think or do the words come out of your mouth on their own?" Athena was glaring at him. "I hope you limp the rest of the damn day."

Harper felt a tiny bit bad for him.

"What?" Calder kept on rubbing. "I'm saying, might be the two of them need to get each other out of their system is all—" He broke off, shouted a curse and held up his hand. "You kicked my damn hand that time." He flexed his fingers.

Harper didn't feel the least bit sorry for him this time—even if Athena *was* wearing steel-toed boots. Thanks to Calder's speculation, last night had gone from special to... something else. The worst part was nothing he'd said was necessarily wrong. She wanted it to be but he'd planted the seed of doubt and, as someone who tended to jump to the worst-case possible scenario, the doubt was spreading.

"What the hell's going on over here? What's with all the yellin'?" Eddy came to the table and pulled out the chair next to hers. "You good, Harper? You're lookin' a little pale." He sat, then turned to frown at Calder. "You better watch your mouth, Calder. Harper's a real lady."

"A real lady," Gabe echoed. "And a pretty one, at that."

Harper was pretty sure Gabe had been sound asleep against the wall not five minutes ago. Now he was here, sitting beside Athena, smiling at her over his piled-high breakfast plate.

These boys can get real competitive.

Eddy draped an arm along the back of her chair. "I won't have anyone disrespectin' her."

"Including you?" Gabe pointed at him. "You're taking liberties without her permission."

Eddy sighed but lifted his arm. "I meant no offense, Harper. Guess I got so excited, I forgot my manners."

Harper looked at Athena.

Athena nodded, her hand sweeping the table as if to say, "See?"

"If you'll excuse me." Harper collected her trash and silverware. "I do have some work I need to finish up."

"But it's Saturday. And I just got here." Gabe's disappointment was sort of sweet.

"Maybe that's why she's taking off." Eddy chuckled.

"Or maybe she's had enough of both you yahoos and is making a break for it. And I don't blame her one bit." Logan toasted her with his coffee cup.

Calder and Athena found this hilarious.

But Harper was just done with all of it. Boring or not, she wanted the peace and quiet of her room. "I really do have some work to do. Have a great day." She carried her plate to the sink, scraped her trash into the trash can, rinsed her plate and loaded it into the dishwasher. When she turned to go, she almost walked right into Brandy. "Excuse me."

"And if I don't?" Brandy had a mean-girl smile.

"Then that's your choice." Harper had never had someone dislike her simply for existing before. But Brandy did—and she was really good at it.

"You hurt one of them and you'll be sorry." Her eyes narrowed to slits.

While she didn't appreciate being threatened, she couldn't fault Brandy's loyalty. "I'd never intentionally hurt anyone. Or try to make enemies."

"We'll see, I guess." But nothing about Brandy's expression softened.

When she finally managed to get out of the kitchen, she was exhausted. She hurried—but didn't run—to her room before anyone or anything else could stop her. As soon as she was inside her room, she locked the door and leaned against it. She closed her eyes and focused on taking slow, deep breaths and calming her heart rate. Slowly, the tension sapped from her shoulders and the thoughts whirling about in her head slowed enough to sort through.

She pushed off from the door and spent the next fifteen minutes straightening her room. Organizing things always made her feel better. She was headed for the bathroom when she heard the barking.

She hesitated, listening.

Copper?

Ames would be along, soon. He'd take care of her.

But five minutes later, Harper had cleaned her bathroom sink and mirror and Copper was still barking. She'd been here for a week and this was the first time the dog had done this. Was something wrong? Did Copper need help? Or Daisy?

Snakes. Cactus. Javelinas.

She had no idea what a javelina was but, since Ames

had lumped it in with a bunch of unsavory things, it couldn't be good.

Plus, there were coyotes. She remembered that video, clearly. And it had her yanking open her door. There was no point in knocking on Ames's door. If he was here, he'd have gone to check on Copper long ago. Instead, she stepped outside.

Copper's barking increased, and she'd started whimpering. She could hear Daisy, too. The little goat's bleats were just as distressing.

Harper hurried to the gate. "Hey, Copper, what's—" She got a good look at the dog and winced. "Oh, sweetie. What happened?" There were several nasty looking things sticking out of Copper's nose and muzzle. Long and white and very definitely poky. Were they porcupine quills? "I bet that hurts."

Daisy bleated.

"I get it, you're worried about your…momma." Harper opened the gate. "Come on. We'll get those nasty things out of you, okay?"

Copper and Daisy hurried inside and straight to the door. She closed the gate and followed, smiling when the two of them stopped outside Ames's door.

"He's not there, girls." She opened her door. "I know I'm not your dad, but I promise I'll do my best to help you."

Daisy trotted into her room without pause, her little tail flicking as she went.

Copper, however, gave Ames's door another look.

"I have beef jerky." Harper pointed into her room. She might need to bribe Copper to get those nasty things out. "You can eat as much as you want. Just remember, I'm trying to help you, not hurt you." She smiled down at Copper. "Deal?" Since the dog ran into her room, Harper assumed that was a yes.

Ames had been surprised when Copper and Daisy hadn't been waiting for him at the stables. He'd checked all the favorite spots on the way back to the Big House. In the shade of the big oak close to Hoss's place. Under the porch by the kitchen French doors to wait for scraps. No Copper. No Daisy. If they didn't show up for dinner, he'd worry. For now, he needed a shower before lunch. The supply order he'd been hoping to place would have to wait until later.

He opened the exterior door that led into his hall, grateful for the silence. Calder hadn't shut up the whole damn time they were out. He had something to say about Miss Janie, Athena, Eddy and Harper and, after a couple of hours, Ames had had more than enough. He rarely pulled rank but desperate times called for desperate measures. A few sharp words had Calder falling in line and pulling his weight. It'd taken longer than he'd wanted, but they'd made sure all the heifers were accounted for and there were no new calves that'd need watching.

"You like that, huh?" Harper's laughter spilled out into the hallway. "I didn't know you were a diva."

He paused. He didn't know who she was talking to. On the phone, maybe? There was still a whole lot he didn't know about her. He could feel a sneeze coming and rubbed at his nose but still wound up sneezing three times.

And from inside Harper's room, there came an awful familiar bark and bleat.

Harper yanked open the door. "You're back. They've

been waiting for you." Sure enough, Daisy and Copper were on Harper's bed, staring at him like they had every right to be there.

"Have you two been bothering Harper this whole time?" He came in, knelt alongside the bed, and gave them each a scratch behind the ear. He shook his head. "I was looking for you two, you know?"

Daisy flicked both her ears and hopped off, then back up on the bed. Copper lay down on the bed so she could press her nose against his face, her tail swishing happily.

"You're not in trouble." He accepted Copper's kisses, noticing the pink marks on her muzzle for the first time. "You hurt?"

"I think it was a porcupine." Harper retrieved the trash can and held it out so he could see inside. "I heard her barking at the gate and knew something was up. She never barks that way. She's such a good girl." Harper's baby voice had Copper wiggling all over. "Yes, you are." She smiled at his dog. "It looked like it hurt so I couldn't leave her that way."

Ames stared up at the woman. It wasn't all that long ago she'd been scared of Copper and Daisy. Now she was doctoring them? He hadn't given her enough credit. She was capable, that was obvious. Smart and caring, too. He'd been too knotted up over how she got to him to see much more than that. Harper could fit here, if she wanted too. He'd been wrong to think otherwise.

"I didn't know if they could come inside but, after all that, I figured Copper could use some pampering." Harper was hesitant to look at him—just like she'd been this morning.

He stood. "It's more than okay, Harper… Thank you."

"Anyone would have done the same, I'm sure. I had to watch a few videos first. It might surprise you to know that my veterinary skills are pretty non-existent. Normally, I'd use books but I didn't want poor Copper to have to wait any longer. Nasty things were in there, too." She set the trash can down. "I hope that porcupine gets what's coming to him."

He smiled at the snap to that last bit.

"I didn't think about whether or not they were allowed inside. I guess I should have asked but I was only thinking about Copper's nose." She gestured to the animals, lying on her nicely made-up bed, watching the two of them. "Anyway, I'm sure you've got things to do… I won't keep you."

There was no way he was leaving. Not until he set things straight between. He wasn't going to let Calder and his damn mouth get in the way of something good with Harper. The way she was fidgeting made him think she was nervous. Over what Calder had said? Or something else? "I've got nowhere to be." In fact, he was exactly where he wanted to be.

"Oh." She shifted from one foot to the other, avoiding his gaze. "You're all done with work for the day?"

Ames sighed and kicked her door shut. "Calder is an asshat." He took off his hat. "I wanted to shut him down this morning but if I'd caused a scene…" He cleared his throat, easing the tightness. "Calder's right about one thing… Eddy and Gabe would have come running." He watched her as he said, "You don't like them fawning all over you—neither do I."

That was enough to have her, finally, looking at him. "You don't?"

"Hell, no." He shook his head. "This isn't a game. And you're not some damn prize." His voice was garbled and thick, but he'd got the words out.

"Is he right about us being hot and bothered, too?" A V formed between her brows.

"Is that what's bothering you?" He tilted her chin up so he could see her clearly.

She shook her head, then nodded, then shrugged. "If that is all this is…yes. I'm not… I don't… I'm don't do casual sex. Hookups. Whatever you call it… That's fine if you are. I'm not judging anyone's choices, I'm simply saying that's not how I…do things. I thought you should know." She took a deep breath and held it, her eyes glued to his face.

"You holding your breath?" He had to smile.

"No." Breath whooshed out of her. "I'm waiting for your thoughts on what I said."

"You think I want sex?" He loved the way her cheeks went scarlet.

"Yes." She frowned. "Of course. Don't you?"

Alright, she had him there. He ran a hand over his face. "You think I *only* want sex?"

"I… I don't know. Last night, it felt like, maybe, something was starting between us—something that would definitely, maybe, include but wasn't all about sex." She took another deep breath. "But then, after hearing Calder, I wondered if it was all about being hot and bothered and I'm being ridiculous and turning nothing into something."

"You're not." He put his hands on her shoulders. "This isn't nothing. It's something." He cleared his throat. "Something good." He smiled. "And Calder? He's a damn fool."

"Okay." Her smile was a thing of beauty. "I won't listen to him anymore."

"Or Eddy." He murmured. "Or Gabe."

"Are you saying I should only listen to you?" She cocked her head to one side and reached for him.

"About us? Yes." He caught her hands in his. "I'm covered in dirt and sweat—you don't wanna get too close."

"I do, thank you very much." She waited for him to let her go before sliding her arms up and around his neck.

"Fine." He grinned and leaned forward to kiss her—

"I've been meaning to ask, what's a javelina?" She pressed two fingers to his lips. "It sounds like something you made up."

"Wild pig. Mean sonsabitches." he murmured around her fingers. "Can I kiss you now?"

"Yes." She moved her hand away and rose on tiptoe, her lips clinging to his.

Damn, but her lips were soft. Truth be told, everything about Harper was soft. Her hair, her skin, her mouth. It almost felt wrong for his work-roughened hands to touch something so fine. Almost. But now that she was in his arms and he was pulling her close, he knew nothing had ever felt this right.

He cupped the back of her head, breathing her in when her lips parted beneath his. It was easy to get lost in her. The soft sounds she made, the way her fingers tightened, the tremor that rolled over her—he wanted to savor her every response to him. He wanted to know what she liked. He wanted to know what set her on fire. What made her… climb him like a tree.

Copper and Daisy, however, decided to kill the mood.

Copper was up, swatting at his thigh with her paw. And Daisy started wailing like she was at death's door.

"What's all the fuss about?" He frowned down at the two animals but didn't let go of Harper.

"You belong to them." Harper eased out of his hold. "I'm sorry. He's yours, I know." She sat on the bed between his dog and his goat. "Here." She doled out a bit of fruit and jerky accordingly. "All better now?"

Whatever irritation he might have felt at being interrupted vanished as the three of them smiled up at him. He wasn't sure a dog or a goat could smile but it sure as hell looked like that's what they were doing.

"What? I need to stay on their good side so they won't mind us spending time together."

"Can't argue that logic." Still, he'd rather put Daisy and Copper in the garden and get back to kissing Harper.

"I'll keep an eye on them if you want to go shower. You don't want to miss lunch." She glanced at the rooster-shaped clock hanging on her wall. "I'm still full from breakfast."

"You sure?" He was disappointed when she nodded, but she had a point about getting cleaned up. And he was starving. "Fine." He couldn't help but notice neither Daisy nor Copper complained when he left them in Harper's room. "Traitors," he murmured.

The shower was cold. Like, ice-cold. Due to the size of the Big House, it had four water heaters. One for the family residence wing, one for the bunkhouse wing—this one, and another for the kitchen. Hopefully, it was only this one acting up. There weren't any spare water heaters lying around—and it took a while to get anything shipped out here. But the cold shower had the benefit of cooling him off after Harper's kisses.

He shouldn't care about what he was wearing. Harper wasn't going to be there. But he tossed the second shirt he'd tried on onto the bed and was putting on the third shirt when he heard Copper scratching at the door.

"About time you started missing me," he said, opening the door. Copper ran past him, tail wagging. Daisy did a happy little hop and bounced into the room behind Copper.

But Harper stood there—staring at his bare chest. Staring and blinking. A whole lot. She blinked a handful more times, took a deep breath, then spun on her heel. Before he realized what she was doing, she was back in her room—shutting the door behind her.

He stared at the closed door. Going after her was a bad idea. They'd just established they were both hoping for something more—something beyond a physical connection. But he'd be lying to himself if he wasn't tempted.

"I didn't see anything." Calder's voice carried down the hallway.

Dammit! Ames turned to see the man, his hand covering his eyes, at the end of the hallway. "Funny." He snapped up his shirt and tucked it into his clean jeans.

"Earlier, you said it's none of my business. But, since what I just *didn't* see happened in a public space, it kinda is my business." Calder leaned against the wall. "What are you thinking? Going to lunch?" Calder pointed over his shoulder with his thumb. "Or no lunch." He pointed at Harper's door.

Ames wasn't going to answer that. Daisy and Copper were cuddled up on the oversize dog-bed in the corner so he pulled the door shut and walked down the hall, past Calder, and headed for the kitchen. But food wasn't foremost in his mind. He *was* hungry—for Harper. And if he didn't rein in his desire, he was going to wind up taking another ice-cold shower real soon.

Chapter Ten

Harper hadn't meant to doze off. She'd worked some on her scarf, considered sending an email to her parents, then propped herself up to read. But the book was on the floor by her bed and her room was full of shadows when she jerked awake. Her dreams had started with Ames. Shirtless. And how, instead of running into her room, she'd grabbed hold of him and... Well, she'd had plenty of reason to stay asleep. But then she and Ames were walking in that park on that day and the screams and the gunfire started, as always. Suddenly, Ames had disappeared and Harper felt the bullets pierce her thigh and side—and woke her up dazed and panting.

She turned on the lamp by the bed, saw the clock and bolted upright. It was five thirty? She'd slept for three hours?

That explained why she was so hungry.

And she wanted to see Ames. Seeing him would chase off her bad dreams so she could focus on the good ones. Ames. *With or without his shirt.* She wasn't picky. The mind-blowing image of his rock-hard abs and chest had given her overzealous imagination all sorts of inspiration. Unfortunately, she knew she'd never try to initiate any of her fantasies. Not because she had loads of self-control—

she was just too shy. Ames, on the other hand, had already proved he was more in control of himself. He'd been the one to separate them at Lookout Point and he'd tried to hold her off because he hadn't wanted to get her dirty.

She stood, stretched and headed into the bathroom. Once the shower was on, she stripped and stepped under the water. It took a few minutes for the water to warm up so she poured a dollop of bodywash onto her loofah and started scrubbing. The fresh scents of tea and eucalyptus perked her up. She'd just washed her body and was soaping up her face when the water went from lukewarm to ice-cold.

The shock of it had her stepping back, slipping on the bodywash, and, with a shriek, she went down, hard, on her rear. "That's going to leave a bruise." She rubbed her backside and turned her face into the water to stop the soap from getting into her eyes.

Too late. "Wonderful." Her eyes were burning and she couldn't see a thing. She was swiping and mumbling and leaning out of the shower to hunt for her towel.

That's when she heard Ames.

"Harper? I heard you yell." He sounded close. "Are you okay?"

Her eyes popped open—and the soap suds flooded in. "Oh, ow-ow-ow." She blinked and blinked, but it didn't help.

"Harper." He knocked on the door. "You hurt?"

"No." She kept blinking as she searched for her towel. There it was, right out of reach. She stood, leaned forward and slipped again. This time she caught herself but she slammed her elbow into the shower frame in the process. "Dammit."

"Need help?" He sort of barked the question, gruff and hard-sounding.

"No." She shook out her tingling arm, grabbed the towel and frantically wiped at her eyes. "I'm okay." And she wanted to keep it that way so she took extra care stepping from the shower onto the mat on the floor. "Sorry I scared you. I'm fine. You can go." *Please, please, go.* "Really." She secured the towel around her chest, counted to fifty, then opened the bathroom door. *Is he gone?* She squeaked. "Ames?"

Then she saw him, walking out her door…

But he spun when he'd heard her, saw her and quickly shut his eyes. "You're good?" His jaw clenched.

"Yes. Sorry. The water was freezing."

"Damn, I forgot to tell you." He opened his eyes, stared at her bare shoulders, then stared up at the ceiling. There it was, another jaw clench. "Water heater is out." He cleared his throat. "I—I'm going." He was so focused on looking up at the ceiling that he walked straight into the wooden doorframe. His head bounced off the frame from the force of impact.

She hissed. "You're going to need an ice pack, Ames—"

"No, stay there," he grumbled and pressed a hand to his forehead. "You stay. I'll go." He practically ran from her room.

She winced at the sound of his door slamming.

Harper dressed for dinner and sat on the side of her bed to wait for Ames. Was his head okay? Did he put any ice on it? She'd found some anti-inflammatories for him. When it was six, she set the bottle of anti-inflammatories on the floor outside his door and headed to the kitchen. If they were going to try to fly under the radar it was probably best if they didn't arrive together.

The kitchen smelled wonderful. While she wasn't familiar with a lot of the food served at Crossroads, most of it was the sort of stick-to-your-ribs fare that was going to stick to her hips and thighs if she wasn't careful. Penny wasn't helping. She seemed to have a vested interest in ensuring Harper ate too much at every meal.

Tonight's meal was corn on the cob, black-eyed peas and collard greens, and what looked like spaghetti but had bacon and sausage and hamburger so, clearly, it wasn't *spaghetti*-spaghetti.

Brandy was in line of front of her. She gave Harper's plate a long look. "That's not gonna fly for Penny, book-girl."

Harper almost smiled at that. Brandy had a nickname for her? And it wasn't an insult. Considering the offensive and colorful the things she called her fellow ranch hands, Harper wasn't sure whether to be flattered or offended by her unoffensive and tame new moniker. Instead of saying as much, she smiled at Brandy and added another small scoop of the whatever spaghetti-pasta-stuff onto her plate. Brandy snorted, then walked to the table. Harper followed, sitting at the first available chair she came to.

"You good, Harper? We missed you at lunch." Eddy was sitting across the table.

She nodded. "I'm embarrassed to admit I slept all afternoon." She took the basket he offered her. "Thank you. I am starving."

"So, I finally get to meet the lovely Harper." Janie Winston stood across the table from her, a smile on her lips that didn't quite reach her eyes. She lacked the warmth and welcome that Hoss and Rooster both radiated. "I'm Miss Janie."

"It's a pleasure to meet you." Intimidated was more like it. Unlike her brothers, Janie's clothes were designer, her platinum-colored hair was a stylish, long pixie cut, and her make-up was flawless. From the looks of it, she was in her fifties and the youngest Winston sibling. "I've heard so much about you." As soon as she said it, she regretted it.

"I just bet you have. I've been getting an earful about you myself." Miss Janie sat in the chair directly across from Harper. "You seem to be real popular with some of the fellas at this table." The woman didn't seem happy about this. "How was your first week here at Crossroads? I guess you worked extra hard to nap the day away." There was a whole lot of judgment in her narrowed eyes. "Good for you for taking care of yourself."

Harper felt like she was teetering on a high wire without a net. Which was probably what Janie Winston wanted her to feel. She'd heard enough about the woman to know she needed to be careful—she was beginning to see why. "I think it went well. There's a lot to see and learn. All of it new."

"Nothing like where you came from?" Miss Janie asked, taking a piece of garlic bread from the basket.

"No. Nothing like it." Harper agreed, twirling a sizable amount of pasta onto her fork and shoving it into her mouth. If her mouth was full, conversation wouldn't be easy.

"Harper, honey." Penny's hand rested on her shoulder. "You go on back for seconds so you don't fall over from hunger, you hear?"

Harper gave her a thumbs-up, her mouth too full of food to do much else.

Penny gave her shoulder a squeeze.

"She's settling right in. But if you need any help, Harper, come find me." Eddy winked at her.

Brandy mumbled, "Are you trying to kill my appetite?" but everyone at the table heard her.

"You haven't taken the full tour, yet. This weekend seems like as good a time as any." Gabe propped his elbow on the table and was leaning so that he was basically blocking—and irritating—Eddy. "We could gas up the four-wheelers, have some fun, too?"

Harper patted her mouth with her napkin. "I appreciate the offer, Gabe, but—"

"This seat taken?" Ames pulled out the chair beside her and sat in it.

"It is now." Miss Janie smiled at him. "How is the handsome foreman for HQ doing? Life treating you well, Ames? We haven't had a chat in ages."

"No complaints." Ames seemed completely at ease with the woman. "You?"

Harper took another, smaller bite of her pasta. She didn't know what it was called, but it was delicious.

"Me? Oh, dear, where should I start?" Miss Janie set her fork down. "I'm on the National Cowgirl Museum & Hall of Fame board now, don't you know?" She listed off several other important-sounding organizations she was involved with. Harper hadn't heard of most of them but the list sounded impressive all the same.

"And I've found myself a new beau." Miss Janie patted her wavy platinum chin-length hair. "He's a doll. I don't even mind he's got a belly or that he enjoys a cigar now and then. I'm thinking he might just suit well enough to be husband number five."

Harper almost choked on her pasta. Five? She swallowed, carefully, and took a sip of the glass of water Ames, thankfully, put beside her plate.

"Does he know this?" Ames asked, a slight smile on his face.

Goodness, he has a handsome profile.

"Of course not, darling. What fun would that be?" Miss Janie laughed.

"I can't say." Ames shrugged.

"No? Come talk to me when some lucky thing catches your eye. I'll tell you how to make her head over heels in love with you." Janie shot him a knowing smile. "I've had plenty of time to figure out how the human heart works. And I'm an excellent judge of character. I knew after ten minutes Franklin would be a part of my future." Miss Janie's sharp gaze shifted back to Harper. "It's a matter of asking the right questions and reading body language. Just now, I was trying to get to know our Miss Harper, here. Give me ten minutes and I'll know if she'll be a part of Crossroads' future." Miss Janie paused. "I might only need eight minutes."

Is that an insult? It felt like an insult. What reason did the woman have to insult her?

"What do you think of our elusive new housekeeper, Ames?" Miss Janie asked, all smiles for Ames.

"Elusive?" Eddy scratched the back of his head.

"I've had a hard time finding her. It's the strangest thing, but, I feel like Miss Harper here has been going out of her way to avoid me?" Miss Janie said this with a smile. "One second she was there, then, poof, I'd turn around and she'd be gone."

"Harper?" Ames asked, letting everyone in the room breathe a little easier. "I think…" He paused, glancing at Harper.

It was unfortunate that he looked at her then—when she was taking another large bite of pasta.

"She's doing fine." He shrugged.

Harper resisted the urge to smile at him. It wouldn't have been a nice smile, considering she'd stuffed her cheeks like a squirrel prepping for winter.

"It takes time for a person to find their footing in a large operation like this. But there's no rush." Hoss was sitting at the head of the table. "From what I've seen and heard, you're living up to Crossroads' standards just fine, Miss Harper."

She smiled.

"I'm sure she is." Janie watched her chew and swallow her food. "She is…a delight." But the distaste on Janie's face said otherwise.

Harper's cheeks were burning then.

"I don't know if I'm allowed to ask but, Ames, what did you do to your head?" Miss Janie made a face. "There's a big ol' swollen red lump over your right eye. It's pretty angry looking—and new."

From this angle, Harper hadn't realized Ames's recent head injury was evident. She felt terrible about it—even worse now that it had become the topic of conversation. Now he was going to have to come up with some plausible explanation that didn't involve her—or her being wrapped in a towel. She took a long sip of water.

Calder chuckled. "You got stung by wasps and a splinter earlier this week, didn't you? Sounds like you're running out of luck."

Poor Ames.

Ames, however, silenced Calder with an icy look.

"Men and their pride." Miss Janie was laughing again. "I think a few scars makes a man even more attractive. Don't you, Harper?"

At the moment, Harper had no reason not to answer the woman. "I do." Ames's sculpted chest was one of the most beautiful things she'd ever seen. The thick, raised scar extending across his right pectoral muscle hadn't detracted from how perfect he was—to her, anyway. But it had hurt to think about how that scar had come to be. Like it hurt when she thought about how she'd got her own scars. "Scars are often a badge of survival, I think."

Ames shifted in his seat as he reached for the bread basket. But, as he offered it to her, he pressed his thigh along hers. Even after he'd set the basket aside, they stayed that way. Thigh to thigh. His solid, warm strength offering her comfort.

She smiled, twirling her fork in the pasta.

"It's always nice to see a girl with a healthy appetite." Miss Janie was watching her with slightly narrowed eyes. "Don't listen to Penny. You don't need to worry about getting seconds."

At least, this time, it was an obvious insult.

Ames froze, then leveled an icy-cold look at Janie Winston.

Harper pretended she was fixing the napkin in her lap—but, really, she gave Ames' knee a quick, reassuring squeeze. His gaze dropped but he was fuming, she could tell.

Harper was a big proponent of the whole "if you can't say something nice, don't say anything at all" philosophy. But Janie, like many others, didn't seem to agree. But why Janie Winston seemed intent on getting to Harper was the question.

Harper, however, was not going to let that happen. She smiled and sat back in her chair, patting her stomach. "Oh, I couldn't eat another bite."

Miss Janie shook her head and turned her attention to the rest of the table. "Is it true that Nick Brewer is getting married? Good for him. I admire how he doesn't let his hardships stop him from living life to the fullest."

Try as she might, Harper couldn't remember who Nick Brewer was.

"Hardships?" Ames rested an elbow on the table, his jaw clenched.

"His face. His..." Janie made a face. "Well, you know."

"No, I don't." Ames waited, his gaze openly challenging.

Harper glanced back and forth with mounting concern.

"Dessert!" Penny announced, jumping to her feet. "Who wants some banana pudding? I know I do."

That was enough to cut the tension and put everyone in motion. Everyone except Ames, Miss Janie and Harper. As much as she wanted to remove herself, leaving Ames to deal with the woman by himself felt wrong.

"My word, Ames, when did you and Nick Brewer get so close?" Janie sighed. "I didn't mean anything by it. No need to get your feathers ruffled." She stood. "I'll get you some banana pudding to make up for it." She carried her plate from the table.

From the look on his face, Harper worried Janie was

going to end up wearing the pudding she brought back to him. Tension was rolling off him in waves.

"Do you think she'll get me some pudding, too?" Harper whispered, hoping to distract him.

Ames's brown eyes went wide and then he burst out laughing.

It felt good to make him laugh. Tonight had been awkward and, at times, horrible, but they'd made it through. She might not get any banana pudding, but his laughter was just as sweet.

Ames had a bowl of banana pudding in hand and was heading for Harper's room when Hoss stopped him. "I know it's late and it's a Saturday but I need you for ten, fifteen minutes."

"Okay." He didn't bother pretending to be happy about it. He'd reached his people quota for the day. All he wanted to do now was to feed Harper some banana pudding and start reading that book she'd found for him. He was hoping he'd get her to read the book to him.

"In the lounge." Hoss's expression was almost apologetic.

Ames sighed. They only ever used the lounge to discuss business. "This Janie's idea?"

He nodded. "Penny's about to blow a gasket so the three of us need to stay calm."

Meaning he, Hoss, and Rooster were supposed to keep Penny and Janie from getting mean and nasty. Ames had seen it happen on more than one occasion. He wasn't sure he had the patience for it tonight. Especially since Janie had already been mean and nasty to Harper. "About?"

"Some fundraiser she wants to host out here." Hoss

held up his hands. "Rooster and I will shoot it down, don't worry."

Unfortunately, Hoss said this a lot. Most times, he and Rooster wound up giving Janie her way. If they didn't, she made their lives hell, which trickled down to everyone on Crossroads. It sucked, yes, but as long as Janie kept coming in here and getting her way, nothing was going to change. But he was in charge of HQ's day-in and day-out operations and making sure the place ran like a well-oiled machine. Navigating volatile sibling relationships and power plays was not part of his job description.

Penny, Rooster, Janie and Micah were already sitting around the round oak table, waiting.

"Glad you could make it, Ames." Janie smiled up at him—like the banana pudding she'd brought him had redeemed her. It hadn't. Nick Brewer had third-degree burns covering the left side of his face. For some people, like Janie, that's all they saw. Ames knew Nick never had a mean word to say about anyone. Nick was a good, hardworking member of the Horse Camp team. He'd suffered a kind of pain no one should. He deserved respect—not to be gossiped about behind his back. Ames didn't like it.

He sat in one of the overstuffed leather chairs, put his pudding on the table and settled in for whatever shit show Janie had planned.

"I asked Micah to join us to get her input." Janie stood, her smile a little too practiced as she said, "Micah will be in charge of the menus and such, of course."

Penny sniffed.

Here we go. Janie was coming out swinging. The kitchen was Penny's domain, Micah was her helper. Janie knew as much. Hell, *everyone* on Crossroads knew it.

"Back up, Janie. What, exactly, are we talking about?" Rooster steepled his fingers together, his brow furrowing deep. "And why, exactly, are we needing this?"

"Um, we're talking about money. For the upgrades the two of you've been wanting to make. Or to get Penny a new industrial washer and dryer. You've been wanting to inject new blood into the herd for a while, too." And, with that, Janie had their undivided attention.

"And?" Ames prompted.

"Let me show you." Janie dimmed the lights and clicked on the small remote in her hand. "I've put together a little something for you."

Ames stayed silent as she flipped through the pictures of fancy place settings, more flowers than a funeral home, high-class and high-dollar food, live band options, a damn fireworks show and more. "I'm confused." He cleared his throat and leaned forward. "They're buying tickets for?"

"The Crossroads Community Charity." Janie smiled, like she'd just announced world peace.

"The what?" Hoss sounded confused.

"How's that now?" Rooster ran a hand over his balding head.

"You don't need to worry about the particulars. I'll run it. We'll do a horse camp for kids once a year—maybe twice, host a couple of scholarship student interns at the Horse Camp, and let environmental studies grad students come out here to do tests and research and the like. Nothing that will get in the way of daily operations *but* just the sort of thing that people love to throw money at."

Ames ran a hand over his face.

"*You* are going to run it?" Penny asked, her tone waspish. "So, when these grad students and interns and campers come stay, you'll be here making sure they're fed, that there's housing for them, transportation to and from? Or you'll show up with a camera crew every now and then to make sure the ranch gets some headlines and *you* get credit."

Janie stared at Penny, her brows rising so high Ames wondered if they'd shoot right off Janie's forehead.

"It sounds like this will need more than one person on the ground floor, Janie. You're already involved in a whole lot back in the DFW area." Rooster stood. "Do you have someone in mind for that? For staffing? Or what you're thinking this is going to cost up front?"

"You know, there are times when I forget this place belongs to me, too." Janie crossed her arms over her chest. "You always go on about smart investing and making sure this place can survive after we're gone. Things like trusts and charities will help with that. When there are no biological Winstons left, we can ensure the ranch goes to those that love and respect the land like we do."

It was true. Rooster and Hoss worried a whole hell of a lot about the ranch's future. Hoss's kids had cut him out of their lives years ago. When Rooster and Penny married, Rooster hadn't adopted her kids because she and her ex were amicable. And Janie, for all her many marriages, had no children.

"I'll leave this here for you all to look at." She tapped the stack of leather dossiers. "You need time to think about it. That's fair." She shook her head. "But it really chaps my hide that you can't acknowledge what I'm saying."

"About?" Hoss managed not to snap—Ames had to give him credit.

"About you two running this place willy-nilly. I get you hiring on people from the prison, I do. I know your time in prison saved you, Hoss, and you want to do the same for others. And I know everyone here works hard and all that. But this new housekeeper isn't from the prison, is she? What did she do before coming here?"

Ames hadn't expected Harper to get dragged into all this. Her past was her business. Janie needed to leave it alone. If she didn't, he wasn't going to keep quiet.

"Miss Lynn was a librarian." Micah spoke up, surprising them all.

"She's highly overqualified for the job she was hired for, don't you think?" Miss Janie shot Hoss a questioning look.

"Well, I, for one, have never seen the bunkhouses so clean." Penny was quick to defend Harper. "That girl is a hard worker."

You tell her, Penny. Ames caught himself before he nodded.

"Mrs. Gable, the schoolteacher? She's has been ready to retire for a couple of years. Rooster and I were thinking Harper could take her place at the school. Our little two-room schoolhouse could benefit from having an educated teacher."

Mrs. Gable—his old teacher? Ames assumed she'd retired long ago.

"She got real excited when we mentioned the GED and college program," Rooster said. "Douglas Greer has been running that on his own. I'm betting he would appreciate the help and, maybe, not having to drive out here twice a month."

"I suppose." Janie paused. "And you checked? She *is*

a real librarian?" She glanced between her two brothers. Their guilty expression was answer enough. "Please tell me you ran a background check on the woman, at least?" The woman was real good at being condescending.

Rooster heard it and scowled at her. "I know what I need to know about the woman."

Hoss nodded and stood a little straighter. "You're gonna need to trust us on this."

"Why? Give me a reason why I should accept that someone you know nothing about is trustworthy?" Miss Janie shook her head. "Why are you so quick to trust a woman that's willing to move to the middle of nowhere and take a substantial pay cut—if she really *is* a librarian—to clean toilets."

"Are you trying to find fault with the girl?" Penny regarded Janie with an icy gaze. "Or your brothers for hiring her."

They'd all been thinking it but he'd never expected Penny to have the nerve to say as much.

"I'm making a point, Penny." Janie didn't seem the least ruffled. "I have every right to ask about who's living and working here. This is my home, too. Long before it was yours, I might add. You're here for this meeting out of courtesy to my brother, Penny."

Micah slammed her hands against the arms of her leather chair and stood. "My momma has poured blood, sweat and tears into this place. She's put her whole heart into making a home here—even when some folks have been less than hospitable. What about Ames?"

What the hell did I do? He braced himself.

"If we're talking about seniority here, he's spent more years actually on the place than *anyone* besides Hoss and Rooster. Including you. Why does that matter? It doesn't." She stared at the three siblings. "What is wrong with all of you? You're family. You're all here, alive and together. You've got this place. You should be grateful every damn day. Instead, you fight. About what? Most times, about nothing." She shook her head. "As far as this fundraiser business, you go on and hire a damn caterer. I don't want any part of it." She stormed out, with Penny hurrying after her.

"I'll leave early in the morning." Janie arranged the dossiers into a neat stack. "Ames, can you fly me home?"

Ames glanced at Hoss, who nodded. "Yes, ma'am."

"I'll be ready at six." She turned to Hoss and Rooster. "You told me to trust you but trust goes both ways, you know? You're my brothers but you have more faith in some stranger than you do in me." She glanced at the door. "I try to contribute and I get lectures and arguments and dramatic exits. Whether you like it or not, a third of this place is mine. I've been a mostly silent partner up until now but I think it's time for a change." She gave Hoss and Rooster a final look before leaving.

Ames could tell how shell-shocked the Winston brothers were. There was a whole minute of silence before Rooster asked, "Anyone else want to drive to Lubbock for a beer? Oh, hell, something strong. Like a shot of whiskey. Or a bottle?"

"Sounds good but you'll have to take a rain check." Hoss clapped Rooster on the shoulder. "It's too far a drive tonight and, after all that, Penny's gonna need you to talk her down."

"Yeah, yeah. Just like every time our sister comes to

visit." Rooster offered them a weak smile and stomped from the room, muttering.

"That was a shit show." Hoss picked up one of the dossiers, opened it and held it at arm's length so he could read it. "And that's a whole lot of big numbers." He tossed it back on the table. "She's not gonna drop it until she gets her way. She's worse than a dog with a bone. Relentless. I got a bad feeling about this." He shook his head. "Poor Harper got caught in the crossfire o' this damn mess. You think she's gonna leave it or do some digging on Harper?"

Ames nodded, studying his boss. "Is she gonna find something?"

"Of course she'll find something." Hoss gave him a long, considering look. "You think someone like Harper Lynn would come out here for no reason? She's running, all right."

Hoss's answer scared the shit out of him. And pissed him off. "What the hell, Hoss! Are you kidding me? Who is she running from? What are we doing about it? I can't protect her if I don't know what we're up against?" And no matter what, he would protect her.

"Cool your jets, son. No need to load your shotgun or get a posse together. It's just ghosts she's running from, that's all. Not much we can do to help her with that." Hoss gave him a thoughtful look. "That was a whole lot of talking. I've never heard you say so much all at once. Ever."

Relief rolled over him. There was no immediate threat against Harper… But he had firsthand experience with fighting inner demons. There'd been plenty of times he'd rather have confronted a living, breathing foe than take on those living in his mind. Being trapped in fear had been the worst kind of nightmare. That's what Harper was dealing with—stuck in her own private hell. And while Hoss might think no one could help Harper, Ames wasn't so sure about that. Might make a difference if she knew she wasn't alone anymore.

"So that's the way it is, huh? You and Harper?"

He glanced at the man he called boss but considered his father. "I'm thinking so."

"Thinking so?" Hoss chuckled.

"It's only been a week, Hoss." And of that week, how much time had they spent together? So, whatever he thought he was feeling, it couldn't be real.

"The moment I laid eyes on my Nan, I knew." Hoss shook his head. "She was sipping on a milkshake, singing along to an ABBA song, and, right then and there, I knew she was the one. Felt it. Right here." He pressed his hand against his chest. "She's been gone for more years than I had her but I feel the same every time I think of her." His smile was sad. "A week, a month, a year, your heart doesn't give a damn. You'll know."

Ames had lived for thirty-four years using his clear and level head to make decisions—that's how he'd survived. This world was hard and unforgiving—that was a fact. He knew better than to want something he couldn't have. Until now, it had never been an issue. Yes, he wanted her to stay her on Crossroads but would that make her happy? Was that best for her? No matter what his heart tried to tell him, those things mattered more.

Chapter Eleven

The second week on the ranch was easier. Now that she knew the layout of the place, there wasn't as much guesswork. And while the washing machine insisted on making an eerie otherworldly groaning when it started the spin cycle, neither machine had given her too much trouble. She'd learned about composting, trash burn-piles, and that Daisy would eat anything. So far, she'd lost a hair scrunchy, one earbud and the bunch of wildflowers Ames had picked and put on her pillow.

Her nightmares hadn't let up but finding ways to steal a bit of time with Ames made every day better. Monday, they'd met in the library and gone through at least three shelves before they'd found a book with the potential to keep him reading all night. But the best part of the book hunt was learning more about Ames. Like the fact that he'd moved to Crossroads when he was twelve, had never worked with animals before then and learned to drive a tractor when he was thirteen.

Tuesday and Wednesday had centered around Copper. She wasn't eating—which worried Ames, thereby worrying her. But a quick visit to Crossroad's resident veterinarian proved Copper was fine and healthy—and pregnant.

Harper was excited about puppies but Ames, however, was struggling with the fact that "his girl" was expecting.

Ames was gone for a windmill repair all day Thursday.

The replacement water heater arrived on Friday so, once again, Ames wasn't around as much as she'd like. After days of sponge baths and icy-cold showers, it was nice to wake up and take a hot shower this morning. It was even nicer to walk into the kitchen and find Ames there. For some reason, her dreams had been extra intense the night before. Somehow the shooting wasn't in the park—it had been here and those at HQ were under fire. She'd woken up with tears on her cheeks and a need to see everyone with her own eyes and know they were safe. The way Ames smiled at her now flooded her with relief and pure happiness.

She was humming as she loaded her plate with breakfast casserole and headed to the table.

"Morning." Penny slipped an arm around her shoulders. "You survived another week."

"And my back isn't killing me this time." She sat in the chair beside Ames. Interestingly enough, the chair beside him had been empty all week. "Good morning," she said to no one in particular even though she glanced at Ames when she said it.

"Good morning to you, Harper." Eddy gave her a wink.

"You're looking like a ray of sunshine." Gabe held out the basket of biscuits. "Hungry?"

Ames took the basket. "Yeah, thanks."

Gabe sputtered, shooting daggers at Ames.

"Forget your manners, Mr. Paxton?" Eddy frowned. "Ladies first, remember?"

Ames turned to face her and held out the basket. "Biscuit?" His eyes were full of mischief.

By now, she should be getting used to that handsome face of his. She wasn't. One look had her toes curling in her boots and her heart slamming into her ribcage. "Yes, please." She took one of the still warm buttermilk biscuits and put it on her plate.

"Got any plans for this weekend?" Eddy asked.

"We do. If the weather cooperates, we're going swimming." Athena gave her two thumbs-up.

"You were going to invite your little brother, right?" Gabe grinned at Athena.

"That sounds like fun." Penny nodded. "We should all go. I can pack up a picnic and we can make an afternoon out of it."

Ames nudged her with his knee, she nudged back.

She hadn't agreed to go swimming with Athena. Her only plans for the weekend had been to spend as much time with Ames as possible. There was no Lookout Point or Miss Janie to complicate things. Just two whole days of doing whatever she and Ames felt like.

When Rooster walked into the kitchen, there was a palpable shift in the air. "Listen up," he announced. "Storm warning. We need to move the herd out of the south pasture. Let's go, let's go."

Ames was up, tossing his napkin onto his plate.

"So far, just a plain ol' thunderstorm." Rooster shot him a look. "We'll see."

Harper saw the look but didn't have time to process it. Everyone was in motion, with a purpose. In a handful of seconds, the overall mood had gone from light and airy to—not. She turned to Ames. Was he worried? Should she be worried?

His warm brown eyes swept over her face before giving her a crooked grin. And then he was gone. The rest of the ranch hands filed out quickly, leaving Penny and Micah to clear the table.

She stacked up some plates and carried them to the counter. "Is there something I should be doing?" she asked.

"We could lose power so making sure there are batteries and flashlights in every room comes first." Micah glanced at the window. "I can't imagine any windows being open, but double check that, too. If the winds get real strong or a tornado drops down, we want everything locked up tight."

Illinois was part of Tornado Alley so she was no stranger to the threat they caused. "I can do that. Back home, we had a storm cellar under our garage."

"You did? Then you know that fretting doesn't do a bit of good." Penny gave her a smile. "This place is rock solid. But we have a storm cellar, too. That door in the middle of the hallways isn't a closet."

"What about the ranch hands?" Harper knew being out in a tornado wasn't a good idea.

"They'll be fine. Remember, no tornado watch or warning has been issued." Penny took the stack of dishes Harper brought her. "I'm thinking Rooster's bringing in the herd because of lightning. It's been so dry, there's a risk of fire."

Micah nodded like there was no reason for concern.

Harper, however, was concerned. *Ames is out there.* But Penny was right. Fretting wouldn't help. She took a deep breath. Ames was out there, doing his job. She needed to do the same. Better to work than sit and let her imagination come up with all the ways Ames could end up maimed or killed. *Stop it. He will be fine.*

"Batteries and flashlights in all the rooms. Making sure the windows are closed and locked. Anything else?"

"No, ma'am. It's just another workday, really." Penny smiled. "We'll have a hearty lunch waiting for them."

"I'll make sure they have a clean bed ready for them to collapse on, if they need it." She'd like to contribute something more than flashlights and freshly made beds but she'd work with what she had.

Harper went from room to room, locating flashlights and making sure they were working before she moved on. When she was done, she'd come up short three flashlights and had two more that needed new batteries. She knew right where she'd find the fresh batteries and spare flashlights, too. The minibarn Penny called the cleaning pantry had plenty of both. The only hiccup was the cleaning pantry's location. It would take her ten to fifteen minutes for her to reach the far side of the tractor barn, past a handful of holding pens, to a fenced-off enclosure full of a variety of sheds and barns full of surplus gear and supplies.

Easy-peasy.

Harper peered out one of the parlor's windows at the sky. It wasn't raining yet but she didn't trust the look of the clouds overhead. She hurried to her room, tugged on her raincoat, tucked a canvas shopping bag into the pocket of her coat and grabbed her flashlight. When she opened the exterior door, Copper and Daisy came running inside.

"You two stay here." She opened her door for them.

Daisy hopped up onto her bed and snorted. Copper flopped on the wooden floor, panting. "I'll be right back."

Harper stepped outside, tugged the exterior door shut and hurried across the garden to the gate. It was a long trek from the Big House to the tractor barn and, even with the gale-like winds and rain imminent, the sweltering heat wasn't helping. She seriously regretted wearing her lined plastic raincoat. All it was doing was sealing in the heat, leaving her sweaty and gross. Even the air she was breathing felt thick and damp.

She came around the corner of the tractor barn and got slammed in the face by a brutal gust of wind. She held up her arm and leaned into it, almost falling to the dirt when the wind suddenly died.

The rain started then. Not some gentle shower, though. These raindrops hit the ground with artillery-style force, big and fat and slapping the hard earth as they hit.

Rain meant they didn't have to worry about fire, right?

She was feeling fine. Until she wasn't.

It was a sudden crack of thunder that had her cowering. A single, burst of sound. Almost an explosion. It rolled across the sky with menace. She pressed her hands over her ears but the noise was still there—echoing.

This was what it had sounded like. Violent, but rapid-fire. Loud and all-encompassing. In her head, the sound wasn't thunder. It was something else. Something horrible. Making the air around her vibrate before the bullet slammed into her side and knocked her off-balance. The second bullet knocked her legs out from under her—knocking her flat against her back to stare up at the clear blue sky overhead. While, all around her, the explosive, staccato shower of bullets and panicked screams continued.

It's over. She closed her eyes—pushing against the memory. *It's over.* She stared up at the dark sky, the rain pelting against her face. It wasn't raining that day. It'd been cool and crisp, a blue sky with white fluffy clouds.

No blue skies, for one thing. She took a deep breath, staring around the empty yard.

This was not her hometown park where every festival or holiday was celebrated. This was Crossroads. And right now, everyone on the ranch was doing something to help get through the storm.

I have a job to do. She pictured Ames on horseback, herding cattle, drenched but focused. He was doing what needed to be done. She needed to, too.

She took a deep breath, glaring up at the dark clouds rumbling overhead. "I hear you!"

You're not going to scare me.

She stood, defiant, until she was sure-footed enough to move, step-by-step—she refused to give up or give in. All she had to do was think of Ames, to ground herself in the here and now, to keep moving. Finally, she reached the minibarn, stepped inside and leaned against the door to catch her breath.

She was here. She'd done it. And she was delighted with herself.

She ignored the thunder rattling the structure around her, wiped the rain from her face and scanned the shelf for flashlights. Once she'd shoved three flashlights into the canvas bag she'd brought, she hunted down the batteries. She found what she needed, slipped the box into place, then closed and locked the doors behind her.

The trip to the cleaning pantry had been a cakewalk compared to her trek back. Visibility was low and the newly muddied ground was sticky and slick. She did slip and land in mud twice, and she almost lost the bag with her supplies to a strong gust of wind, but the roar of thunder wasn't crippling anymore. It made her jump but that seemed like a perfectly normal reaction to thunder.

All in all, she was feeling proud by the time she'd reached the Big House. She ran up the steps to the door leading onto her hall and paused. Instead of messing up her clean floors, she sat on the top step, tugged off her mud-coated boots and hung them upside down so they wouldn't fill up with water. She couldn't wait to tell Ames about today. He'd seen her lock up with fear, and he wouldn't belittle her victory over the thunder. Hopefully, he'd give her that look he always gave her and tell her he was proud of her. And, maybe, he'd pull her close and kiss her, too. She'd like that very much.

Ames held open the door to the storm cellar and let the others pass. He brought up the rear—that was his job. It was up to him to keep account of his people. On days like today, when the tornado siren sounded, it was the most important part of his job. Luckily, where the tornado touched down was nowhere close to HQ but, once the cattle were moved, Rooster had them all head right back to the Big House anyway. If the damn funnel cloud pivoted and decided to head their way, Rooster would feel better being close to Penny. No one ever said as much out loud, but it was no secret that the man adored his wife.

For the first time, Ames thought he might understand what Rooster was feeling. All morning, Harper had been on his mind. When he'd saddled up his horse, Tango, he thought about the smile she'd given him this morning. When he'd been rounding up a few stubborn stray heifers that'd been hiding in the prairie tallgrass, he'd been wondering how best to introduce her to Tango so they could go for a ride together. And when he'd been double-checking every gate was secure on the ride back, he found himself wondering how she was handling the storm. Out here, weather was a force to be reckoned with. Days like today served as a good reminder that there was no predicting or controlling Mother Nature. She was mighty fierce.

There was no reason for him to worry about Harper. She was safe with Penny and Micah—far from danger. But there was a tiny part of him that couldn't relax, either. He figured, once he saw her with his own two eyes, that'd would go away.

"Virgil walkie'd." Hoss's voice carried up the stairs to him. "Funnel cloud shifted. Says it's headed this way."

If a tornado was coming their way, there was no safer place to be. Ames remembered when the Winstons had the basement converted into a storm cellar. He hadn't been at the ranch all that long so he'd been fascinated by the construction work, tools and watching it all come together. It wasn't all bare bones, either. There was a tiny half-bathroom, plenty of comfortable seating, a mini-fridge and snacks, and all the basic necessities one might need if trapped in a basement for a couple of days. Since then, he'd spent more than a few hours down here playing chess or darts, reading or dozing off in the steel-reinforced space.

Did Harper play chess? If she didn't, he could teach her.

He came down the stairs two at a time, greeted Copper and Daisy with some scratches behind the ear, then did his best to act like he wasn't looking for anyone or anything in particular so as not to draw attention to himself—or Harper.

"Thank you." He took the cup of steaming coffee Micah offered him. He took a sip, gazing over the rim of the mug looking for Harper. She wasn't sitting on one of the couches. She wasn't helping Penny or Micah with coffee. Gabe and Eddy hadn't cornered her—in fact, he didn't see her.

"Ames, you're here." Penny's smile faded when she looked behind him. "Harper isn't with you?"

"No. Why would she… Where is Harper?" He turned, slowly, to scan the faces now staring at him. The instant he realized she really wasn't there, the hair along the back of his neck stood straight up.

"Ames, honey." Penny's tone was soothing. "Try not to panic but she isn't here."

"I can see that." Ames swallowed, tightness settling into his chest. He was panicking all right. "Where the hell is she?"

"I thought she'd be with you all." Penny shrugged, looking at Micah in confusion. "Earlier, she wanted to know what she could do and I said—"

"I said." Micah interrupted her mother, her eyes going round as she said, "You don't think she—"

"Where is she?" The roaring in his ears wasn't from the thunder outside, it was his blood—pounding louder and louder as he waited for an answer.

"I told her we needed flashlights and batteries in each room." Micah had a hard time meeting his gaze, which amped up the pressure in Ames's chest. "Maybe…could she have gone to get some extras?"

"Harper went out in this?" Eddy was up.

"To the cleaning pantry?" Gabe stood, too.

"She said they had tornadoes where she came from. I'm certain she'll take shelter, Ames. She's a smart girl." But Penny's smile wobbled.

"So we don't need to worry." Logan rested his elbows on his knees. "Sound like she knows what to do—" He broke off and held up his hands when Ames rounded on him. "Okay, we are going to worry."

There was no time for this. For all he knew, she was in trouble. Ames spun on his heel and headed for the stairs.

"Sorry, son." Hoss stepped in his path. "You heard what Rooster said. You can't go out there with a tornado—"

"I'm going. Please don't try to stop me, Hoss." Ames had never disrespected Hoss or Rooster—not once in twenty-two years. But there was no way—no way—he was going to sit here when Harper was out there.

"Ames, you've got a good head on your shoulders." Hoss frowned. "Harper is a smart woman—"

"I'm going." Ames met Hoss's gaze. "You can fire me later." He brushed past the man and ran back up the stairs.

"I'm going, too—" Gabe said.

"Sit your ass down," Athena snapped.

Ames closed the door to the storm cellar behind him. There was an unnerving shriek to the wind but nothing like the roar of a freight train that signified an approaching tornado.

He headed toward the Foreman Hall, calling out her name as he went, his heart damn near thumping its way through his chest. Harper wasn't in the living room, study, library or ranch hands' hangout. He knew where she was then, and he *would* bring her home. He'd grab his headlamp and rain gear and head out after her. And he wouldn't give up until he'd found her. By the time he came around the corner of Foreman Hall, desperation was pressing in on him.

And there she was…

Harper. Standing right outside her room, talking to herself, shivering, soaking wet and dripping.

Ames headed straight for her. He was feeling—a whole lot. Terror and relief, anger and joy, panic and a million other things he rarely experienced crowded in, overwhelming him.

"Where the hell have you been?" He was relieved and happy and grateful that she was back, but he sure as hell didn't sound like it. He sounded like an asshole. An asshole who was grabbing her shoulders and turning her to face him because he was frantic to make sure she was okay. A quick head-to-toe sweep revealed no blood or sign of injury so he could breathe.

That's when the feel of her, solid and real beneath his hands, registered.

She smiled at him. How could she look so damn happy to see him—excited almost? Didn't she know she'd worried folk? Worried him? Didn't she know today could have ended differently? That she could have been hurt… or worse? He swallowed, shoving that thought aside. He couldn't think that way—he'd never let anything happen to her. Period. He needed to see her smile at him, like this, every damn day.

"Harper." But that was all he got out. There were so

many things he wanted to say to her but, in his current state of mind, he wasn't sure he could trust himself to say the right ones.

"We…we were missing flashlights." She held up a still-dripping canvas bag and offered him a weak smile.

It was the smile that broke him. There was no holding back his desperation, not anymore. "Dammit, Harper." He groaned, then pulled her into his arms.

"Wait, Ames, I'm muddy and soaking wet." Her voice was muffled.

"It's fine," he murmured, adjusting his arms until she was pressed flush against him. Even then, it wasn't close enough.

"What's wrong?" she whispered, sliding her arms around his waist.

"A whole hell of a lot," he ground out. "Why the hell didn't you tell Penny or Micah where you were going? You can't do that, Harper. You can't take off without someone knowing. Everyone is worried about you." He gripped her shoulders and held her back, scanning her face. "What made you think you needed to risk going out in this?"

"I was doing my job." She frowned, put a hand in the middle of his chest and pushed. "We were three flashlights short and out of batteries—"

"I don't give a rat's ass about flashlights or batteries!" He was basically yelling at her, refusing to let her go.

"Well, I did!" She pushed harder, yelling back. "Everyone else had something important to do. I couldn't sit here worrying about you all morning. I had to do something." She gripped his shirtfront, her eyes clear and shining.

There was a sudden, quiet stillness all around them

that reminded Ames this was not the time or place to have this conversation.

"We need to get to shelter." He didn't offer up more of an explanation—there wasn't time. Instead, he grabbed her hand and pulled her behind him, all the way to the other side of the house to the storm cellar.

There was total silence when he and Harper descended the stairs. Worse, every single person in the room was looking at them.

"Oh, honey." Penny burst into tears and pulled Harper in for a hug. "Where on earth did you go? I… I was so worried." Penny held Harper away from her. "Micah, hurry and get a towel for Harper here."

"I'm sorry, Penny." Harper watched as Penny took the towel Micah offered. "I… I brought the flashlights." She looked downright dejected as Penny wrapped the towel around her. "And the batteries, too," she murmured, every word laden with regret.

"Of course you did." Penny patted Harper on the cheek. "I'm sure Ames has already given you a talking-to so I won't add my two cents worth."

"I will." This from Hoss, whose expression was anything but forgiving.

Ames wasn't sure how this was going to play out. Hoss had every right to be pissed at Harper for taking unnecessary risks and pissed at him for disobeying orders. Ames would take whatever consequences Hoss doled out. Likely, Hoss would give Harper a talking-to, too. And while it was deserved—and he was still upset about her going out in the storm—he wanted to step between Harper and Hoss Winston and offer to take Harper's punishment, along with his own.

"Miss Lynn, while I appreciate your dedication to your job, I need you to understand that what happened today is unacceptable. Of all the resources on the ranch, it's our employees—our family—that are most valuable." He gestured to the canvas bag, still dripping, in her hand. "While they're handy to have on hand, we can make do without the flashlights. I can't say the same about you."

"Ames, especially." Logan snorted.

For the first time, Ames looked at his team of ranch hands. Well, now they all knew. So much for keeping him and Harper a secret. And he had no one to blame but himself. Finding her missing had split him open so that every damn one of them knew what he was feeling on the inside. There was no undoing that. But he wasn't upset over it, not really. He'd rather they all knew—maybe now Gabe and Eddy would leave her be.

"I apologize." Harper hung her head. "I… I was feeling superfluous. Everyone had something important to do and I… It was wrong. I am sorry for worrying you—"

"*Us?* Ames's head was about to explode." Brandy shook her head. "He was all riled up. The bulging eyes. The neck thing." She flexed so the tendons of her neck went taut. "Snapping at folks—and threatening Hoss."

Ames pretended he didn't notice Harper's surprise as she stared at him.

"I don't know about *all* that." Eddy tried to downplay Brandy's description.

"Well, you've been kicked in the head a lot so you don't know about much." Brandy sat back against the couch. "You two doing the four-legged foxtrot, or what?"

Harper's brows dipped. "What's a four-legged—"

"Nothing. Forget it." Ames scowled at Brandy. "If you don't want extra stall duty, you'll stop. Now."

This made Brandy smile. "You mean, if Hoss and Rooster don't fire your ass for disobeying an order?"

There was a chance, sure. But it wasn't a big one. He knew he was essential to Crossroads. He knew Rooster and Hoss—even Miss Janie—knew as much. But, even if it cost him his job, he didn't regret going after Harper. From now on, no matter where the future led them, Ames wasn't going to waste one more minute of their time together.

Chapter Twelve

Ames could get fired? Because of her? *No.* Her heart went into triple-speed. This was Ames's home. He belonged here.

"No," she said, holding up her hands. "Oh, Hoss, Rooster, please don't fire Ames." She stepped in front of him, holding her arms wide like she could shield him. "This is my fault." And she felt sick about it. "He meant well. He's a protector by nature. He can't help it. And he would have done the same for any one of you. It's commendable, really. That he is so protective of his… coworkers."

"Is that what you think?" Hoss was half smiling now.

"Yes." She had no doubt that Ames would have gone after any one of them.

"In twenty-two years I have never seen the version of Ames Paxton I saw today." Rooster had his arm draped around Penny's shoulder. "Miss Harper, I think you and Ames might want to have a heart-to-heart and see about gettin' on the same page."

"Let's keep this professional." Ames cleared his throat, his tone all business. "I screwed up." He paused, his throat still tight. "I own that. I expect there to be consequences and, no matter what you two decide, I'll accept it."

"Like firing his disrespectful ass—and kicking him off the place." Brandy's whisper wasn't a whisper at all.

Why does Brandy sound so amused? Harper glared at the woman. What she was suggesting was awful. This place wasn't just Ames's job. This was his home and the people in this room were his family. This wasn't a joke—this was Ames's life they were talking about.

"Except that." Harper spoke up, turning to Ames. "This is my fault." What was he doing? Why wasn't he defending himself? Or blaming her—since it was her fault. She turned to Hoss and Rooser, willing to speak up on his behalf. "If you have to fire someone, fire me. I'm the one that went out there. He went after me—that deserves a promotion, not a pink slip."

Emotions were high, sure, but she had to believe Hoss and Rooster wouldn't do something out of anger—something they'd regret. Letting Ames go would be a huge mistake.

"They're like some ranching Romeo and Juliet," Calder mumbled. "Willing to make a sacrifice for the other."

"Only, thankfully, they're not actually killing themselves." Micah glanced at her brother.

Harper ignored them, irritated. Shouldn't they be rallying behind their foreman right about now? Shouldn't they be speaking up instead of talking nonsense?

"They're more like Jack and Rose from *Titanic*." Athena leaned in to join the conversation.

"Yeah, that fits better." Calder shrugged. "I bet Harper would share the board-thingy with Ames, though. Not let him freeze to death."

Both Micah and Athena nodded.

Harper frowned, glancing at Ames. They were talking

about them? She had the urge to smile. But she shouldn't, should she? She didn't know how to react.

"Nah, Ames is more like..." Logan snapped his fingers. "What's that old black-and-white movie. With the guy and the bar and the piano player. At the end, the guy lets the girl leave with her husband on the airplane—and the bad guys are coming after them."

"Wait, the main chick is married? To someone else?" Eddy frowned. "So she's a cheater?"

"They were a couple back from before, when she thought her husband was dead." Logan sighed.

"So the guy, not her husband, is *the* one from her past? If they were still into each other, why'd they split up?" Eddy shook his head.

"There was a war on, Eddy. They were separated but never forgot one another." Harper slammed her mouth shut. Now she was taking part in this ludicrous conversation?

"Also, her husband was alive so there was that. The movie is called *Casablanca*." Penny sighed. "It's one of my favorites."

"But they *just* met." Gabe pointed at Ames, then Harper. "So that movie doesn't work."

"Well, they're not on a sinking boat but I still think *Titanic* works." Athena nudged her brother. "Ames is the boy from the wrong side of the tracks. Harper is some fancy, educated librarian."

Harper sneezed, drawing all eyes her way. She knew what she looked like and it was anything but fancy. Her raincoat was too big, her hair was a tangled mess and the mud coating her jeans was forming a thick crust—some had crumbled off onto the floor already.

"Oh, yeah, I see it." Calder laughed. "Fancy."

"Seriously, Hoss." Ames pinched the bridge of his nose. "I can't take much more of this."

As amusing as all the back-and-forth was, there was a very serious matter that needed to be addressed. Ames's job. Did no one care about him? She was offended and hurt and beyond perplexed by the others' behavior. She almost reached for his hand.

"You can't?" Hoss crossed his arms over his chest. "Y'all keep it going then. Sounds like a pretty good punishment to me."

Ames stared at the older man.

"Um… I'm confused. Ames's job isn't in trouble?" Harper asked.

"Hoss never said that. Neither did I. More like we'll dock him a week's worth of pay." Rooster chuckled. "But it is kinda fun to see him squirm some, too."

Harper wasn't a fan of this sort of humor. Or the fact that everyone in the room seemed to be amused. "Laughter at other's people's expense is called Schadenfreude. It literally translates to the two words harm and joy. Another word for it is bullying." She knew a lot about bullying, how it could hurt and isolate. Her stepmother had been the first to bully her but she hadn't been the last.

Ames's hand rested, briefly, on her shoulder. She glanced up at him—and his waiting smile kicked aside her frustration and confusion and irritation. If Ames was fine, then so was she. Not that she minded the shamefaced looks of the others after she'd called them out. Not one bit.

"Harper." Micah waved for Harper to follow her. "I found you some dry clothes."

"Go on," Ames murmured, his gaze sweeping over her face. "You don't want to get sick."

"Oh, come on, now." Gabe sounded like a whiny five-year-old. "We get it, okay. Stop with all this…this whisperin'." He pointed at her, then Ames. "And the…that."

"Chill, Gabe." Eddy clapped a hand on his shoulder. "We know Ames. We know he's not the hearts-and-flowers kinda man. You might still have a chance."

"She's the one that said they were coworkers." Brandy pointed at Harper. "Maybe she's not interested in Ames but she feels guilty because she's going to get him fired."

"You are…" Harper stopped herself from insulting the woman. From Brandy's defensive posture and defiant narrow-eyed stare, it was obvious the woman hoped to instigate something. "I *won't* get him fired—though you might want to ask yourself why you're so set on seeing Ames fired." She faced Ames, who was watching her with the slightest smile on his face. She kept looking at him as she said, "Ames is more than my coworker… I am very interested in him."

There was an audible *ooh* from the ranch hands. Athena, however, said, "Oh my gosh, you two are so cute."

"Whatever. I give it a month." Logan turned to Gabe, then Eddy.

"Two weeks." Brandy snorted. "A lot is going to depend on the sex. Once they start, you know, knocking boots?" Brandy asked, her brows going up.

"Doing the bedroom rodeo?" Logan grinned. "Planting the parsnip."

"Good one." Eddy clapped his hands together. "Shagging. That's one, right?"

"See, too many head injuries." Brandy made a face.

"Charming the one-eyed snake is one. Oh—shaking sheets."

"Banging. Boning. Or boinking." Eddy listed each off on his fingers.

As horrified as she was by this whole discussion, Harper could at least appreciate the alliteration of Eddy's last round of suggestions, if not the terms themselves.

"Are y'all done?" Ames cut in, his tone steady and calm.

"They're done," Hoss barked, no longer looking amused.

"I guess?" Logan looked at the others, who shrugged or nodded. "Yeah, I think so."

"That wasn't an actual question." Ames went back to pinching the bridge of his nose.

"You're playing with fire, son." Rooster shook his head at Logan. "You keep that up, your foreman might not take too kindly to it."

Their foreman. Ames. Harper was glad to see the Winston brothers siding with Ames now. *It's about time.*

"I'll say this once. From here on out, there will be no more talk about me or Harper's personal life. I don't pull rank often but, on this, I will. You hear me?" Ames made sure to look at each and every one of them.

There was a lot of mumbled *yeah*'s, grunts, as well as a "Yes, sir" from Calder.

Harper was surprised. No arguing or pushing back or teasing? Just like that? She'd never seen Ames in authoritative mode but it was sort of…hot. She could feel the heat creeping into her cheeks and decided now was a good time to give herself a minute.

"I'm going…to change." She hurried across to Micah,

took the clothes from the woman and headed into the small bathroom with the blinding fluorescent light. "Oh my gosh." Her reflection was more appalling that she'd imagined.

"You can wash up some—and once the storm passes you can take a shower." Micah paused before she closed the door. "I am glad you're okay, Harper. We all are."

Harper was still staring at the door after Micah closed it. She hugged the clean clothes to her chest and smiled. For the first time, she didn't feel like an outsider. She'd been part of the banter and teasing. Heck, Brandy hadn't spared her from her jokes. That had to be some sort of rite of passage, didn't it?

She'd also pushed back—something she never would have done in her old life. But, man, it felt good.

She set the clean clothes on the edge of the sink, stripped down to her bra and underwear. But the cotton T-shirt bra and dancing-avocado-print cotton panties were just as wet as the rest of her clothes so she pulled them off, too. She washed her face and chest, hands and arms, then tugged on the dry clothes. She could hear a lot of muffled conversation happening outside—hopefully it was Ames working things out with Hoss and Rooster?

The dry clothes consisted of a pair of men's sweatpants and a men's plaid flannel button-down shirt. She was swimming in fabric but the drawstring waist of the pants kept them secure and the shirt was too big to tell she was braless. She rolled up the wet clothes into a ball and pushed open the bathroom door.

It was nice to see she was no longer the center of attention.

Athena, Gabe, Logan, Brandy, and Eddy were huddled

around a board game. Micah sat opposite Hoss, playing dominoes, while Rooster and Penny were cuddled up on the loveseat.

Ames, however, stood by himself, scanning the shelf of books along the wall.

She rolled the too-long sleeves up and joined Ames at the bookshelf. "Hi."

He didn't look at her. "Feel better?"

"Are things okay with you and Hoss and Rooster?" She shoved at her sleeves, which had unrolled.

Ames folded over the cuffs on her shirt, then rolled up the sleeves. This time, they stayed. "Fine." He smiled at her.

"So your job isn't in jeopardy?"

"Never was." Ames shook his head, his eyes searching hers. "All Brandy."

"Who I am no longer a fan of." She tried to smile. "Are you mad at me for telling everyone about us?" It felt like he was keeping his distance and she wanted to know why.

"How about we talk later?" He glanced, pointedly, around the room.

The CB radio crackled. "North Camp to HQ, this is Kent. Over?"

Hoss stood and picked up the CB. "Hoss, here. How's it look?"

"Clear skies from here. You?"

That was good news, wasn't it? Harper hoped that meant the storm had passed.

"Waitin' it out a bit." Hoss glanced at his wristwatch. "Sensors aren't going off anymore but we'll give it another ten."

"Check back in fifteen, then. Over and out," Kent said, the CB crackling again.

Hoss was smiling as he sat and went back to his game of dominoes. "Ten minutes, people."

"You play chess?" Ames asked.

"I do. Chess club in high school." She paused, then decided not to add she'd gone to college on a partial chess scholarship. The whole Schadenfreude scolding-thing had been nerdy enough without her adding to it.

"So, you're good?" Ames seemed impressed. "Good-like-I-don't-stand-a-chance?"

She laughed. "Oh, I'm pretty rusty. Last time I played, Matt almost beat…" *Nope.* Thoughts of her brother or anything to do with him or why she'd come here were not welcome. All things considered, today had been a good day and she wanted to keep it that way. "You *might* stand a chance."

"Let's find out." His crooked grin made her stomach clench tight.

And when his gaze met hers, there was a shift in the air. The pull between them was undeniable. A live wire of sensation that melted her insides and left her dizzy. The look in his eyes was warm, gentle, tender—with just enough hunger to make her flush and tingle. But he hadn't just woken up her body—he'd resuscitated her heart, too. For the first time in a long time, grief didn't have her in a bruising vise. Because of Ames, her heart was healing and lighter and full of hope and possibilities. With Ames, right here on Crossroads.

If Ames didn't know Harper, he'd have thought he'd been hustled. Harper wasn't so-so at chess—she was really good. He lost to Harper, twice, even though he could tell she was trying to go easy on him, too—which was sweet. Watching her get all focused and confident had been fascinating. It was a whole new side of Harper. She was so damn cute he didn't mind losing to her.

They were still getting to know one another and he was in no rush to fast-forward the process. He'd rather let things come out naturally, when the time was right for her to share.

With one exception.

Matt.

He wanted to know who this Matt was and how he figured into Harper's life.

As soon as she'd said his name, that thing had happened. It'd only lasted a split second but it had been enough. Some memory, some trauma, tripped a sort of mental-shutdown for Harper. Everything about her locked up before she tried to pull in on herself as if she could hide. Today, she'd stopped it from happening. He'd seen it—watched her push back until she'd boxed whatever was tormenting her back up.

Now he knew: Matt was in the same box as her fear of guns. For that reason alone, Ames wasn't sure how he should feel about the man. Was he a victim, like Harper? Or someone bad?

That's what he'd been thinking about when Harper had beat him at chess and what he was thinking about now—while he was riding the south pasture scouting for damage left by the storm.

"You look like you're trying to solve the world's problems." Rooster rode his horse alongside Ames's. "What's eating you, son?"

Ames shrugged. He'd told the others to stay out of his business—Harper's business, too. Talking to Rooster about her was no better. He wanted to keep their relationship private, to protect it from gossip and ridicule.

"Wanna talk about it?" Rooster offered.

Ames glanced his way. "Nothing to talk about."

"You still pissed?" Rooster clicked his tongue and steered his horse around a sizable clump of cactus. "Lettin' off steam is all. You know that."

Ames nodded. He did know. Normally, it wouldn't have bothered him. But that was when Harper hadn't been part of it.

Maybe his face gave away what he was thinking because Rooster said, "But it sure riled up Harper something fierce."

Ames remembered—it'd be a memory he'd cherish. The way she'd scolded the others for teasing him put a smile on his face. He'd liked seeing her trying to protect him today. Harper, feisty, was a mighty fine sight.

"Guess she doesn't know that Brandy was just being Brandy. If anything it's a sign she's starting to like Harper. She's hardest on the ones she likes." Rooster chuckled. "Still, I was impressed to see Miss Harper come to your rescue like that. I'd take it as a good sign, son. It doesn't matter how angry Penny might get with me. If someone else wrongs me—she'll make them regret it." He looked Ames's way, smiling. "As long as she does that, I know she still loves me."

Ames knew better than to think Harper was in love with him. He figured his heart had been so quick to jump ship because he lived a small, quiet life. He didn't have a lot of fancy learning or time away at college—he'd done all that online right here on Crossroads.

Harper had lived in a whole other world before she came here. But there was no denying the mutual attraction between them. Hell, the word attraction wasn't big enough to describe how powerfully he wanted Harper. He was pretty sure she felt the same. Yes, she was interested in him—she'd said as much before everyone at HQ. But even with his limited experience, he knew interest and attraction didn't equate to loving him. For all he knew, she could've felt this way before for some other fella. It was possible she didn't think this thing between them was special, the way he did. That realization put a bad taste in his mouth and a knot in his gut.

"Just remember, women are mysterious creatures," Rooster said. "I think they like keeping it that way, too."

Ames was almost relieved to see a wide swath of tallgrass had been torn up, turning up the dirt as cleanly as a tractor before planting season. "See that?" He pointed at the path the tornado had left behind.

"Let's hope that's the worst of it." Rooster tipped his hat back on his head. "Sure would hate to miss out on tomorrow's rodeo."

Tomorrow was the rodeo? It would be a damn shame if they had to miss it. Harper would probably enjoy getting out… Though she might be uncertain about going to a prison rodeo. And seeing as how it was three hours, round-trip, to reach Pardon, Texas—where Graves Prison was located—she'd be giving up her Sunday to go. It took time and effort to go anywhere from Crossroads, so the destination needed to be worth it. For him, the rodeo was worth it but Harper might see it differently.

For Ames, the Prison Rodeo Rehabilitation Program was just another part of life on Crossroads. Hoss and Rooster were advocates and volunteers for the program. They believed taking care of animals and engaging in healthy competition gave the inmates something constructive to do with their time and energy. Hoss would know.

Fifteen years before Ames came to the ranch, Hoss had done some time for disorderly conduct, among other things. To this day, Hoss swore it was the rodeo program that had saved his life. When Hoss was released, drinking, using drugs and raising hell were no longer part of his life and Rooster had given his brother another chance. The two had been mostly inseparable since then.

When Ames had first arrived, he'd followed the Winston brothers everywhere—including the prison. Over the years, Hoss and Rooster had developed a baseline to help them recognize the inmates who felt remorse for their crimes and were committed to change over those saying all the right things to get out but, more than likely, would end up back inside within a year. As a result, more than a dozen ranch hands currently working the ranch had come from the Graves Prison Rodeo Rehabilitation Program.

"Looks like something lit a fire under that boy." Rooster slowed his horse to a stop, waiting as Calder rode up, fast.

Calder shook his head. "The windmill lost two blades and the tail."

Not great news but it could have been a whole hell of a lot worse. When he turned to Rooster, the older man gestured for him to handle it. So Ames did. "Parts are at HQ." He sat back in his saddle. "Take Logan and Brandy."

"Should I bring the crane truck?" Calder asked, his horse dancing sideways with nervous energy.

The ground was so muddy that the added weight of the crane might get the vehicle stuck so he shook his head. "Service truck." He tipped his cowboy hat back and looked up at the sky. "Should be done before dark."

With that, Calder nudged his horse into a canter back in the direction he'd come.

"I swear, that boy only has one gear—and it's overdrive." Rooster smiled. "Just like his mother."

It would take a while for Calder and the others to get back with everything they'd need so Ames and Rooster finished looping through the pasture. While there were a handful of trees torn up from the roots and great patches of missing native tallgrass, there was nothing too alarming. They circled back to the windmill and started clearing the area. The closer they could get the truck, the easier this would be.

He climbed up the twenty-foot ladder to the platform at the top of the windmill. From up there, the view of Crossroads made him think of the ocean. He'd never seen it himself but this was how he pictured it. Endless, rolling and peaceful—calming him. No matter how rough his life had started out, he'd been grateful every damn day since he got here that this was the place he now called home.

Work wasn't going to wait so he assessed what needed to be done. Wiggling and pushing on the other blades showed they were solid. He stomped around on the platform to make sure it was secure enough to hold their weight so they could work safely. He gave the rotor motor a quick inspection but it seemed no worse for wear.

The tornado had wound a large plastic tarp around

the metal below the blades so he used his pocketknife to cut it free and tossed it down to the others. Below, Gabe, Eddy and Athena were piling up trash and anything else that needed disposing of. Things should be dry enough to set up a burn pile for all the trash and debris on Monday.

As the service truck pulled up, Ames was halfway down the ladder.

It had taken a while for Ames to get his crew to work together. Brandy and Logan had resisted the most—they were loners. But that wasn't how it worked on a ranch. Ames had made it perfectly clear that they were part of the team or they weren't a part of Crossroads. After a whole lot of time and patience and effort, he was proud of how far the HQ hands worked together. Every now and then, they'd hit a rough patch but it'd never been so bad that it interfered with their work or lasted so long it'd jeopardized the team as a whole. Times like this, it made him proud—and happy—to see them all working so efficiently together. Happier still that Rooster was here to see it.

It was getting dark when they headed back to the ranch. Rooster, Athena and Brandy had taken the service truck back while Ames and the others rode home on horseback. He was content—even if the others were griping about how late it was and how hungry they were and that it was a Saturday.

"Rodeo tomorrow," Ames said the first time there was a pause in their bellyaching.

"Is it?" Logan perked up. "Well, damn."

"It'll be Harper's first…" Gabe mumbled off, shooting Ames a dark look.

"Let it go." Eddy chuckled.

"I am. I have." Gabe nudged his horse forward. "I will." His horse took off at a canter.

"Poor kid." Logan shook his head. "I think you broke his heart, Ames."

Ames was feeling bad about Gabe. Five years ago, nineteen-year-old Gabe and his twenty-one-year-old sister, Athena, arrived at Crossroads. Gabe had followed Ames everywhere, asking more questions than Ames could answer in a day. But the boy's interest in all things ranching made it easy for Ames to teach and mentor young Gabe. It didn't take long for Gabe to become more than capable in his duties. In all that time, there had never been any tension or awkwardness between them. Until now.

"He'll get over it." Eddy sighed. "He's so damn young—too damn young to stay out here. That boy is going to need to get some living under his belt or he'll get restless."

"And by living you mean *women*?" Logan chuckled.

"Partly. Yeah. He's too young and inexperienced to know the difference between love and lust." Eddy paused. "Not his fault. Out here, there's not much chance for either. It's your call, Ames, but, might see about him going along next time there's a trip to Lubbock or Amarillo."

"I can hear it now." Logan cleared his throat. "Y'all take Gabe with you and make sure he gets good and laid while you're at it. He's too innocent and we need to fix that."

"Hold on, now." Eddy laughed. "All I'm saying is it might not hurt for Gabe to see there are other women out there—besides Harper. Only way to do that is get off the ranch for a bit. And if he winds up having a little...*fun*, too, what's the harm in that?"

Ames could see where Eddy was coming from. Not about getting the kid laid, that was bullshit, but about giving Gabe a break. There were times he forgot just how young Gabe was or how small Crossroads could get, at times. This was one of those times.

When Ames became foreman, he'd worked hard to get Hoss and Rooster to agree to his annual extra-week off policy. He felt strongly that each of the cowboys should take a week away from the ranch. He didn't care where they went or what they did, only that they came back relaxed and ready to work. In that time, only two ranch hands had decided they were ready to move on and didn't want to come back to Crossroads.

Ames figured that was a good thing.

Not everyone was meant to live on Crossroads their whole life. Some folk came because they needed time and a place where they could puzzle over the big decisions facing them. Others came because they didn't want to make any decisions—they wanted a safe place to live and work and be without thinking beyond that. And, for others, it was a place to regroup—a passing-through point before they went on to the next stage of their life.

An image of Harper popped into his head. At one time, he'd assumed she fit into that last category. She'd come to make peace with herself and move on. He hoped like hell he'd been wrong. Maybe it was selfish of him to want her to fall in love with this place enough to stay, but he did. If she stayed, there'd be time for her to fall in love with him, too. There was no guarantee that'd happen—he knew that—but if she left, that guaranteed it wouldn't.

The thought of her leaving Crossroads, of losing her, damn near split his heart in two.

Chapter Thirteen

Harper had been pacing her room for a solid thirty minutes. It was dark out but she had yet to hear the boot-clad footsteps of Ames making his way to his room. She couldn't shake off the feeling that something was… off. They'd had fun playing chess earlier but Ames had seemed distracted. Then they'd left to inspect the property and Harper had been left with hours to read all sorts of things into their interactions—but she was almost scared by how great things were going. Okay, she was scared.

She'd stayed busy, starting with a long shower. Once she was mud-free, she'd put on clean clothes and headed to the kitchen. Penny and Micah were making dinner and tolerated her asking questions and attempting to help. Penny couldn't wrap her mind around the fact that she couldn't even boil an egg. By dinner, there was a new easiness between them. Micah wasn't much of a talker but her icy exterior seemed to have thawed some. When it was clear the others weren't going to be back for dinner, they assembled barbecue sandwiches for a quick and easy meal once the ranch hands finally got home. After cleaning up, she said good night, selected a new book from the library, took another shower and attempted to read—only to give up and pace.

How about we talk later.

"It is later," she said, sighing. "Sorry," she whispered when both Daisy and Copper jolted awake to stare at her with heavy-lidded eyes. "It's okay. You sleep." She smiled as the two of them curled up again, occupying the bottom half of her bed. Not that she minded. It made her happy that they liked spending time with her—or her bed.

She sat in the small chair by the window, grabbed her book and read the same page four times. It was a good thing she heard him coming before she could throw the book at the door. How would she have explained that?

Finally. She hurried to the door. It only occurred to after she'd flung her door open to greet him, smiling from ear to ear, that her behavior wasn't exactly…subtle.

She'd startled Ames, and he was staring at her with a mix of shock and surprise on his face.

But now that she was standing in her open door like a ninny, she couldn't exactly go back inside, close the door and pretend this hadn't happened. More importantly, she didn't want to. Seeing him now smoothed out the knots in her stomach—and triggered an instantaneous thundering in her chest.

"Hi." She waved, then dropped her hand. Why did she have to act this way? *I really am a ninny.*

"Hi." The corner of his mouth kicked up. "I'm surprised you're awake."

That crooked smile turned up the heat a good five degrees. "Is it late?" Yes, it was late. She'd been checking the clock every five minutes for the last hour or two…or three. It was almost eleven. That wasn't late in the non-ranching world. In the ranching world, that was equivalent to two in the morning. Harper was now fully appreciative of the phrase "early to bed and early to rise." As long as the sun was up, it was working hours on the ranch.

"Did I wake you?" His gaze dipped to her shoulder, the muscle in his jaw clenched tight, and he went back to looking at her face.

"No." She glanced down at her nightgown. None of her simple cotton nightgowns could be considered…alluring. Not that she was trying to be alluring at the moment. Did she want to be? The longer his gaze lingered on her mouth, the harder it was to breathe or think or do anything but stand here and want. "I was waiting for you."

He swallowed. "Good." He started towards her—

Harper ran to him, delighted at the feel of his hands gripping her waist. Even more delighted by the way he ran his nose along the side of her ear. She gasped, tilting her head to the side so his lips could reach her neck. And when he dropped slow, clinging kisses all the way up to the skin behind her ear, her breath had gone ragged.

He smiled down at her. "Damn, you are beautiful."

"I am?" She frowned up at him. She was breathing hard, her face was hot, and she was in a full-length, shapeless white nightgown with a messy bun. Frumpy, maybe. Beautiful? No. He, however, was beautiful—in a very manly way, of course.

"You are." He shook his head, running his fingers along her jaw before leaning in to kiss her.

His mouth brushed hers. It was a light kiss. Sweet and gentle. She twined her arms around his neck, wanting more. He seemed to be of the same mindset because the next kiss was firmer. More intense. Turning into a lingering, clinging, hungry kiss that had her leaning against him so she didn't slide to the floor.

He lifted his head. “I need a shower,” he ground out. “I’m a mess.”

Don’t say it. She swallowed. She couldn’t say it. She couldn’t. She wasn’t brazen—at all. But today, it seemed she was. “Is that a statement or an invitation?” she whispered.

He stared at her, startled all over again. “Harper—”

“We agreed we’d wait until we were both ready.” Why had she said anything? “I…am ready.” What if he wasn’t ready? Or he rejected her altogether?

He swallowed, his voice gruff and broken. “You sure?”

“Yes.” She paused. Was he? “Unless you don’t want to—”

Ames grabbed her around the waist and lifted her. His mouth sought hers, parting her lips as he carried her to his door. Somehow, he managed to get them inside before kicking it shut behind them. “I want to.”

His words made every bit of her clench with anticipation. He turned, pressing her against the door, bracing her so he could lift her high enough to grip her hips.

Harper wrapped her legs around his waist, moaning softly when he arched against her. She’d never felt desire like this. The need to feel him, all of him, was urgent and all-consuming. With a tug, she pulled his shirt open, popping the snaps free. It was ridiculously satisfying. And sliding her fingers over his bare chest turned her insides molten. But it was the feel of Ames’s full-body shudder that had her twining her fingers in his hair and pulling his head to her. Her touch was soft and hesitant but her kiss was all fire and hunger. She wanted him to know she wanted him. Oh, so much.

He trailed kisses from her jaw down the length of her

neck, then back up to nuzzle and suck her earlobe into his mouth.

Her moan was equal parts pleasure and impatience. Thankfully, her moan was just the encouragement he needed. He carried her to his bed and laid her down, propping himself over her.

"Wait." Harper gasped.

Ames stopped and pushed himself off the bed. He was flushed and breathing hard but he didn't argue with her.

She sat up on her knees and crawled across the bed to reach for him. "You are wearing too many…clothes." If she hadn't been fully invested in taking off Ames's clothes, she might have commented on how admirable his restraint was. She had none.

Ames smiled then, doing his best to help her rid himself of his clothes.

When he was standing in front of her in a pair of heather gray boxer briefs, Harper felt a moment's hesitation. He was basically naked, and she would be soon enough. And then there was no hiding her scars. They told a story. And it wasn't pretty. "I have scars, too, Ames."

"We all do." Ames stepped forward to cradle her face in his hands. "If you're having second thoughts, we'll wait."

"About you? No." She shook her head. "About this? Absolutely not."

He took her hand in his and rested it against the elevated, jagged line that ran along his shoulder and chest. "You don't think any less of me for this."

"No." She frowned then, smoothing her fingers over the long-healed wound as if she could ease the scars on his body and his heart. "I think you're the most gorgeous man I've ever seen. This isn't who you are but it is a part of your story."

He nodded, his gaze holding hers. His jaw was clenched tight, his nostrils were flared and the fire in his eyes was all for her. But he was letting her choose what happened next and it gave her the courage to keep going.

"I want you, Ames." She took a deep breath and reached down, tugging up her nightgown and pulling it over her head.

There was nothing but the sound of their labored breathing then.

Ames was staring at her, exploring her with his eyes—but not touching her. In fact, his hands were fisted at his side. "Harper." He moaned her name.

She slid her arms around his neck and leaned into him. The crush of her breasts against his chest had them both groaning. He was all muscle. Warm and strong.

"Touch me, please, Ames," she whispered.

He did. His arms wrapped around her waist like steel bands and his big hands pressed against her bare back. Seconds later, she was on her back with him over her.

She savored the feel of his work-roughened fingers on her skin. His strong hand was surprisingly gentle as it slid down her side to cup her hip. When his hands had explored, his mouth followed. As much as she wanted to give, she hadn't prepared for how relentless and thorough he was. Her body was on fire. Aching. Desperate. But Ames was in no hurry.

He knelt on the floor between her legs, nuzzling the bend of her knee, then kissing his way up her thigh—

"Ames." She gasped, looking down at him. "Kiss me."

He stared up at her and grinned. "I was about to."

Her eyes widened. "Oh…"

"Oh, no?" He waited. "Oh, yes?"

Yes. No. "Oh… I can't breathe." She sat up, her mind spinning. This was really happening. "Birth control."

"Hell." He sat on the bed beside her. "I don't have anything." He ran a hand over his face. "Dammit. I wasn't thinking."

"No, I'm on birth control." She held out her arm. "It's an implant that lasts three years. Well, two since I've had it for a year. Not that I've needed it once…until now." Why had she said all of that? Why would he possibly want to know that? "I mean, we can…do this."

He was watching her. "You okay?"

"Yes." She was getting there. "It's a lot. For me."

"Me, too." He smiled at her. "There's no rush, Harper. Tell me what feels good. I want you to feel good. Okay?"

She was beyond flustered. "Everything feels good. Too good."

He was still smiling.

She loved that smile. She loved the angle of his jaw. She loved that his hair was mussed and he was staring at her mouth like she was dessert. "Kiss me. Here." She tapped her mouth.

He buried his hand in her hair, tipped her head back and kissed her. Devoured her was more like it. The kiss went on and on until her nervousness had melted into pure, white hunger. He sucked her lower lip into his mouth and a desperate little sound slipped from her.

"I want to make this last," he whispered.

"Next time," she moaned. "Next time we can make it last." Or the time after that.

For five seconds, he was gone. Then he was back,

warm and hard atop of her, nudging her knees apart. Harper obliged, sliding her fingers along the muscle of his back. So many muscles… Then she realized—there was no cotton boxer briefs separating them. The skin-on-skin contact knocked the breath out of her.

Ames kissed her, featherlight—and eased his way inside her.

Harper was done for. It was agonizing and blissful. Pressure-building. Intense. Consuming. Shattering her in the best possible way.

"Okay?" he whispered, the strain in his voice telling.

"Mmm-hmm." It was all she could manage. She was not *okay*, she was…wonderful. This was wonderful. And then he started moving and Harper realized she only thought she understood what wonderful meant. This? This was wonderful and so much more.

Harper held on, her fingers biting into his back as sensation took over. Her body grew tighter and weightless and electrified all at once. But that yearning, deep inside, spread until it was unbearable and euphoric.

Watching Ames heightened every sensation. The set of his jaw, the hiss of his breath, the struggle for control was the sexiest thing she had ever seen. He was the sexiest thing she'd ever seen. It was enough to push her over the edge into what had to be an orgasm. An out-of-body experience that pulled every muscle tighter and tighter until she exploded and collapsed back on the mattress. She'd never made such noises before—but she'd never experienced anything like this.

She was still free-falling when Ames's rhythm quickened. He lifted her hips and his whole body went rigid.

She watched as his head fell back and a long, broken groan tore out of him.

He was panting when he collapsed on the bed beside her.

She smiled at him, awash with shudders and tingles and little sparks of pleasure.

He smiled back, a slight sheen of sweat on his brow.

This was real. This had happened. She and Ames… It—they had been better than anything her overactive imagination could ever have come up with. "Today has been amazing," she whispered. "First, I didn't let the storm and thunder send me into a PTSD episode. I'm not sure why I never noticed thunder can sound like a gunshot. Today, it was hard to miss. But I didn't let it stop me." She took a deep breath and went on. "And now, this. *This* is even better than overcoming my fear. I mean, I know there was a tornado and things were a bit scary for a while but this…this is my favorite day ever. My first orgasm. And it was…wow. You…this… Thank you." She sighed, still smiling. Hopefully, he felt a sliver of the happiness she was feeling. And, hopefully, their day wasn't over yet.

Ames's heart rate had yet to fall within normal range and now that Harper had said all that, it wasn't going to happen anytime soon. He'd never met anyone like Harper. She came across as soft and uncertain—almost timid. But that's not who she was. Haunted or not, she was braver and stronger than anyone he'd ever known.

Today's storm had been loud and for Harper, it had been hell.

Thunder. Gunfire. PTSD.

He reached over and pulled her against him. Everything had turned out fine but the panic that'd grabbed him by the neck and damn near brought him to his knees was too recent a nightmare for him to already have forgotten. He hadn't been able to think—to breathe. He'd had to find her. There'd been no alternative.

All the while she'd been battling her demons—alone.

He buried his nose in her hair and breathed in her scent. It helped to feel her, warm and solid, in his arms. As long as he kept Harper safe, he'd never have to worry about getting swallowed up by such godawful helplessness ever again.

"You're really quiet," she whispered.

He swallowed. "Well..." He ran his fingers through her hair and let it fall against his arm. "I'm working through what you just said." He kept playing with her hair, willing his heart to steady.

"That's fair." She burrowed closer to him. "Your heart is going really fast."

He smiled. "You said it... Wow."

She giggled. "Glad it wasn't just me."

"It wasn't." He was still trying to make sense of the rest of what she'd said. If he was being honest with himself, he took great satisfaction in knowing he was the only man who'd ever heard her cry out that way. He, alone, had watched her arch off the bed and felt her nails rake down his back. And, dammit all, he wanted it to stay that way.

He was happy. Happy in a way that was new. And it was all because of Harper. He loved her. It was that simple. In time, he'd tell her as much. But, for now, he was content to hold her.

She pressed a hand over his scar. "I'm sorry this happened to you."

He covered her hand with his. "It was a long time ago."

"I know." She tilted her head back to meet his gaze. "But if you ever want to talk about it, I'm here." She took a sudden breath, shook her head and hurried on to say, "Or not. You don't ever have to talk about it. I'd understand. Either way, I'm here—if you want. That's all I meant."

He didn't talk about his past much—he'd never felt the need. But Harper's offer felt like an opportunity. If there was a chance baring his soul might help Harper open up to him, he'd do it. Ames had been so broken when he arrived on Crossroads, the Winston brothers had been relentless about finding him a counselor. Hoss thought highly of Doc Klein, who worked with the prison inmates. And since Doc had stayed on the ranch Ames's first month here, Ames had come to like and respect the man, too. Doc Klein had made it okay for Ames to talk through his past. Getting it out there and working through it had been hell but it had helped. So much so that the Winston brothers paid Doc to drop by the ranch twice a month to talk to anyone here who might need an ear. Maybe that's all Harper needed—someone to talk to. He'd be that someone if she'd let him be.

He cleared his throat. He'd tell her the nuts and bolts of it—but spare her the details. The goal was for her to feel safe enough to share, not get worked up or upset on his behalf.

"My dad was a mean SOB. He drank a lot, had a temper and used words like knives." He felt her go stiff against him. "But he didn't do this to me. He went to jail for neglect and I was sent to my uncle. My uncle drank a lot, had a temper and used his belt and fists instead of words."

Harper slid her arms around his waist and held him, tightly.

"No matter how drunk he got, he was careful. Any evidence was covered by my clothes. He knew what he was doing." He cleared his throat and pressed a kiss to her temple. "Two years in, our water got cut off so I snuck into the boys' locker room at school to shower. A coach saw me. I said I'd fallen off a dirt bike and ran home. But my uncle was waiting and he was pissed. We went to a motel so CPS or police couldn't find us. That's when this happened." He ran his fingers over his scar. "Broken bottle landed me with stitches. A stomp to the throat crushed the vocal cords. A few weeks later, the cops showed up and I was taken to the hospital."

"A week or so *after* you were hurt?" She eased back enough to look at him. "You didn't get any medical treatment?"

"My uncle sewed me up as best he could." Ames glanced down at the jagged scar on his chest and shrugged. "Then Hoss Winston showed up at the hospital and told me I was going with him." He chuckled. "That's when I was most scared." He cleared his throat. "Was Hoss Winston worse than my uncle? I was never going to talk right but I knew what to expect from my uncle. With Hoss, there was no way of knowing what'd happen next."

Harper's mossy eyes searched his. "Thankfully, Hoss is a good man."

"The best." Ames agreed. "He'll be the first to tell you

he's made plenty of mistakes but he's trying to make up for that with the time he has left."

She turned onto her stomach and propped herself on her elbows. "I'm glad he found you and brought you here." She glanced from him to the sheet.

He nodded. "A lot of people come here to get away, to heal. Crossroads is good for that."

She stared at him for a long time. So long, he was about to ask her what she was thinking. But then she said, "I came here to get away." She stared down at the sheet. "I had to."

He rested his hand on her back, giving them both courage, but stayed silent.

"Eight months ago." She shook her head. "Only eight months… My hometown is close to where they filmed the movie Groundhog Day so, every year, there a mini-Groundhog Day festival. Family-friendly stuff. Musical chairs, cakewalk, bouncy castles—all that."

"Sounds nice." He covered her hand with his.

"After work, I left the library and walked through the park where the festival was held. It was on my way home." She sat up, pulled her knees to her chest and wrapped her arms around them. "I heard a popping… Really loud. I thought it was a game until… Everyone was screaming and crying and everyone was running." She blinked rapidly. "I saw two men. They had those big guns that can fire lots of bullets?" Her gaze darted to him. "They were *laughing* and shooting."

Hearing that gutted him. And pissed him off. But he had to keep it together—for Harper. He sat up, moving closer.

"And I saw… I knew them—him. Matt." Her voice broke. "Mattie. My little brother."

Matt. Ames had not been prepared. There was no way to prepare for this. And he knew… He knew what she was going to say. A cold, hollow pit formed in his belly as he waited.

"He ran over to me, smiling." Her voice was shaking. "He said, 'Hey Harper,' and he shot…me. Twice. I laid there, I couldn't move. My leg was…" She broke off, shrugging.

No. No. No. Ames closed his eyes.

"Then he got this weird look on his face. He asked me why was I bleeding?" Tears slid down her cheeks. "I told him and he was so…so shocked. He started crying, saying he was sorry over and over, looking around at… what he'd done." She wiped at her tears. "When the police came, they told him to lay down his weapons but he was confused. He turned, they fired."

She was shivering now so he pulled her into his arms and tugged the blankets up, cocooning them together.

"My poor dad. He can't let go. He's looking for answers that make sense to him. He can't admit Mattie did this. None of us want to. But I was *there*." She broke off, then murmured, "My stepmom…" Her expression grew shuttered. "Matt was her only kid—her everything. She needed someone to blame. Since Matt and I were so close, she mostly blames me. Anyone *but* Matt, you know? And I get it, I do. Mattie was Mattie. And his death broke her heart. Broke her."

He couldn't imagine it. He didn't want to. But, right or wrong, he was angry that the people who should have loved Harper—been grateful she'd survived—had left her to grieve and suffer on her own.

No. She wasn't on her own now. He was here.

"It felt like I lost my life. My friends faded away. Walt, my boyfriend of two years, couldn't take it anymore. But I appreciated he was honest when he broke up with me."

So she had shitty family *and* shitty friends. And this Walt character? Ames hoped he never ran into the bastard. It wouldn't go well. For Walt.

"The day I left, there were still whispers and gossip, phone calls from tabloids, even reporters waiting outside my house or work. There was no getting away from it. No moving on." She faced him, a crease forming between her brows. "At work, they moved me to the back of the library so I didn't make people uncomfortable or remind them of the tragedy." She took a deep breath. "It had taken over my entire life. I was existing, but not really living. If that makes sense?"

"It does."

"And I got scared, Ames. If I stayed, would I eventually hate my baby brother, too? To the world, my twenty-one-year-old brother is a monster. No one cared that his blood alcohol level was twice the legal limit or that the toxicology report showed both cocaine and fentanyl in his system. No one talked about that, how he got the drugs or why Pete's father's gun safe had been open. It was easier for Matt and Pete to be evil." She frowned. "I was furious with him for taking the drugs and drinking but, in an odd way, it was a relief. Mattie hadn't been in his right mind—that's why it happened. It doesn't make it any less awful, but it's something." She waited for him to nod. "Now you know. Maybe running away makes me a coward—"

"No." He pulled her into his lap and rocked her. "That's the last thing you are, Harper."

She drew in a wavering breath. "But I… I *should* have known."

He tilted her face back so he could look at her. "Why you, Harper? Why not your stepmom? Or your dad? Don't take that on. That's not fair. The only person to blame is…" He stopped.

"Mattie. And Pete," she whispered. "Rationally, I know that. And my counselor, Dr. Weisbaum, reminds me every session. But in my heart, I wonder if I missed…*something.* Seven people died, Ames. Nine, with Pete and Matt. And eleven injured."

It twisted him up inside to picture her alone and afraid. He'd never forget how she'd reacted to the rifle that night, how pure terror had rendered her immobile. But today she'd got herself through it. It wouldn't have been easy to stand tall against the storm, but she'd done it. She had every reason to look so accomplished and happy.

He was so damn proud of her. Ames swallowed hard, a million thoughts and feelings kicking around his heart. He'd no idea what she'd been through. The tension eased some when she said she was in counseling—this wasn't the sort of thing to try to navigate on her own. She was smart. So damn brave. *And vulnerable.* The look on her face had him hurrying to say, "Thank you for trusting me with this."

She rested her head on his shoulder. "I shouldn't have dumped that on you."

"I'm glad you did." He kissed the top of her head. "I'm

so sorry, Harper." It wasn't enough, he knew that. But nothing he could say would ever be enough. "I'm grateful you're startin' over here."

She looked up at him, her eyes full of sadness. "Even after everything I just told you—"

"None of it was your fault." He said each word clearly. "What you've been through doesn't change how I see you. I *see* you, Harper. You're a survivor. A badass." He swallowed again. "And I love you."

The shock on her face had him kicking himself.

"Bad timing. I should have waited to tell you." He needed to shut the hell up.

"It's not that..." She frowned, her eyes intent on his face. "When things seem to be too good to be true, they probably are. I guess I'm scared."

Her words made his heart ache. "Scared of me?"

"Not you. But coming here, making friends, learning so much, being able to share everything with you." She paused, her cheeks going pink before she said, "*And* falling in love. All of it is too good to be true. I didn't have anything left to lose. Now, I do. *That* scares me."

He liked that answer. He liked it a whole hell of a lot. So much so that he kissed her. "Falling in love with who?" He kissed her again—he could feel her smile against his lips.

"The man who gave me my first orgasm." She tangled her fingers in his hair.

He liked that answer even better. "Seems like a good reason to fall for him." He slid his hands beneath the blankets. Her skin was silky smooth beneath his caress. And the slight swell of her hip was made for holding onto. "But make sure it wasn't a one-time thing." He bent low to capture her nipple in his mouth. The sound she made had him hard as a rock and, with one adjustment, he had her straddling him—so close he could feel her heat.

"Only fall for him—" she broke off, moaning when he moved to her other breast "—if…if he can deliver regular, multiple orgasms?"

"Mmm-hmm." He pulled her closer, gripped her hips as he angled just right, and thrust up and into her. "Damn…" he hissed. She was made for him. But when she moaned his name, he had to remind himself he was going to take his time with her—to make her forget everything but him.

Chapter Fourteen

Harper woke up buried in pillows and blankets and pressed right against Ames's side. She smiled and closed her eyes, content to stay as they were. It was Sunday. A free day. As far as she was concerned, this was the perfect way to spend the day. Considering the amount of energy and calories they'd been happily expending on one another, they would need food at some point today but… Maybe they could skip breakfast.

"You're smiling," Ames murmured.

"I'm sleeping. And having good dreams," she whispered back, wriggling against him.

"That would do it." He stretched, his arms tightening around her so she was squeezed tight. "You're so damn soft." She was pleased when his hands slid down her back to cup her rear.

"See, good dreams," she murmured.

"I'm dreaming, too?" He nuzzled the sensitive skin behind her ear. "Fine by me. It's Sunday. I say we dream *all* day."

She laughed at that. "You won't get hungry?" Her eyes opened. Ames with sleepy eyes and mussed hair was her new favorite view to wake up to. The crooked grin he gave her instantly woke her up—and turned her insides molten. “We have sort of expended a lot of energy in the last several hours… It’s been lovely.” Which was the understatement of the century.

“Lovely?” His grin widened. “I’ve worked up an appetite but not so much that I wanna get out of bed.” He gave her rear a squeeze.

Harper giggled. “No?”

“No.” He dropped a kiss on her shoulder and rolled over her.

Harper was sore in places she didn’t know she could be sore. And when Ames settled between her legs, the feeling of him sliding deep inside her was achingly sweet and enflaming all at once.

“Mmm,” Ames moaned. “Damn, Harper. How can I want you even more?”

Harper was too caught up in the exquisite stretch of her body around him to form a coherent sentence. But she nodded—she got it. After last night, they should both be worn out. If anything, she felt the opposite. She stared up at him, the pressure in her chest doubling when he started to move.

He’d spent hours getting to know her body. Now he knew how to please her. His mouth, his hands, the sweep of his tongue and the hot sweep of his breath across her skin—all of it drove her out of her mind with want. And she gave in to each and every sensation he stirred within her. The rising pleasure in her body had her holding onto him. And then, it happened. Her climax rolled over her, sending a million jolts of pleasure down all her limbs and pressing the air from her lungs.

Ames was smiling when she opened her eyes.

She was still panting but she managed to say, "You're proud of yourself, aren't you?"

"Yes, ma'am." He dropped a kiss on the tip of her nose. "I didn't hear any complaints."

She wrapped her arms around him. "I have *none*." She smiled. "Good morning."

He laughed.

She loved the way he laughed—loved the way his whole face relaxed. "You really don't have anything to do today?" She rolled onto her side to face him. "I know this place would fall apart without you."

His brows rose. "You think so?"

She nodded. "I know so."

"Nice. You believing in me." The tenderness on his face sent her heart rate into the stratosphere.

"I do," she whispered. Something stopped her from saying *I love you*. Instead, she said, "That's why I don't want to hold you hostage in your bed. I don't want to put you behind on work—or get the others to give you grief."

"They do that on the daily." He leaned over her. "It's not too late. If we hurry, we could get breakfast. Pretty sure Hoss and Rooster won't be handing out any extra duties today." He paused, running his fingers between her breasts. He sighed and smiled up at her. "There's a rodeo in Pardon this afternoon. Most of Crossroads will be going. It's something to do and all."

"Are we going?" As tempting as it was to think about spending the day in bed with Ames, she knew better.

"Do you want to go?" He ran his fingers through his tousled hair. "We can. Or we can stay." He leaned forward to drop a kiss on her collarbone. "I'm sure we can find plenty to do right here."

She cradled his face. "We should go eat. And go to the rodeo. When we come home tonight, we can do whatever you'd like."

"I have ideas." He patted his bed.

"Already?" She grinned. "I'd offer up my room but your bed is a lot bigger than mine." She sat up and stared around her. "Your room is probably four times the size of mine."

"The previous foreman had a family. He and his wife used this room, the kids used yours and the one next to it. There's a door at the end of the hall—so they could have some privacy. Hoss and Rooster are always looking for ways to make this place a place people want to stay."

"That's smart. Hoss and Rooster are very considerate of their employees."

"Probably because they think of us more like family." He smoothed her hair from her shoulder. "They've been more of a family to me than my own blood kin ever was."

Harper took his hand in hers. She was grateful they'd been able to share with one another. Both of them had endured more than their fair share of heartache. But she felt lighter today—stronger. She'd told Ames what had happened and he hadn't judged her or turned away from her. Instead…he loved her. And she loved him.

"What?" he asked, his gave sweeping over her face.

"Nothing." She squeezed his hand. "I'm just happy." As long as she ignored that little voice warning her that this was all going to fall apart, she'd never been so happy.

It was the first time she'd taken the time to look around his room. Last night, she'd only had eyes for Ames. But now, she could appreciate the foreman's quarters. Like the rest of the Big House, it was all stone and wood. Wood paneling lined the bottom half of the walls and a large stone fireplace took up the far wall. The windows lining the exterior wall were trimmed with the same thick wood as the beams running across the high ceiling. Solid. That's how it felt.

"Did you get to decorate it?" Harper asked.

"Decorate?" He shook his head. "I took what they gave me—and I was happy for it."

Which was a very Ames thing to say. "I was going to compliment you on your style."

"Oh? Yeah, I picked all this out." He chuckled. "The bed and the chest and that table, too." He pointed at the bedside table.

She laughed.

"You like it?" he asked, pushing off the bed to stretch, then standing there.

All she could do was stare. Ames naked was… Well, she'd never get used to the way she responded to this man. "I think you're naked." She patted the corner of her mouth. "Was I drooling?"

He shook his head. "Nope. Guess I'll have to try harder, then. Tonight." He sighed. "Guess I'll get dressed so we can go to breakfast."

"Good idea." She didn't hide the fact that she was studying his body. When he was staring at her body, it was empowering—and a huge turn-on. It was her turn to make sure he felt the same way.

"You're makin' me want to skip breakfast." The gruffness edging his voice was all promise.

She glanced up at his face, smiled, then flopped back onto the bed and covered her face with a pillow. "Go on."

She waved him away. "Before I change my mind and we both starve."

He was laughing as he went into the bathroom and turned on the shower.

She considered joining him in the shower but…she was starving. After tugging on her shirt, she grabbed her clothes and ran across the hall to her room. After she'd showered and dressed, she headed for the kitchen.

Ames was already there, serving himself breakfast. He looked especially handsome in his pale blue button-down and straw cowboy hat. A real cowboy.

My cowboy.

"Morning." Athena joined her at the buffet line. "How's your Sunday starting off?"

"Ah, g-good." She swallowed. Stay calm. It's not like anyone knew what she and Ames had been up to all night. And as long as she didn't act strange, they would never know. That's the way she'd prefer it. Last night hadn't just been about sex—it had been about opening themselves up to one another. What happened between her and Ames would stay between her and Ames.

"Alright." Athena gave her an odd smile. "Well, you better hurry because they're all about to come back for seconds."

"Oh." She'd seen the ranch hands eat so there was no time to dawdle. Three biscuits and an extralarge portion of breakfast casserole should ease the ache of her empty belly. She sat at the table, poured herself a glass of orange juice, and picked up her utensils, beyond starving now.

"That is the most food I have ever seen you eat." Brandy made this observation loudly enough to catch everyone's attention.

"Oh." Harper stared at her plate. It was a lot of food. "I brought extra biscuits…" She held her plate out. "In case…anyone wanted one."

"Mighty kind of you." Logan grabbed one.

"They are extra good this morning." Eddy took one, too. "Extraflaky."

"Don't mind if I do." Brandy swiped the last biscuit from her plate.

Harper stared down at her biscuitless plate. It was probably for the best. Carbs settled in her hips and rear. And since she'd developed a real fondness for Penny's fresh-baked breads—in all forms—she probably should cut back.

"Here." Ames sat a basket of biscuits on the table in front of her. "Asshats," he grumbled, glaring at the three who'd taken her food. He sat in the chair beside her—which had somehow unofficially become his chair over the last week.

"Aw, you're such a good boyfriend." Brandy's voice was extrasarcastic and she added an eye roll just in case anyone missed it.

Harper stared at the woman, at a loss. As far as she knew, there was no reason for the woman to be so caustic toward Ames—or her.

Harper almost jumped when Ames reached over and took her hand in his. "I'm tryin' to be."

The total silence in the room was unnerving—but then the table erupted with questions and laughter. Logan said something to Eddy about paying up, Brandy choked on her food—so Penny came running around the table to pound on her back, and Athena announced, "I knew it," while smiling.

Even Hoss and Rooster looked pleased—which was a relief. She knew how special Hoss and Rooster were to Ames. She'd never want to do something that would drive a wedge between them. If they'd been against the two of them being together, she'd have respected their wishes. It would have been horrible but…she didn't have to worry about it.

"Now, that's settled." Penny stopped patting Brandy's back. "I need a head count of who's going today? We need to get the buses rolling by nine."

And just like that, she and Ames were no longer the topic of conversation. She listened as the talk shifted to who was favored to win and what events were slated for the day, and that's how she learned about Hoss and Rooster's involvement with the Graves Prison Rodeo Rehabilitation Program.

"Here." Ames placed a buttered biscuit on her plate.

"You're full of surprises." She smiled.

"Just wait until tonight." He took a sip of his coffee, his eyes locking with hers over the rim.

She swallowed. He really shouldn't be looking at her like that. In the kitchen, in front of everyone… It wasn't fair. "I was… I was talking about the prison. I didn't know you volunteered there, too."

"Oh." He smiled, taking a bite of breakfast.

"Harper." Hoss called from his place at the head of the table. "Rooster and I were hoping to get you squared away with the GED program this week? If you're still open to lending a hand?"

"I would love to." She nodded enthusiastically.

"Good, good. Doug will likely be there today so I'll

make sure to introduce the two of you." Rooster took a sip of his coffee.

"Doug is good-looking, Harper. More your type, I'm thinking. You know, book smarts and fancy degrees and stuff." Brandy kept on eating.

"It sounds like you know a lot about him. Does that mean *you* might be interested in him." Harper smiled at Brandy. "Don't worry, I won't get in your way."

"Can you imagine?" Eddy gave Brandy some serious side-eye. "I can't."

"How about we all get along today." Hoss sounded irritated. Like a father at the end of his rope. "Knock it off with the teasing or it's gonna be a hell of a long drive to Pardon."

Harper felt bad for participating. But Brandy seemed intent on poking at Ames, and Harper did not like it. Not one bit.

"Eat," Ames murmured, pressing his leg against hers. "You're going to need your energy later." There was mischief in his warm brown eyes—and fire, too.

Harper scooped up a bite of breakfast casserole and started eating. She'd learned that everything Penny and Micah prepared was delicious, which made eating everything on her plate easy. And since Ames clearly had ideas about what would happen later tonight, she did need to refuel. But, as delicious as the food was and as excited as she was for the day's trip, there was a part of her that wished they'd decided to stay in Ames's bed, happy and tangled up in one another. The only consolation was knowing they'd have all night to be together. Until then, she'd have to be patient… And Ames needed to stop looking at her like she was something to eat. If he didn't, she couldn't be held accountable for what might happen.

For the last couple of weeks, Ames's daily life had been undergoing all sorts of changes. He'd been content before—his work was fulfilling and it served a purpose and that had been enough. Technically, he had never wanted for anything. He had a roof over his head and company when he wanted it, and there was always plenty to eat. He might not have been happy every damn day but who was?

Except… Now that he was kissing Harper in his bed every night before falling asleep and waking up to her in his arms every morning, he was pretty damn happy. Every day.

It was all the little things in-between, too. The way Harper took an interest in his day, the way she wanted to learn all about "ranch-y" things and how to do them—but she also wanted to understand why things were done the way they were. She was smart—he'd already known that—but she was curious, too. And he loved seeing everyday things through her eyes.

One day, he'd volunteered to feed the chickens for Micah. Harper, curious as ever, had gone with him. Initially, she kept her distance but something about the birds made her smile and laugh until Ames had been smiling and laughing, too. She had that effect on him. He liked it.

After that, Harper took over feeding the chickens and collecting the eggs every day. And, damn it all, if the birds didn't see or hear her coming and they'd start clucking and hopping and running out to greet her. It was like they were excited to see her.

Not that he blamed them. He was excited every time he saw her, too.

It didn't matter if she was sitting on Tango's back, listening attentively as Ames led her around one of the corrals or if she was reading aloud to him in bed—she was fully invested in whatever she did.

And she was rubbing off on him. He'd never thought to learn to knit but, since Harper wanted to teach him, he was learning. Her love of books had him reading things he'd never considered before. He's always been a both-feet-firmly-on-the-ground kinda man. Biographies, spy thrillers or some historical fiction once in a while. But now she'd got him reading some dragon-fighter series that he was enjoying the hell out of. It didn't hurt that she liked to cuddle up next to him, with her head on his chest, when they were reading together.

Daisy and Copper had picked up on this new dynamic and how to use it to their advantage real quick. If they didn't get what they wanted from him, they went to her—she almost always gave in. It made her so happy, he didn't have the heart to stop her. Besides, it wasn't a bad thing that Daisy and Copper were getting showered them with treats and affection.

When Harper started helping out with the GED classes, he found himself helping out, too. Doug was a good guy but, dammit, Brandy's digs about Harper and Doug being better suited than he and Harper were had stirred up a feeling he'd thought he was above. Turns out, nope, he was not above feeling jealousy. Or insecurity.

There were times he'd be in bed and he'd look over at her, sleeping or reading or cooing over Copper or Daisy, and he'd wonder how long this could last? How long could

Harper be happy with someone who wasn't well-read or well-traveled? He tried not to think about it too much, but when those doubts and questions snuck in, it was a lot to shake off.

The truth was, he still struggled to believe she'd picked him.

He'd never say as much but he understood what Harper meant about things being too good to be true. This, them, Harper was too good to be true.

Last night had been rough. Since their talk, Harper's nightmares had eased some. But last night? Last night, she'd jolted awake with tears on her cheeks and her heart pounding away. He'd held her close until she'd dozed off into a restless sleep, but he worried she'd be tuckered out before the day was up.

That was why he'd come to find her in the washhouse and found her armed with a wrench. He leaned against the doorway, watching.

"You are a machine," she said, whacking the side panel with impressive force. "Do your job…dammit." Another whack.

The machine clicked and sputtered—then slowly started filling with water.

"Thank you." She patted the side of the machine. "Hopefully, next time I won't have to get rough with you."

Ames found just about every damn thing Harper did adorable. That included her having full-blown one-sided conversations with inanimate objects.

"You telling it who's boss?" he asked, grinning.

"Hi." She sort of half skipped, half ran to him and slid her arms around his waist. "This is a lovely surprise."

"Lovely, huh?" He hugged her tightly.

"Yes." She sighed. "You are lovely."

He chuckled. No one had ever called him lovely before. Or gorgeous. Or beautiful. Harper had called him all that and more. "You good?"

She looked up at him. "I'm fine." She wrinkled up her nose. "I'm sorry about last night. I didn't mean to wake you up—"

"Don't apologize." He smiled. "I wish I could do… something, is all."

"You did—you do." She blinked. "They rarely happen now. I think it's because I know you're there and you'd keep me safe."

Hearing her say that made him feel like a real ass for getting insecure. She'd never said or done a thing but look at him like she was now—with trust and affection. "That's the plan." He kissed her forehead, wanting nothing more than to steal a few minutes of time with her every day. She had no idea how important she was to him.

"You'll be happy to hear I fixed the machine all by myself." She beamed up at him.

"I saw." He glanced at the massive turquoise machine shimmying as it spun through its wash cycles. "Intimidating a washing machine." He cleared his throat. "Didn't know that was possible."

She giggled. "I was mad, I'm not gonna lie. And I know I could have come to you for help but, I don't know, I didn't want it to think it had the upper hand."

"It? The washing machine?" Ames chuckled.

"Yes, the washing machine." She smiled.

"It was the same panel. The one you fixed last week?" She looked so damn cute when she was proud of herself. "I remembered what you'd done and, sure enough, that rubber washer had slipped out just like last time." She tucked a strand of hair behind her ear. "I screwed it back together, gave it a whack and it started up again." She held up the wrench, looking triumphant.

"Looks like I'm going to have to start coming up with excuses to come see you, now that you're figuring everything out on your own."

"You can come see me anytime you want." She stopped and stood on tiptoe to slide her arms around his neck. "Seeing you always makes my day better."

He liked hearing that. He liked kissing her, too. He especially liked the way she felt pressed close like this. "Got time for a walk?"

"I do." She glanced at the washing machine. "Fifteen minutes." She let go of him, set the wrench next to the machine, checked the timer and turned back to him. "Let's walk."

He took her hand and led her from the washhouse, down the stone path, to the paddock fences that surrounded the HQ horse barn. It was another hot day but he made sure to keep them in the shade of the oak trees lining the path. Harper was so fair, she'd get sunburned easily.

"I think that is the prettiest horse on Crossroads, Ames." She paused by the fence line.

Ames looked in the direction she pointed. "The gray one?"

She nodded.

"That's Clover. She's sweet-tempered and docile. She's Miss Janie's mare." Ames saw her smile dip. "Next time she needs to be exercised, I'll let you ride her."

She shook her head. "No way. I wouldn't want to get

you in trouble. Plus, I'm not sure I'm ready to ride on my own. You're still leading me around when I ride Tango."

"I won't get in trouble for doing my job, Harper. Clover doesn't get ridden enough. I'm sure she'd appreciate the attention—even if it's a couple of slow turns around the arena." This was the first time he'd seen her take an interest in a horse. That was progress. He'd figure out a way to get her up on Clover's back. He had a feeling Clover and Harper would be a good fit.

"Maybe." Harper shrugged. "Tomorrow is Lookout Point. That means I've been here a whole month." She shook her head and looked up at him. "How can it only be a month?"

"A lot has happened."

She smiled. "You mean all the orgasms?" she whispered.

He laughed.

"I have had a lot of them." She sighed.

"Happy to hear it." He was still laughing. "That is part of it." A part he was mighty fond of, too.

"What's the other part?" She squeezed his hand. "You mean that you are blissfully in love with me? That you're happy we share a bed every night? Or that you feel complete now that you've stayed up reading all night?"

"I wasn't *reading* all night." He pulled her close. "Remember? Orgasms?"

Her eyes widened. "I *do* remember. You're right. So, you still haven't read all night." She covered his heart with her hand. "But you're happy we share a bed every night."

He nodded.

"And…that, maybe, you are…" She swallowed, the sudden tension in her posture told him he wasn't the only one struggling with insecurity. "You're blissfully in love with me?"

He nodded again. But, because he didn't want her ever to doubt it, he said, "I am."

She relaxed, her smile growing until he had no choice but to smile back at her. "Had to make sure."

"It's not going to change." For him, his love for her was instinct, ingrained—a part of him. Like breathing or blinking or needing sleep.

She rested her head against his chest.

He was still getting used to this. He'd tended to ignore his feelings for things that were more concrete and tangible. But how he felt about Harper was concrete and tangible. And those feelings were too consuming to be ignored. Tenderness, satisfaction, joy, protectiveness, belonging, safety, hunger and love—all at once, all the time. Even now, standing beside the paddocks, holding her close under the scorching afternoon sun.

"Will you dance with me tomorrow night?" She giggled. "I'll try not to trip over you or stomp on you this time. If you promise not to look at me like…well, you know."

He knew. "I don't." He grinned.

"Like you want to… Like I'm… Like you want me to yourself so you can do whatever you want to me?" She looked up at him. "You do know."

He nodded. "Can't help it. It's the way I feel."

She sucked in a sharp breath. "Ames Paxton, behave yourself."

"For now." His gaze shifted to her lower lip. "But, yes, I'll dance with you." He swallowed. "I don't care if you stomp on me."

"I figure I need practice before the Charity Ball. I don't want to embarrass Hoss or Rooster by damaging their HQ foreman." She stared up at him. "You're still not on board with the whole charity thing?"

"I get it. The Winstons are looking for ways to secure their legacy, a charity trust—all that." He cleared his throat. "When Janie delivers on the staff for the camps and such, I'll be on board."

In his experience, Janie loved to plan and talk and promote but the actual doing? She wasn't the type of person to "do" much when it came to work. HQ and the other quadrants on Crossroads had solid infrastructure but none of them had any manpower to spare. Janie's fancy dossier full of numbers and quotes and research studies and impressive projected investments was all well and good but those things required people with the knowledge to make it all happen—and no one on Crossroads had those skills.

"You're worrying." Harper was frowning up at him.

"I am?"

"We've spent a lot of time together, Ames. Some of it talking." She smiled. "When you talk, I listen. What you don't say with words, I can see here." She pressed her hand against his cheek. "You love this place. You want what's best for the land and the people that live here. Even though Janie is a Winston, you don't fully trust her. But, for Hoss and Rooster, you follow orders and hope for the best. Because, for Hoss and Rooster, you'd do just about anything. Am I right?"

He couldn't have said it better himself. "Yes, ma'am." He could get lost in those clear hazel eyes for hours. "You reading my thoughts?"

"I am. I can read them clearly." She nodded. "But you

can't think those things right now, Ames. We have at least six hours before you can take my panties off with your teeth so don't tease yourself." And, with that, she slipped out of his arms and ran back to the washhouse, giggling.

Ames stood there for a solid five minutes, stunned by Harper's hotter-than-hell invitation. He could make it six hours. He could. Now, if she lingered a second longer than that at the dinner table tonight, there was a good chance he'd end up picking her up and carrying her straight to his room to do exactly what she'd said. But the excitement on her face and her husky giggle told him she was just as eager for tonight as he was. Tonight was going to be a very good night.

Chapter Fifteen

Harper pushed the wheeled mop-bucket into the men's bunkhouse bathroom. After she'd mopped in here, she was done with work. She'd have plenty of time to get cleaned up for Lookout Point. Even though everyone on Crossroads would be there, she still felt like it was a date. Their third date. The last two Sundays, they'd gone to the Graves rodeo in Pardon. It had been nice to get away from the ranch but Harper wasn't much of a rodeo person. She wasn't sure who she should cheer for—the men or the animals? The idea of either getting hurt made her so tense, it was hard to enjoy any of it. But, for Ames, she'd put on a smile and tried. Her favorite part of both rodeos had been the drive up and back, beside Ames, holding hands and talking softly. The more time she spent with Ames, the more she loved him—so going to the rodeo was worth it.

"Hello?" There was a knock on the bedroom door. "Harper?" The click-click of heels on the wooden floor announced the imminent arrival of Janie Winston.

Harper turned, mop in hand, right as Janie came into the bathroom. She'd expected to see Miss Janie tonight at Lookout Point—not here, in the men's bunkhouse bathroom.

Janie stopped and made a big production of turning

around and looking at everything. "My goodness, look at this bathroom." Janie Winston stood in the bathroom door. "Penny was right. You're quite the little housekeeper, aren't you?" She gave Harper a long, narrow-eyed look.

"Thank you." A trickle of apprehension ran down the length of her spine.

"I'm glad I found you." Janie's smile was brittle. "I wanted to have a little chat before tonight, just the two of us."

"I'm not quite done in here—"

"It won't take too long. Then you can get right back to it." Janie waved her into the men's bunkhouse and pulled two chairs together, sitting in one and patting the other.

Harper rested the mop against the wall, wiped her hands on her the towel tucked into her belt, and went to sit beside the woman. She hated the coil of apprehension twisting up her insides but, really, what could she and Janie have to talk about?

"Isn't this nice?" Janie crossed her legs and rested her hands on her knees. Her fingers sparkled with rings and her nails had been filed to points and painted a deep, glossy red. "Rooster mentioned you'd had a few ideas about the Charity Ball."

Relief hit Harper in the chest. There was one thing they could talk about. "Yes. Well, not many but I did help out with special events in my old job and I thought there might be—"

"Your old job? At the Lake Mayfair Library?" Janie cut in, her voice upbeat.

"Yes." Harper swallowed. She'd never mentioned the

name of her hometown—not once. Not even to Ames. And, suddenly, she was more anxious than ever.

"I see, go on."

"I… Auctions were always a big success." She cleared her throat but a knot had formed, large enough to make it difficult for her to speak. "Especially if—if you could find people willing to donate items that would appeal to the crowd participating in the fundraiser. Limited edition books signed by authors or rare collectible books were very popular auction items."

"Interesting but I'm not sure how that applies to our event?" Janie's brows rose. "It seems like a large demotion to go from being someone who organized fundraisers to someone who cleans toilets. Is there a reason for that?"

Harper studied the woman, knowing to be careful. "I wanted a fresh start."

"That is understandable." Janie nodded. "I'm curious why you picked Crossroads? Surely there are other places closer to Illinois to start fresh?"

"I suppose." She swallowed but that knot didn't budge.

"I'm thinking the appeal was the distance from Lake Mayfair? The further, the better?" Janie glanced at her nails, then back at her. "The last time I was here there was something…not right about you. You don't fit or belong here. I *feel* it. So when I went back to Fort Worth, I did some digging. After all, you are living under the same roof as my brothers. For all I knew, you could be an axe murderer. Thankfully, you're not."

Harper understood then. Janie knew.

"But, you are a threat to the ranch and the people that live here. The people that live on Crossroads came here because they had no other place to start over. They needed to forget about who they were before they came here so they could work on bettering themselves. They deserve that, don't they?" Janie didn't wait for her to respond. "But you…you're different. Hoss and Rooster make sure no one comes to Crossroads with a violent criminal record. It's the one rule we all agree on. Which means you don't belong here."

She didn't have a violent criminal record—she didn't have *any* criminal record. "I don't have—"

"This might sound personal, but it's not. My family and this ranch come first. I need you to understand that. And what happens if the press finds you're here, Harper?" Janie interrupted her, acting as if Harper hadn't said a thing. "You think they'd stop at exposing all your dirty laundry? No. Once they learned Hoss and Rooster had harbored you, it'd be like blood in the water—and all the tabloid sharks would come here. They would dig up every skeleton, every wrongdoing, conviction or tidbit about every one of Crossroads employees. All the work they'd done to move on, gone in an instant. It would put them through hell—who knows what sort of damage that stress might lead to?"

"No one knows I'm here. I'd never do anything to draw attention to myself." She shook her head, hoping the woman would give her a chance to explain her side of the story. "I don't want to hurt anyone, Miss Janie. Especially the people on Crossroads. They are important to me—they've become my family. I'm like everyone else. I want to forget and move forward—"

"Honey, you can't forget and move forward when the police are looking for you." Janie tsk-tsked. "I guess you were too caught up in playing housekeeper and warming Ames's bed to keep up with your family back home."

"No." *What? The police?* "The investigation was closed, Janie. No one is looking for me."

"It's being reopened." Janie sat back in her chair, watching Harper. "Apparently, there are allegations that *you* put the drugs into those boys' drinks. That would make you an accessory to all those murders."

Harper stared at the other woman. "What?" Her voice cracked. Allegations? How was that possible? From who? "Where did you hear—"

"You see? I don't think you understand the severity of you being here. Do you know what kind of trouble Hoss and Rooster could get into for harboring a fugitive? Crossroads has some ranch hands that have served time but the ranch has never, ever harbored a fugitive or broken the law. You want Hoss or Rooster arrested?" She sat up straight and peered down her nose at Harper. "That's why I know you'll agree that it's best if you pack your things and leave here."

Harper couldn't speak. Her head was buzzing from all the horrible things Janie Winston had said. Was it true? She'd left her cell phone at home so, even if someone had tried to get in touch with her, they couldn't. The few times she'd been on the computer to help out with the GED classes, she hadn't looked up Lake Mayfair, her family or anything to do with home. She wasn't ready. Not yet. She had no way of knowing the truth.

"Did you hear what I said?" Janie snapped her fingers in front of Harper's face.

Harper blinked, glancing at the other woman.

"I will not stand by and let you bring hurt or ruin to my family or this ranch."

"Janie, I promise you I wasn't involved. I was shot but I didn't—"

"No? That's up to the police to decide." Janie paused, but there was no sympathy on her face. "Being a victim makes you less likely to be a suspect, I suppose."

For a moment, Harper was too stunned to respond. What was she saying?

"I blame my brothers for this." She took a deep breath. "If they'd done their due diligence and bothered to look into your roots, this could have been avoided. This place is a business, not a halfway house."

"Hoss was being kind—"

"Hoss is a damn fool." Janie snapped. "It would serve the both of them right to have the police *and* the press show up. The only reason I'm not calling the press right this minute is because of the impact it would have on the ranch. A third of this place is mine and I have plans for it, too." She stared at Harper. "I'm giving you until Sunday to leave. Without making a fuss or getting Ames riled up about it. This is the only home and family he has, after all." She paused. "If you don't leave by Sunday, I *will* call the law myself. Whatever happens to my brothers will be on you." For a minute, Janie softened. "So, if you really care about them like you say you do, you'll go. You won't make me do this."

Harper felt like she'd been punched in the gut. No, it was more like the day she'd been shot. How she'd been slammed to the ground and had the air knocked from her lungs. That was what this felt like.

"Am I clear?" Janie asked, standing and putting her chair back.

Harper nodded.

"Good. Now, I'll get out of your hair and you can finish mopping." Janie pointed at the bathroom with one long bloodred- tipped finger. "And I'll see you at Lookout Point."

As soon as Janie left, Harper ran to the bathroom and threw up. She couldn't help it. This was one of her worst fears, coming to pass. The idea of her past, threatening Crossroads, her new friends… Ames, was unbearable.

But leaving Ames? She was gasping for air. There were no secrets between her and Ames anymore. She had told him everything. She could tell him this… But if she did, he'd tell her to stay. He'd tell her it would be okay. Because he didn't know how awful it would get.

She knew what it was like to live under a microscope, to be picked apart and eviscerated until, little by little, she'd started to think she had done something wrong—something to deserve this. Her time here had made her strong enough to see she'd had no hand in what had happened but it had been a long, hellish journey to get here. If she hadn't had Ames, there was no guarantee she would have reached this point.

She wouldn't hurt her friends or disrupt their lives.

She wouldn't do that to Logan, Brandy, Eddy, Gabe or Athena. She wouldn't do that to Penny, Micah, Calder or Rooster or Hoss. And, most of all, she wouldn't do that to Ames. This was their sanctuary. She wouldn't take that away from them.

She'd tell them she had to go, face whatever inquiry was waiting for her back home, and, maybe, she would come back. But she'd only come back if she was certain her past wouldn't follow her here. If there was a question? She couldn't come back. It was a terrible plan but she was still reeling from the whole horrible encounter.

She mopped the bathroom, put away all her cleaning supplies and headed to her room. Thankfully, there was no sign of Ames. She'd have caved if she saw him, she knew it. She wasn't strong enough to act okay yet. It was a relief to close her bedroom door and lean against it. She slid down the flat surface to sit on the floor and sobbed.

She'd always known this would happen. It had to. Finding this place, falling in love, feeling alive again—it was just as she'd feared. All too good to be true. And even though it felt like her heart was being torn into tiny pieces, she was thankful for every precious second she'd spent here. The memories she'd made would get her through the dark days ahead—when Ames could no longer be at her side offering her his strength.

As soon as he saw Harper, he knew something was wrong. She looked beautiful—she always did. But her posture was tense and she was playing with the straps of her purse—like she had her first day on the ranch. Since Gabe's truck wouldn't start, they had Gabe and Athena in the truck with them for the drive to Lookout Point. He hated not knowing what she was thinking, what was weighing on her. But he'd have to wait until it was just the two of them.

"Are we going swimming tomorrow?" Athena asked. "It's supposed to be *q*-hot."

"Like it is every day?" Gabe asked.

"Even hotter." Athena leaned forward to put her hand

on Harper's shoulder. "Will you go? It's Saturday. Free time. Free time is me time. And I can't think of anything I'd rather do than cool down and float."

"Maybe." Harper's attempt at a smile was pinched.

"You okay?" Athena asked. "You seem… I don't know. Less sunshine-y."

Ames glanced at Harper. As far as descriptions went, it was spot-on. Harper had this internal glow about her—like a human ray of sunshine. But not now.

"I am feeling a little under the weather." Harper sighed. "My stomach."

Ames reached over and took her hand. "We can drop them off and head back to the house, if you want. So you can rest?"

"Oh, no. I'll be fine." Harper took a deep breath. "Tonight will be fun."

Ames wasn't buying it. Her hands were clammy and… well, she wasn't acting like herself. He didn't like it. And he especially didn't like not knowing what the hell was going on.

"Are you pregnant?" Athena asked. "I mean, you and Ames have been together for a while—"

"I am going to jump out of the truck." Gabe moaned.

Ames laughed at that.

"What?" Athena slapped her brother on the shoulder. "It could happen. Why are you acting like such a child?"

"Call me whatever you want. I do not want to hear this."

Ames glanced at Harper, who looked at him and they smiled at one another. It was the first real smile he'd seen all evening.

"No. I'm not." Harper was smiling now. "Please don't throw yourself out of the truck, Gabe."

"Fine." Gabe sighed. "But, seriously, Athena. If you're going to ask her that sort of stuff, can you wait until I'm not around?"

"Can do." Athena laughed. "But you are a child."

"Whatever," Gabe grumbled.

The rest of the drive, Athena gave Harper tips on riding. She said riding horses was an essential part of living on a ranch and, since Harper had picked up on everything else, there was no reason Harper couldn't be a pro rider in a month or so.

"I was thinking about putting her on Clover," Ames said, glad to have the opportunity to bring up the horse again.

"Yes." Athena clapped her hands. "Clover is the sweetest mare, Harper. She is the perfect horse to learn to ride on. No offense to Tango, Ames."

"No offense taken." Ames knew his horse could be a little stubborn from time to time. For Harper to really fall in love with riding, she'd need the right horse to win her over. "Clover is a better fit."

"And that genius insight is why you're the foreman," Athena said.

"Laying it on a little thick, there, aren't you, sis?" Gabe asked. "If Brandy was here, she'd say you were sucking up."

Ames tried to enjoy their back-and-forth but, with Harper a ball of stress, he couldn't. When they finally parked the truck, he hoped to keep Harper back—but she was out of the truck before he'd even unbuckled his seat belt.

"You two fighting?" Gabe asked when Ames got out of the truck.

Ames gave him a look.

"Athena can ask about babies but I can't ask if y'all are fighting?" Gabe shrugged. "She seems upset is all. Geez. Forget it." He spun on his heel and walked off.

He adjusted his straw cowboy hat and scanned the crowd for Harper. When he found her, she was helping Penny get the buffet tables set up. Harper liked helping out—she said feeling useful on the ranch made her feel like she belonged here. Maybe working with Penny would cheer her up? Besides, if she'd wanted to talk to him, she wouldn't have bailed out of the truck as soon as he parked. Instead of crowding her and plying her with questions, he'd give her space.

"Ames Paxton." Miss Janie hooked her arm through his. "You're looking a little long in the face. Trouble in paradise?"

"No, ma'am." He led her toward the tables being set up in the pavilion.

"No?" Janie sounded surprised.

He glanced at her—in time to see Janie's narrow-eyed sneer directed at Harper. What the hell was that about? He stopped, dislodging her arm from his. "Is there a problem?"

"Problem?" But the way she said it was a little too contrived for his liking. "Look at you getting all grumpy for nothing." She sighed, rolling her eyes. "Be careful about getting territorial, Ames. A woman doesn't like to feel smothered—it can come across like you don't trust her."

Ames wasn't in the mood for Janie Winston or whatever mischief she was trying to stir up.

"You sure you're okay?" Janie asked again.

"Is there a reason I shouldn't be okay?" He put his hands on his hips and waited.

"How would I know? You've always been as prickly as a cactus toward me—I do my best to stay out of your personal life." She shrugged. "You go on and be a grumpy sourpuss and I'll go find someone who doesn't think I'm always up to something."

Good luck with that. But he didn't say a word.

At dinner, he sat across the table from Harper. She answered questions and attempted to laugh a time or two, but he wasn't sure she heard a word that was being said. She wasn't eating, either. It'd taken Harper a week after arrival before her appetite had kicked in but, since then, she didn't miss meals. Watching her push her macaroni and cheese, brisket and yeast rolls around on her plate without actually eating a thing was reason for concern.

After the tables were cleaned off and the music started, he couldn't take it anymore.

"Harper." He took her hand. "You wanted to dance."

Her big hazel eyes swept over his face. "Okay."

As soon as they were on the dance floor and she was in his arms, he was a little steadier. "What's wrong?"

She stared up at him and swallowed. "I need to do something."

"Okay." He nodded. "Whatever it is, we'll do it."

"I need to…" She took a deep breath and closed her eyes. "I need to go home. I need to see my dad. And Valerie."

They'd talked about her dad a lot. She loved him—she missed him. But she knew that until he was in a better place, he wasn't in a position to think about anyone beyond himself. But Valerie? Harper rarely mentioned the woman. What little she had said was enough to make Ames not like or trust the woman.

"You've said I should face my fears. I'm stronger now." She looked at him again. "I need to see my dad… Make sure he is okay. Make sure everything if okay with the… investigation, too."

That threw him. "I thought it was closed."

"Apparently, not." She didn't look at him. "It's important."

He couldn't argue with any of what she'd just said. She had every right to feel this way—every right to go and set things straight with her father. "You've always been strong, Harper. You know it now." He smiled at her, willing himself to ask the question that flooded him with dread. "When will you come back?"

Her gaze focused on the middle of his chest. "I'm not sure."

He stared at the top of her head. "When are you thinking about going?"

"Tomorrow." She cleared her throat. "Penny is going in to Winston Creek so I thought I could get a ride, rent a car and go to the airport."

Ames listened, doing his best to stay calm. "I could fly you there. It'd be less time—"

"No." She shook her head. "I'd rather say goodbye here." She glanced at him, then back at his chest. "Please."

Every instinct told him this was wrong. All of this was wrong. "Harper—"

"Ames." Her hand tightened on his. "I'm really not feeling all that well. Do you mind taking me back to the house?"

"I don't mind." He kept hold of her hand as he led her off the dance floor. He spied Athena and stopped long enough to make sure she and Gabe could get a ride back with Logan. He was acutely aware of the way his team of ranch hands was looking back and forth between him and Harper.

"Get some rest, Harper." Athena gave her a quick hug.

The others said their good nights and Ames led her to his truck. A few minutes into the drive, she scooted to the middle of the bench seat and rested her head on his shoulder. He draped his arm along the back of the seat so she could get closer—and she did.

By the time he'd gotten up the courage to ask her why she was doing all this so quickly, he realized she'd fallen asleep. She wasn't feeling well so sleep was a good thing. But it gave him too much time to think about what was going to happen tomorrow morning. Maybe if he'd had more time to prepare, it wouldn't feel this way. But…it hurt. A whole hell of a lot.

He parked and came around to the passenger side. She was sleeping so peacefully, he couldn't bear to wake her. He scooped her up, nudged the truck door closed and carried her inside.

"Are we home?" she murmured, her voice thick with sleep.

"Yes." He opened his bedroom door.

"I can walk." She pushed against him. "Really. I know I'm heavy."

"You're not." But he set her on her feet. "How are you feeling?" He pressed the back of his hand to her forehead. "You're warm."

"I'm fine." Her gaze locked with his. "I'd be better

if you'd take me to bed, Ames. Please. I need you." She twined her arms around his neck and kissed him.

There were so many things he needed to say, to ask, to understand. But there was an urgency about her that drew him in. Her mouth was soft against his, clinging to his bottom lip until his lips parted and their tongues touched. Her little moan was all it took to put her physical needs before everything else. If she was leaving tomorrow, he'd make sure she left knowing how much he loved her. First with his body and, later, with his words.

When they fell back on his bed, she rolled over him to tug her shirt up and over her head.

He loved the way her hair fell about his when she leaned forward. He groaned from the brush of her nipples against his chest. His hands gripped her hips when she slid onto him and began to move. Whatever she wanted, he'd give it to her. No matter what. And when they both fell apart, moaning and crying out together, he allowed himself to doze off. Knowing them, he'd wake up wanting her all over again and he'd make damn sure to say what needed to be said before they got lost in one another again.

But when Ames opened his eyes, sunlight was streaming into his room and the bed beside him was empty. He sat up, scanning the room. "Harper?" he called out. The silence had him jumping out of the bed, winding the sheet around his hips, and running across the hall to her room. Her room, which was empty. The bed was stripped, the pile of books she'd been reading was gone, as well as the bag full of her knitting supplies. Her toothbrush wasn't in the bathroom.

"Sonofabitch."

But then he saw the envelope on her pillow. His hand

was shaking as he reached for it. He knew, he knew what he'd find and his heart was already aching. He sat on her bed and opened the letter, each word slicing his heart wide.

> Ames, I am grateful for the memories we have made together. Crossroads is a special place that I'll hold in my heart forever. I will picture you on Tango, with Copper and Daisy, with affection—always. Thank you for giving me the strength to move forward, face my fears and see where life takes me next. If I hurt you, I am sorry. Be happy. You deserve to be happy. – Harper

He dropped the paper to the floor. It didn't make sense. None of it. She'd been happy here, he knew it. He'd felt it. What had changed that? Why had she left? Her note hadn't explained a damn thing. But it had made one thing clear. Harper was gone and she wasn't planning on coming back.

Chapter Sixteen

Harper stood on the sidewalk in front of her childhood home. It, like the rest of Lake Mayfair, looked exactly the same as the day she'd left. The two-story white house was neat, the grass was cut and the flower beds were blooming with color. It was a stark contrast to the more earthy tones at Crossroads. And the temperature was almost cold now that she'd become so acclimated to the heat.

She'd half expected there to be a patrol car waiting for her. Not finding one offered a sliver of comfort.

Her father appeared from around the side of the house, a watering can in one hand. He was assessing the state of each flower bed as he moved, pouring water where he saw the need. It was such a normal thing for her father to do that, for a minute, it felt like she'd stepped back in time and she was coming home after working at the library.

She gripped the handle of her wheeled suitcase and headed up the path. "Dad?"

Her father paused, his body going rigid, before he turned to her. "Harper?"

She let go of her suitcase. "I'm home." She swallowed, watching the shift of emotions on his face. Shock, concern, happiness, then concern all over again.

He dropped the watering can and hurried to her, pulling her into his arms and hugging her tightly. "You're here." His words were thick. "You're really here." He was crying now, his body shaking.

"Oh, Dad." She hugged him back. "I'm sorry I left—"

"No. Don't be." He sniffed and pulled back to look at her. "I can't believe you're here." His voice was unsteady. He wiped the tears from his cheeks and pulled her back into his embrace. "My girl."

His tears gutted her and his words sliced deep. Leaving had been a way to save herself, not hurt him. She hadn't thought he'd notice her absence. But she'd been wrong and she was sad she'd hurt him.

He sighed, then said, "Let's go inside to catch up." He released her and took her suitcase.

Once they were inside and her father poured them both some lemonade, they sat at the kitchen table. He kept reaching over to pat her hands and smile at her. It was the first time he'd truly *seen* her in a long time. It was a relief. Being here, with him, eased the ache in her chest some, too. This was home, after all.

But she couldn't relax, not yet. Valerie was nowhere to be seen—or heard.

"How have you been?" she asked, sipping her lemonade.

"Good." He nodded. "Working again. They've been holding down the fort long enough without me. I can't keep doing that to them so… I'm back a couple of days a week." He patted her hand. "I'm back in the land of the living most of the time." His smile dimmed.

"That is great, Dad." Harper was genuinely pleased. Moore Plumbing was her father's company and he'd loved his work. Luckily, he had a capable staff, who had kept the business up and running. She took his hand and gave it a squeeze. "I know it's hard. I do." She met his gaze. "Day by day."

"Day by day." He stared at her for a moment. "For one, I owe you an apology, Harper." He cleared his throat. "Not just for checking out after Matt... Well, you know. That's not what a father should do. I let you down and I'm sorry."

She squeezed his hand again. "We were all grieving in our own way, Dad."

"And then... A lot of things have come out in the last couple of weeks. Things I had no idea about—but I should have." His eyes welled up with tears. "I had no idea how things were between you and Valerie. I know she was upset after Matt's death. We all were, so I chalked up what she said as that—her lashing out because of what happened. I never thought... I never thought she blamed you." He swallowed. "Someone called for references last week—"

"I know." She took a deep breath. "Are they reopening Matt's case?"

He propped his elbow on the table and rested his forehead in his hand. "No. They're not. There is nothing to investigate. It's done. But Valerie can't let go... She can't accept it..." He broke off. "She's not in her right mind, Harper. She's not. When I heard her on the phone, telling whoever it was that you were implicated in that whole mess, it was a wake-up call. I knew she wasn't okay but I hadn't understood how much she needed help. We had a serious discussion. She decided—not me—that it was time for her to check herself into Bright Horizons for some help."

Harper was stunned—and beyond relieved. Bright Horizons was an inpatient mental health hospital. "She did?"

He nodded.

"Are you okay with that?" The tears in his eyes tore at her heart.

"I am." He nodded. "It is the right decision. It's hard since she won't let me visit and won't take any of my calls but I can't blame her, really. What happened..." He shook his head. "There might be no coming back from it for her."

She held onto his hand. "I'm sorry you had to deal with this alone, Dad."

He sniffed. "That's my girl."

She leaned closer to rest her head on his shoulder.

"You think you'll stay for a while?" his voice wobbled.

How could she leave? If she did, he'd be alone. *Alone*-alone. As much as she wanted to go back to Crossroads and Ames, she wasn't convinced that—somehow, some way—her past would catch up to her and hurt those she'd come to love so much. Janie had alluded to the bad press it might cause simply because she was related to Matt. There was a chance. The press did love to sensationalize and exploit. She couldn't let that happen to Ames—to Crossroads.

When she was ready and confident her past wouldn't affect Crossroads' future, she'd go back. But, for now, this was where she needed to be.

It was easy slipping back into old patterns. Morning coffee with her father, grocery shopping, family counseling sessions, individual counseling sessions. Driving with her father to visit Valerie, who refused to see him, but he wouldn't give up.

Three weeks went by in the blink of an eye but the ache

in her heart grew until it was hard to ignore the pain pressing in on her. Every night, she missed being in Ames's arms. And every morning, she missed his heavy-lidded smile as he woke up beside her. She missed his uneven voice and steady gaze. She missed how he was with Daisy and Copper—she missed Daisy and Copper, too. And the others. All of them. Even Brandy, a little.

But her dad was happier. She could see it. He was putting on weight, working more often and taking interest in things like the upcoming Best Roses of Lake Mayfair competition. It offered some consolation.

Another Wednesday rolled around, another morning of bringing the mail to her father and sitting down with her coffee.

He flipped through the mail, paused, lifted an envelope and offered it to her. "Looks awful fancy. Maybe it's an invite to cousin Marie's wedding?"

Harper made a noncommittal sound. There was no way they were getting invited to cousin Marie's wedding. But it was a fancy envelope and… Her heart stopped and she dropped the envelope to the table.

"What's wrong?" Her father stopped sorting the mail. "Harper?"

She stared down at the Crossroads Ranch address on the back of the envelope. "It's…nothing."

"It looks like something." Her father reached for the envelope. "You're shaking like a leaf."

She held her breath and watched as he used his letter opener on the thick cream stationery.

"It's an invitation for a charity ball." Her father scanned the invitation, his eyes widening. "This is from the ranch?

Where you worked?" He looked at her then—studying her closely.

She nodded.

"Where that fella is?" Her father sighed when she nodded. "Are you going to go?"

Was she? Could she? As much as she wanted to, she hesitated.

"Harper, I can explain to them about Valerie. That all those things she said about you, blaming you, saying the police were after you—that all of that was a lie." He swallowed, hard.

"It's okay, Dad." The last thing she'd wanted was to upset him this morning.

"They should know, Harper. I don't want anyone thinking my daughter is a wanted fugitive."

Harper tried to give him a reassuring smile. "And I appreciate that. I'm just…" She shrugged. *Scared.* Not just that she'd somehow negatively affect Ames and the others, but that, maybe, Ames had moved on. It was possible. As much as she wanted to believe he loved her, it had all happened so fast. "I'm not sure it's the right time. Yet."

"I am. I know you miss him. I see it." Her father grabbed her hand. "I can't stand it, Harper. You being back here isn't right. I want you to have a future without the shadows of our past getting in the way. Leave them here. You deserve better."

"And you don't?" She squeezed his hand. "You can stay but I can't?"

He shook his head. "I can't leave her." He handed her the invitation. "You have plenty of reasons to go. One in particular."

Harper took the invitation. The event was this weekend—three days from now. A note slid out and onto the table. She stared at it, her heart pounding away.

"You gonna read it?" Her father glanced from her to the note.

"I don't think so." If it was from Ames… In the note she'd left for him she'd told him she was strong. But that wasn't true. If she was strong, she wouldn't be terrified of how she'd react to a note. If it was from Ames… She grabbed the note and opened it.

Harper, please come back to Crossroads. You are family and family stands together, supports one another, no matter what. – H. Winston

Her father sat, watching her. "What did the note say?"

She handed her father the note.

Her father's chin wobbled some and he sniffed. "I'm sorry, Harper." He looked at her. "Whoever this H. Winston is, he's right. Family should stand together and support one another, no matter what. I should have been there for you. I wasn't. But, thankfully, these people were." He held up the note.

"Dad, we were all grieving—"

"I lost my son. But I also lost my daughter." He shook his head. "The least I can do is drag you back to the place where you found happiness again." He tapped the letter. "If they're willing to stand with you, why aren't you willing to let them?"

"Because I'm scared." She swallowed. "I'm scared they'll find out and be like everyone here—that I'll lose everyone all over again."

"But Ames knows." Her father smiled at her. "You

didn't lose him over what Mattie did. You lost him because you thought leaving him was what was best for him. I'm not so sure he'd agree with the choice you made."

She frowned. He was right. She and Ames had agreed to face everything together. Instead of facing her fears, she'd run from them—again. She'd run from Ames and the unconditional love he'd given her. She'd even gone so far as to let her doubt shake her belief in his love. That was unforgivable. Her heart hadn't forgiven her. But, hopefully, Ames would. "Will you go with me?"

"I will." He stood. "Guess I need to see if my good suit still fits. What are you going to wear?"

She shook her head. "Most of my clothes are from my Harper the Mouse stage."

"What stage are we in now?"

"Harper the Badass." She glanced at her dad. "At least, I thought I was. But it turns out I was only a badass when…when I was with Ames."

"You're a badass without him. You left him to come back here. That took no small amount of strength and… badassery. I'm not saying it was the right thing to do, but, knowing how you feel about him, it couldn't have been easy."

She could still remember the way he looked, sound asleep, his arm draped across her. She'd tried to memorize his scent, the feel of him, the sound of his breathing, all of him, so she could take him with her. But nothing could soothe the hollow ache that had taken up residence in her chest the moment she'd slipped from bed and gone with Penny to Winston Creek—long before Ames woke.

"No, it wasn't easy." Her eyes were stinging. "And it won't be easy to go back, either."

"But Harper the Badass can handle it." Her father patted her shoulder.

"Thanks, Dad." She smiled up at him. "I might need you to say that a couple more times between now and then."

"I can't wait to meet your fella." Her father patted her on the back and let her go.

"You'll love him." She swallowed. In three days, she'd see Ames. She'd hold him and kiss him and beg him to forgive her leaving him. There was no guarantee everyone on Crossroads would be as accepting as Ames but she had to try. She missed the heat and the wide-open spaces. She missed Copper and Daisy. She missed everyone—even Brandy. But mostly, she missed Ames. Talking to him. Holding his hand. Sleeping beside him. And seeing him look at her the way only he looked at her. *I love you, Ames. I'll be there soon.*

Ames put two clean pairs of starched jeans and three pressed button-down shirts into the duffel bag on his bed. He had everything he needed. He didn't know how long he'd be gone but he wasn't coming back until he'd convinced Harper to come back with him.

All he had to do was think about Janie Winston and he wanted to punch something. What sort of person set out to hurt and slander someone else—then have the nerve to say she was doing what was best for Crossroads.

"What?" He stared down at Copper and Daisy, who were both watching him. "I'm going to her, okay? I can't take you with me. But I will bring her home."

Copper pawed at his calf.

Ames stooped. "I know." He scratched behind her ear.

"I'll let you give her a talking-to when she gets back, okay?"

Daisy bleated, then snorted, stomping one hoofed foot.

"Yes, I'll make sure you get to speak your mind, too." He gave the goat a scratch, too.

He stood, grabbed his bag and headed out the side door.

He had never seen Crossroads this busy. As pissed as he was over Janie's interference, he had to give her credit for pulling this whole charity ball thing together in record time. He'd never seen so many limousines and fancy cars on Crossroads. And, he hoped, he never would again. It was entirely too loud—too crowded—for his preference.

He walked across the gravel lot, threw his bag in the back of the truck and climbed in. After last night's hollering match between the Winston siblings, Hoss had told Ames he could take the Cessna and go after Harper the very next day. And that's exactly what he was going to do.

He backed up and headed toward the main gate when a car drove in. He paused, blinking, but the car drove past before he could confirm what he'd seen.

Harper? He was seein' things, he had to be. He was so eager to get to her, that's all. But he pulled off to the side and turned and waited until the small black rental car parked before he moved.

Harper.

She stepped out of the car in a long burgundy dress and heels. She was the most beautiful thing he'd ever seen. And she was here. Not in Illinois, but right here. She took a step, leaned against the car and lifted the hem of her dress to reveal high heels.

He frowned. What was she thinking? If she wasn't careful, she'd wind up tripping in that getup.

She was talking to someone so Ames turned to see who. The man was older, handsome enough—and familiar. Harper's Dad. It had to be. The family resemblance was too strong. Harper hooked arms with her father and the two of them headed for the house.

Ames slammed the truck into reverse and spun around, driving back to park—and run after her.

He pushed through the front door. "Harper," he called out, breathless, but headed straight for her.

Harper spun and, sure enough, she wobbled.

But he got there in time.

She smiled up at him. "Hi."

"Hi?" He steadied her. "You… You're here." He pulled her into his arms. He had to, he had to know she was real. The feel of her arms wrapping around his waist was real enough. So was her scent—so sweet he damn near groaned as it filled his nostrils.

"You're not dressed up?" Her voice was muffled.

Ames loosened his hold, his gaze sweeping over her face. "No." He shook his head, blown away by how gorgeous she looked.

"Why?" she asked. "You're not going to the ball?"

"I was coming after you." He frowned. "You've lost weight."

"I'm not as good a cook as Penny." She shrugged.

"But you're okay?" He heard the gruffness in his voice but she only smiled.

"I am more than okay. Now." Her clear hazel eyes locked with his.

The not-so-subtle sound of a man clearing his throat reminded Ames they weren't alone. It hurt to let go of

Harper, but he managed it. The man was her father. Ames needed to show the man some respect. “Ames Paxton, sir.”

“Steve Moore.” He shook Ames’s hand. “This is him?” He asked Harper.

“This is him.” Harper took Ames’s other hand and rested her head on his shoulder.

“I’d like to explain some of the misunderstanding that led to Harper’s quick departure.” Steve Moore shook his head. “My wife, Harper’s stepmother, isn’t well. It seems she spoke with someone here and led them to believe certain things about Harper that were not true. Harper didn’t know who’d said what or what was true. I didn’t know. Valerie…” He broke off.

“It’s okay, Dad.” Harper’s tone was soothing and warm. “You don’t have to do this. I can talk to Ames later.”

Ames saw the struggle on the man’s face. He’d lost his son, almost lost his daughter, and the woman he was married to seemed determined to make Harper suffer. Steve Moore had come here to help Harper. That meant he was trying to make things better with his daughter. For Harper’s sake, Ames wished this had happened a lot sooner, but it least the man was here, now. And Ames had nothing but sympathy for the man standing before him.

But, hearing all this only confirmed what Ames had put together. The only mystery left had been who had told Janie all of those horrible things? The hypocrisy of Janie being so peeved at her brothers for not checking into Harper’s background more thoroughly but quickly believing what she’d heard—without verifying a single word herself—had been impossible to miss.

It didn’t matter. None of it did. Harper was back. That

was all he cared about. He threaded their fingers together, needing a more concrete hold on her.

"I also wanted to thank you." The man was giving Ames a thorough inspection. "I had to meet the man who put the spark back in my daughter's eyes. She lit up whenever she talked about you. Then she'd cry." Steve chuckled. "I wanted to say thank you for helping her feel something other than grief. What you've given her is a real gift."

Ames was thrown off by how hard those words hit. All he'd done was love Harper. Because Harper deserved to be loved. "Thank you for your daughter. I've been missing her since I woke up…" He stopped. He was pretty sure admitting he was sleeping with Harper might change the man's first impression of him. "Since I realized she was gone." He frowned down at Harper, then. "You left me. Why were you crying? You don't get to cry."

"I didn't want to leave you, Ames." She swallowed. "I thought I was protecting you."

"I… I know." And, as much as he wanted to be mad at her, he couldn't. He'd likely have done the same thing. No, he would have talked to her first and then done whatever he needed to do to protect her. But knowing that didn't erase the last few weeks of hell. It had been hell. The sort of relentless ache that gnawed at him from the inside and left him on edge and raw. Until last night, he thought he'd lost her forever. "Harper…" He pulled her back into his arms.

"Hello." Penny called out, walking toward them. "Harper, so glad you're back, sugar. Is this handsome fellow your father?" She patted Harper on the back but didn't try to pull her out of his arms. For that, Ames was grateful.

"Steve Moore." Harper's father held out his hand.

"Penny Winston." She smiled. "How about we find some drinks and I can show you around the place while these two…sort things out."

"Lead the way." Steve Moore gave them a parting look and followed Penny.

"Dammit, Harper." He groaned. She felt so good in his arms. "You should have talked to me. You should have told me what was going on. We're all on your side. Janie told Hoss and Rooster everything and they were pissed—at her for putting that on you. At you for thinking they needed your protection." He buried his face against the side of her neck.

"I honestly thought the law was looking for me, Ames—"

"Because Janie was blackmailing you. She used what Valerie had said to scare you into leaving." He lifted his head to stare down at her. "I knew something was wrong. I could feel it. We talked about everything. If you'd been thinking about going home, we'd have talked about that, too." He cradled her face in his hands. "At Lookout Point, I knew you were hiding something from me. And then last night, she said she wanted to be a part of the hiring process from now so that no other wanted fugitives were put on the payroll." He sighed.

"Oh." Harper wrinkled up her nose.

"I started asking questions. The others caught on pretty quick. Hoss and Rooster were so mad, Harper. They sent her packing—told her to leave. And I was coming to get you to bring you home." He ran his thumbs along her jawline.

"What if I'd really been on the run from the law?" she asked.

"I knew better." He shook his head. "We all did. But, if it had been true, all of HQ had voted for you to come back anyway. Hoss and Rooster were ready to lawyer up to prove your innocence. And Brandy? She said she'd never forgive Janie for using your past against you. She said if Janie ever tries to sleep in the women's bunkhouse again, she's going to put a skunk in her bed—that way Janie is certain to get sprayed. It's the least she deserves." His attempt to tease didn't work. "What hurt most was you not talking to me, Harper."

"I know. I am so sorry for leaving." She rested her hands on his chest, her gaze imploring. "Please, understand. You know… I couldn't bear the thought of my nightmare hurting anyone here. Crossroads was free from all the hate and pain of my past—I wanted to keep it that way. If I told you what was going on, you'd have tried to convince me to stay."

"I understand you were doing what you thought was best." He rested his forehead against hers. "But you're right, if you'd talked to me, I would have tried to come up with another way. One that didn't have you leaving me… One that didn't tear my heart apart."

"Oh, Ames." She shook her head. "I'm so sorry I hurt you."

"You're here." He took a deep breath. "We agreed we are a team, didn't we?" He waited for her to nod. "Then we need to make big decisions together from now on."

She smiled. "I promise."

"I promise I can handle anything, face anything, as long you're at my side." He took a deep breath. "Together, we can handle anything, Harper."

"That's a big promise to make, Ames." There was a flicker of hesitation in her voice.

"I've never made a promise I didn't keep. I'm not going to start now." He kissed her, breathing her in. "I missed you, so much. I don't ever want to feel that kind of emptiness again."

"I couldn't sleep. I don't think I've slept more than a couple of hours since I left. I kept reaching for you in the dark." Her hands covered his, holding onto him.

"There's one way to fix this." He tilted her head back so he could see her clearly.

"Tell me." She leaned into his hand.

"You stay here, at Crossroads, with me. From now on." He paused. "If things get hard, we talk—we work it out. Will you stay, Harper? Please."

"Yes, Ames." She nodded. "There is nothing I want more. The only good thing that came out of my leaving is knowing, beyond a shadow of a doubt, that this is where I belong."

"Crossroads?" He smiled, happy to know she'd found her place here.

"No." She shook her head. "Here. In your arms. Wherever you go, Ames, that is where I belong."

"Dammit, Harper." He was grinning like a fool and it didn't bother him a bit. After what she'd said, how could it? "Just when I think you can't make me any happier, you say something like that and prove me wrong."

"Then I guess I'll have to do my best to keep proving

you wrong." She wrapped her arms around his neck. "I love you, Ames. So much."

"I like the sound of that." He looked at her, hoping she could see the hope and joy and wholeness she stirred inside him. But, in case she didn't, he said, "I love you, Harper. I will always love you."

* * * * *

Be sure to look for Sasha Summers's next book in the Crossroads Ranch series, available soon wherever Harlequin Special Edition books are sold!